The Privacy of Storm

SELECTED STORIES BY

JAMES C. SCHAAP

THE PRIVACY
OF STORM

ISBN 0-932-914-21-7

Printed in the United States of America

FOR BARBARA

Some of the stories first appeared as follows:
"The Privacy of Storm" in *Minnesota Monthly*
"Furloughed" in *Military Chaplain's Review*
"Learning to Speak" in *Farmer's Market*
"Pirouettes" in *Today's Christian Woman*
"So Far From Home" in *The Banner*
"The Facts of Life" in *The Church Herald*
"Paternity" in *The Reformed Journal*
"Harmony" in *Great River Review*
"November's Thursday" in *Today's Christian Woman*
"The Gift" in *The Banner*

Contents

The Privacy of Storm

That January blizzard was one of those storms people talk about two days before it hits, but one of those that comes in anyway—despite all the hoopla. Glenda thought most of the highly touted storms swooped north to dump themselves on the Twin Cities. Others, heavy-bellied, never made it up the prairie to Siouxland; they lumbered along through Missouri instead, taking slow but sure aim on Chicago. The ones people talked a lot about rarely came—it could have been a rule, like February's groundhog.

But the weatherman said this one was all geared up to get them, and this time, after two long gray days, he was right. Glenda wished Nicky was still young enough to forecast storms. When he'd been a toddler, she swore she could tell when the storms were coming by the way he'd crowd her, upstairs and downstairs, even in the basement—never begging attention really, just a bit squeamish about leaving her side. He seemed to have this sixth sense as a baby, but he was older now. Every night his father had him out in the barn for chores, even though he was still too young to help much.

She thought her baby could feel storms because he was, back then, so fresh from God. It was something he lost once his eyes started dancing at the sight of the snowbanks Mark raised in the yard with the loader.

That baby Nicky should be able to feel storms coming wasn't such an odd notion either, she thought. Hank Lemmons bought buffalo one summer when he got sick of beef prices, and he kept them on his place, a mile north and a half west. Lemmons became a true believer in buffalo, singing their praises whenever he could, as if he was sure the whole world would be better off going back to the days of Yankton Sioux. It was Lemmons who told her that a buffalo could smell blizzards—how they bunched up around whatever shelter they could find maybe a whole day before a storm. "Better even than arthritis," Lemmons told her one winter morning, a clear bead of some kind of moisture at the very tip of his nose. "I don't need a radio."

If buffalo could do it, why not Nicky? She just figured it was one of those things you lose when you get older and begin to understand about how life is.

When Mark and Nicky came in for supper, she heard the rustle of their jackets in the back hall, the zing of their zippers, and Nicky's heels banging against the basement step. "Careful there," Mark told him. "You'll ram a hole in those boots sure thing, and your mom won't let you hear the end of it."

She disliked the way Mark cast her as the villain.

The two of them came up the steps into the kitchen. "See how dark it is out there," he said. "She's starting to roll now. It's going to be a big one." He bit on a raw carrot from the relish tray, then pulled out a chair and sat.

Glenda dried her hands and looked out beneath the shade she had drawn earlier in the afternoon to cut out the draft. The barn seemed less than a shadow in the mist of snow. "Doesn't seem so bad really," she told him.

She broke a stick of margarine in half and dropped it in a dessert dish, knowing full well Mark wouldn't like it so hard and cold, just out of the fridge. He picked up a roll and split it with his fingers. His cheeks burned from the lines of his chin to his temples, where the imprint of his cap pressed his straight hair up around his forehead.

Winter storms excited him, even though he knew they were dangerous. She could feel it in his quick movements, the way he buttered the roll up near his eyes.

"You can plan on storms whenever things are happening in the barn," he said. "If I've got sows farrowing, we get dumped on. It'll be late tonight probably."

When she put down the bowl of pea soup, Nicky's nose scrunched up, just as she knew it would. "You think you're not going to like it, don't you?" she asked him.

He crossed his arms over his chest.

"I can't help thinking about Rachel up there in that trailer," Mark said. "Can you imagine what it must be like to hear that wind howl if you lived your whole life in Florida?'' He jerked Nicky's chair up close to the table and pointed at the soup. ''That stuff'll put hair on your chest,'' he said. ''Just eat it.''

She had known the moment she reached for the split peas that Nicky would hate the soup. Mark didn't care for it much himself. But her mother always said that in life you didn't necessarily have to like some things that, plain and simple, had to be done. Glenda knew that kids wouldn't understand—she never did herself until after she was married for awhile. It wasn't until you got older that you really started to understand how much life was like cod liver oil or something.

''Come on, Nicky—no dessert otherwise,'' she said.

''Feels so icky in your mouth,'' he said.

That angelic blond look was long gone. Second grade already and his dad had bought him a BB gun to shoot sparrows in the barn.

''You going to check on Rachel?'' Mark said. ''Give her a ring.''

''She's just a kid,'' Glenda said. ''She doesn't worry yet.'' She cradled a spoonful of soup and blew on it gently, while behind them the radio voice ran down the hog prices and talked about open gilts. With the wind outside, she thought it was the right kind of night for pea soup.

''You got everything ready just in case we got to stay put for awhile?'' he said.

She knew Mark didn't mean it to sound like he was her supervisor. It was only his way of checking. For eight years she had heard him say things that way, and there were times she disliked the radiant voice of his authority, the purity that shown from his eyes like a shiny Sunday School badge.

* * * * *

When she had finished the dishes, she turned off the radio and picked up the phone, because Mark was right about calling Rachel. They were newlyweds, little Rachel and her husband, Hilbert—a nice kid, a serious kid that everybody on the ridge called Hibby. ''Hibby and Rachel'' it had said on the napkins they had printed up for their wedding reception in Siouxland. They had been married in Florida, of course, where Rachel's father was a preacher. Her maiden name was Bleyenberg, and most people knew her father because he was a preacher who had been born and reared not too far south of town.

Now his daughter, a sugary blond, perfectly tan, had come back to make a home where her own father had once lived, a pretty Florida girl with Siouxland roots. She and Hibby had met at the preacher's alma mater. They got married and bought a trailer on an acreage. The place had an old barn, a machine shed in pretty good shape, and a couple of run-down buildings not much use to anybody. Hibby worked in town on the kill floor of a packing plant, but he raised some hogs in the barn. Mark helped him nail up a pen outside the east wall to get him started, because Hibby wanted to farm. He was like Mark that way. They both wanted to farm in the worst way.

"Rachel?" she said, "this is Glenda. You're in for your first big storm, you know that?"

Rachel whined slightly, as if she were already scared.

"What's the matter?" Glenda said.

"Hibby's in town on second shift," Rachel said. "I was thinking how nice it would be, locked up for a couple days together—you know?—and he's in town. It's like a bad joke."

Glenda remembered the way a northwest wind made the windows of their own trailer sing when she and Mark were first married. She tried not to remember the trailer anymore, the first place they lived, because it seemed so terribly far behind them. All of that honeymoon time seemed so very long ago.

"It would be funnier if I wasn't all alone," she said, her voice coming up through the receiver in twists of emotion—humor like frosting over everything else.

"Maybe you ought to walk over here if you think—"

"Then Hibby comes in and I'm gone?—"

"I mean, if you're going to be sick about being alone—"

"He's coming yet, I'm sure of that. You know how men are."

She and Mark had them over to play cards when they first moved in down the road. Ten years difference there was between them, and Mark claimed at first he didn't know how to talk to them—whether Hibby should be a little brother or a friend. Glenda knew what she thought of Rachel. There was still so much such a young thing had to know about.

"If you get lonely or something, come on over."

"Maybe I'll just call."

The silence between them stretched on uncomfortably long. She and Mark used to hang on like that before they were married, when Mark was away at Tech. It was expensive, but sometimes they would just stand there and breathe into the silence, as if there were some part of each other reaching all the way through the wire and touching.

"Just give me a ring then, Rachel—anytime," Glenda said.

"How long do these things last anyway?"

"Maybe just overnight." She knew better.

"What happens if he doesn't get home anymore?"

"He'll stay in town. He'll be all right."

Rachel took one long breath into the mouthpiece.

"You got power, and you got food," Glenda said. "It's going to be—"

"What happens if my furnace goes out?"

"Burn down the trailer," Glenda said.

Rachel's laugh stumbled out slowly.

"Just keep in touch. Call me every half hour if it gets bad—you promise?"

"You think I'm helpless up here?" she said.

"You've never been through one of these things, Rachel."

"Back in the dorm—"

"Look around—you're not in the dorm anymore."

Glenda remembered how it was when they were in the trailer. She and Mark would sit across from the wall where the gusts hit, even change the position of the television just to stay away from the wind sneaking through the thin walls. Once Mark lit a candle just to show her the draft.

She didn't even like to have coffee at Rachel's—that's how much she disliked trailers.

* * * * *

No matter when they played Rook, Mark always insisted it should be the men against the women, like some silly playground game, "Boys Catch Girls." Glenda guessed Hibby didn't like the pairings, because he'd always sit there and bid against his wife, his cards fanned out in one hand, his other hand down on his Rachel's thigh. It wasn't principle or anything with Mark, only habit—as if teaming with his wife would be silly when two women and two men made such natural rivals.

One night in late fall Hibby and Rachel came over for pizza. "Thirty-five," Mark bid, his cards in one neat stack on the table. She had no patience for his bidding so ridiculously low, even though she'd heard him say a hundred times how low bids are the only way partners have of communicating. She didn't have a bad hand, but there wasn't enough for a real trump suit.

"Pass," she said, even though she knew Mark would have hiked up the bid if he held her hand. He always gambled on the blind.

"Oh, Glenda," Rachel said, "I can't take anything."

Hibby bid fifty, and Mark took the first-hand bid cheap at 125 when Rachel pulled up her nose and quit. Mark was a merciless killer; he had this way of slapping down cards with a flick of the wrist, every time smacking the table with the heel of his hand, as if the two or three really important tricks were stunning blows.

"Been over at Senard's yet?" Hibby asked him, in the middle of the third hand.

Glenda didn't like anyone talking when she was trying to choose which card to play. She tried to concentrate on the trick out in front of her.

"I'm not going to do it anymore this year," Mark said. "It's a shame too. I got this big, absolutely useless barn out there. Senard could build me a pretty decent setup for the money, but I guess it's not going to happen yet."

She knew very well what Mark was saying.

"You going to hatch those cards or what?" He looked at her and rapped the edge of a card against the table.

Glenda tried to remember what had been laid.

"Hog prices aren't hurting anybody right now," Hibby said. "Some people say they're still going up."

"I know," Mark said. "It's not money that's holding me back either—" and he stopped right there, leaving the truth standing naked before them. It was perfectly clear that she was the one holding him back. He left this gaping hole in his dreams—big enough for Hibby to know who was at fault for there being no new steel building this year.

She dropped down a big counter, and Mark swept it up with a low trump, just as if he knew exactly what she would lay.

Mark had a way of doing those things.

* * * * *

"You wouldn't believe what happened," Rachel said when she called a little before nine. "He took off work early in order to get home, because they were going to close up anyway—because of the storm, you know?—but he slid in the ditch between here and town, so he's walking. I love it. It's so romantic. He called from the Hermanson place."

Laughing came easier to Rachel now. "He was alone in the car?" Glenda asked.

"I guess so."

She knew she could slay Rachel with worry if she wanted to. She tried to figure out what she could say.

"So what's the big deal?" Rachel said.

"I just hope he doesn't try to be a hero about it—"

"He said it's pretty bad out there, so he's going to stop at every farm place and call me—just to tell me how he's doing."

Glenda had the telephone company put in a long cord so that she could look out in the yard while she talked on the phone. She raised the shade and stared at the vapor light above the machine shed, its blur cut and stretched by the wave of snow running almost horizontally through the bright blue of its glow.

"Don't worry about it, Rachel," she said.

"I'm not worried," she said. "He said he was coming."

* * * * *

Mark sat with his holey gray socks up in front of the TV. He wore two pairs, so at least his toes weren't sticking out. Nicky was already asleep because most of the day he'd been outside. Mark had put him up to bed without a fuss.

The sound of the wind maintained a siege. It was like a train of railroad cars so long it never quite made it past you, its low rumbling moan so constant that you heard it only when you remembered that there was a time when it wasn't there.

Mark wasn't really watching the television. His wrist bounced slightly off the arm of the chair as if he was listening to music that Glenda didn't hear.

"You think she knows what it's like for him to walk home on a night like this?" he said.

Glenda looked up from the catalog as if his question had awakened her. "I don't know. I don't think so."

He brought his hands up in front of him and took little careful bites around the ends of his fingers. "Must be a lonely thing for a girl like that, being up there alone most the time." He pulled his hands away from his face and curled his fingers up to check his nails.

"You sure are worried about her—"

He turned to her. "I mean, the waiting. That girl's just waiting to get pregnant, isn't she? Have herself a little kid."

Mark was right. In December Rachel had Glenda over to help make Christmas candy, and she told her as much in no uncertain terms. "We're trying to have a baby," she said, while both of them stood there with sticky fingers. "It's something I've always wanted, I think," she said. "Not many of my college friends understand it, but you know what I mean, don't you?"

With a smile and a nod, Glenda tried to say that she knew.

"That's a full-time job in my book," Rachel had said. "I want to get just royally pregnant."

Glenda put a fold in the catalog page and put it down next to her. "How is it you think you know something that personal about those two kids?" she said.

He yawned and rubbed the heels of his hands through his eyes. "You're not going to believe this, but I got sows that got the same look in their eyes."

"How can you say such a thing, Mark?" she said.

"Didn't think you'd like it," he said.

She kept her eyes down on the catalog. Someday she thought she'd have courage enough to tell him how much she hated his hogs. "How many other women you see in those sows?" she said.

"Never did a census." He lifted his feet from the hassock and slid himself forward in the leather chair, arms braced up, his back leaning forward.

"What an awful thing to say," she said.

He twisted his head as if to say that she could take it or leave it, then he got to his feet and stretched, his arms rising in an arch up toward the ceiling.

"Where you going?" she said.

"Don't ask," he said, his back toward her, both arms extended straight out to the side. He turned his upper body at the waist like an athlete loosening up. "I don't want you telling me that I'm getting old." Then he turned and faced her, his hands up on his waist.

"Some things don't need to be said, Mark," she told him, picking up the catalog again.

"I'm going outside to put up ropes," he said. "I know you're thinking that too much worry is a sign of old age."

"Sometimes I like the thought of you being old," she said.

He stood there above her and put his holey sock on her knee, then gave her leg a little shove and walked away.

It was already close to ten. She guessed it would take him an hour or more to string the ropes between the house and the barn, to give himself some direction if the storm grew as bad as the howling made it sound. In a couple minutes she could watch the TV weather, alone.

* * * * *

"He just called me from De Bey's," Rachel told her when she called again, just after ten. "Two miles to go."

"Could he see all right?"

"He said it was the cold that was getting to him more than the snow. Arnie gave him another sweater."

"Why don't you call your Dad?" Glenda said.

"What on earth for?"

"Just to talk—"

"You think I want to hear how nice it is in Florida?"

"Maybe it's a dumb idea."

"He'd get a kick out of it, all right."

"I mean—maybe, if you get bored."

"It's kind of exciting right now, to think of Hibby out there bucking snowbanks just to get home to his honey."

She wanted to tell Rachel about the danger—make her grow up a little. "You got heat and everything yet?" she said.

"Really, Glenda, what happens if my furnace goes?"

"Put on the oven."

Rachel's laugh came in a blur over the wire. "Sounds like Hansel and Gretel or something—having your oven open."

Glenda twirled the cord through her fingers, something she never allowed Nicky to do.

"How we going to get the bedroom warm if the furnace goes out?" she said. "It's all the way on the other side of the trailer."

"You been married six months—do I have to draw pictures?"

"It was a dumb question."

"You just be waiting at the door and give him a squeeze for me too," Glenda said.

* * * * *

It had become all the rage for Siouxland young couples to have wedding receptions in restaurants or taverns. For years, they had been held in churches, but the old ways were gradually falling, like the old barns people used to rely on. But Rachel was a preacher's daughter, and Hibby's folks weren't the type to spend big money on a splash, so their Siouxland reception had been in the Fellowship Hall of the church. Glenda thought that was nice.

Hibby and Rachel were already married for a month, and that made the reception a little different, maybe a bit more quiet. All evening, it seemed, the newlyweds held hands, and when they looked at each other, somehow there was less of that embarrassed teenage passion other couples have when they cut the cake right after the ceremony. They'd already spent a month together. Not that they weren't in love. But even a month of marriage had aged them, made them exhange glances in a way that seemed less sly than the normal newlywed peeking. Their smiles were rooted in a month of experience.

For lunch the people marched up in rows toward three tables set with fruit, cheese, and salads. Maybe it was a Florida touch in the middle of Siouxland, a refreshing change from ham buns, potato chips, and dixie cups full of freshly cut cole slaw. Of course there was no liquor.

Mark himself started rapping his glass with his fork, the old way of telling the young-and-in-love that it was time for a full-fledged, married kiss. Hibby honored the request with great passion. But later, maybe the fourth or fifth time the glasses started tinkling, Hibby directed the request back at their neighbors, pointing directly at Mark with nothing less than the knife for the wedding cake. Suddenly, a church full of eyes turned on them. Glenda didn't know what to do with her hands when Mark picked her up by the shoulders, kissed her firmly on the lips and held it for what seemed forever, while all around them folks were oohing and aahing as if some perfect bronze foal had just been paraded before half the town at the 4-H fair.

"You know, you haven't kissed me like that for maybe five years," she told him before bed that night.

"That's a record that needs to be broken," he told her.

He didn't need to ask her—not that night.

One afternoon on their honeymoon, Mark had told her how before they were married he used to have such great fantasies about her in church. That was what she felt on the night of Hibby and Rachel's reception. The way they stood there together, the way they played with all the jokes, the way the two of them kissed in the chorus of ringing glasses—the two of them in that kind of love that people struggle not to outgrow—all of it affected her that night, the night of the old kisses.

* * * * *

Mark was still outside when Rachel called again at 11:30 to say that Hibby had just been at Hank Lemmons' and was on his last leg. Rachel said she was so excited after Hibby said goodbye that she had forgotten to call them for awhile. When she finally remembered, she worried that she'd wake them, because after all it was so late she figured they would be snuggled up in bed.

"No one's sleeping here yet, except Nicky," Glenda told her. She didn't tell her that Mark was out stringing ropes.

"I'm so excited," Rachel said. "This is so great. Nothing like this ever happens in Florida."

Years ago, Mark's roommate at Tech had tried to make it home one Friday night with a carload of kids, when he should have stayed put in the middle of a storm. They went in the ditch, and with little gas in the tank, they decided to try foot it to the nearest farm house. In the driving snow they could see no lights, but they walked, arm in arm, down what they thought was the road, changing directions whenever their steps fell off into ditches on either side. Blinded, they walked too close to death, and some went crazy in snowbound panic. Some had to be carried, half-laughing, half-wailing, almost against their will. Finally, they spotted a light in an old barn just off the road, on a deserted farm place. It was a horror story that everyone talked about back then, but Glenda didn't tell Rachel any of that.

"Maybe a half hour yet, you guess?" she asked.

"I expect him any minute," Rachel said. "He's anxious to get here. I can feel it in my bones."

"Try to remember to call when he gets home," Glenda said. "I mean, just to let me know that everything's all right."

"Once he gets in the door, I'll probably forget," she told her, with a growly laugh. "You know what I mean, don't you?"

"I wasn't born yesterday," Glenda said.

When she put down the receiver, she wondered whether it wouldn't be better if people never grew up, never lost Rachel's enthusiasm.

She pulled a kitchen chair up next to the refrigerator and took down all the candles she could find from the cupboard where she kept stuff she rarely used. She laid them on the counter between the kitchen and the dining room, along with matches, then picked up a little around them, so that if she had to grope in the dark they would be there.

It was more than an hour since Mark left to put up the ropes.

Tomorrow it would be calm and cold, she told herself. Tomorrow drifts would run like waves between the buildings, curl around the corners of the house and stand there between barn and house as if they'd been there since the beginning of time. Tomorrow the temperature in the stillness would drop below freezing, and the snow would crack beneath Mark's boots when he stepped in the back hall.

Out in the grove a kingly ringneck pheasant paraded around on some winter mornings, as if it were a pet. Sometimes she would see him out back, his feathers rich with gaudy coloring, from the green of his neck through the rich brown that lay beneath the march of chevrons down his tail. Against the blinding white, he seemed almost painted, like a cartoon drawing strutting over the crust of frozen snow, some piece of tapestry forgotten in a world without color, as if only God could have left him there. She wondered how he would suffer the storm.

Once Mark caught Nicky shooting at the pheasant with his little air rifle, and he scolded his own son for what seemed to her less naughty than horrifying.

When she raised the curtain, she saw only a blur of light from the shed in the shredding lines of blowing snow. She wondered how much longer it should take him to string the ropes.

She realized once upstairs that she had no reason to check up on Nicky. There was no reason to think he shouldn't be fast asleep, and he was, his body only half-covered with blankets, one foot, warmly covered with a boot from his favorite football pajamas, hanging over the edge of the bed as if it were mid-summer.

Mark would sleep in nothing but his briefs all summer, and most of the time he would need no covers, not even a sheet. Nicky was like his father that way. Always hot, even in winter.

She closed the door to the closet he had left open on the northeast side of the room, where the brunt of the storm was punishing the outside walls. A closed closet door would take the edge off the cold. In the dim light from the bathroom, she could just see the innocence on his face. She picked up his foot, completely limp in her hand, and edged it back beneath the blankets, then smoothed back the hair from his forehead, as if she were preparing him for church.

She stood there and let the silence of the house surround her, the blizzard's low siren rising and falling. The snow was too light to sound against the window; the temperature had fallen already. Beneath the closet door, cold air inched out from the outside wall and swept across the wood floor, sneaking through the worn edges of her house slippers.

In winter she loved to put her cold feet up against Mark's calves when they lay, their backs together, in bed. He never seemed to mind.

It was nearly twelve when she came down from Nicky's bedroom, and Rachel still hadn't called. Lemmons probably told Hibby to take a lesson from his buffalos and stay overnight. But Hibby wouldn't have listened, not with Rachel waiting for him as she was.

Glenda picked up her carpetbag from the bottom drawer of the bureau in the dining room, and pulled out some of Mark's gray socks, but before she started mending, she went around the house putting on lights as if she were expecting visitors after church. She sat in the kitchen in a padded chair with the socks out in front of her, then rose and pulled up the shade so Mark could see the kitchen lights through the storm.

She wondered if he had worn enough clothing when he went out to string up the ropes.

Farm socks were gray because there was no reason for them to be pretty. They wore like iron, kept his feet warm, and ran up above his ankles high enough to cover the bottoms of his long johns, but they looked forever dirty, even on Monday afternoon after a wash, when she lined his upstairs drawer with clean pairs. It took years to wear them through, but when they did they usually gave out right at the point of his toes. She told him he bought them too tight, but it was one of those things that he never seemed to hear. Every piece of dress clothing he owned she had bought for him at some time, but coveralls and socks were two things he bought for himself in town.

There was a time when she enjoyed mending them. That first year in the trailer, when everything was new to her, when watching him shave and strut around in his underwear seemed naughty and sweet, back then she loved sitting there with him in front of the TV, her fingers twirling needles for him. Everything was different then—making him lunch as if she would be getting a grade, buying him ties, feeling him next to her, asleep, with his hand over her breast, feeling desire run through her so spontaneously, any hour of the day.

One summer afternoon he had come in from walking beans. It wasn't hot, and he wasn't sweaty. But maybe he was. Maybe she didn't think of it then. More than a month already they had been married. She had made turkey sandwiches, because her own mother said turkey was a good thing to cook—cheap and usually good for a lot of different meals. He came in without his shirt, his neck and back and chest bronzed, and they had dessert in the bedroom.

They heard the doorbell but had never heard any car come on the yard, and there they lay as if caught in the act. It rang again and again.

"Let it go," Mark said.

"You left the TV on out there," she whispered.

"Who cares?"

It rang again.

"Mark—" she said. "They'll know we're here—"

He put his finger up to her lips.

Some guy on the TV was trying to sell used cars.

Four times it rang, then twice in succession. All the windows were open, and she'd left the salad on the table, right there in front of the door. In the middle of it—in the very middle of it—he reached over and kissed her, and she was powerless even to move, afraid of making a sound. With her chin she pushed him away, fighting back giggles.

It rang again, then there was a blast of fists on the screen door.

"We've got to answer—"

"Sshhhhhhh—besides, what's it going to look like now? He's been there for five minutes." He grabbed at her ribs, and she turned her face into the pillow to stop from laughing aloud.

When they heard the car pull away, Mark stood there naked, looking out through the window. "It's the preacher," he said.

"You got to be kidding—"

"At least he knows we got a good marriage," Mark had said.

She sat there remembering, her hands full of gray socks. It was after twelve already. Through the kitchen window she could see the snow swirl as if in clouds. Mark had been gone for two hours. Sometimes pheasants died in frigid blizzards when their eyes froze shut.

She thought of calling Rachel herself. The walk from Lemmons couldn't have taken so very long; by now Hibby must have made it. She could call and find out. She wanted to know for sure that eveything was all right with them. She stuck the socks back in the carpetbag and sat at the desk near the phone, running her finger around the circle in the middle where they'd printed their number.

Mark should have been in by now, and Rachel should have called. Maybe Hibby was home. She could call, but then she'd disturb them— she could catch them in bed, like the preacher. It shouldn't be hard to know what was happening, just from the number of rings—if Rachel was sitting there waiting, the phone wouldn't ring more than twice. If she wasn't waiting, it would go on and on—five rings and she would know what was happening.

She picked up the receiver and listened for the buzz. The phone wasn't dead. She dialed six digits then waited to be sure she was doing the right thing. Even four rings and she would know what was happening. This time she would be the preacher. "At least he knows we've got a good marriage," Mark had said.

Mark was still outside, of course. She put down the phone because she wasn't ready to talk yet, wasn't ready to hear Rachel's voice puffing from the run through the trailer from the bedroom.

And she wasn't ready to tell her that she was worried sick about Mark right now, because her worry would destroy them, Hibby and Rachel. Her worry would break them completely, get them both up and send Hibby back into his parka. Hibby would think he'd have to come over, and Rachel would be alone again. She couldn't be responsible for that. Maybe Rachel would insist on coming along. That would be worse.

For the first time, it dawned on her that it wasn't Rachel who needed her, it was she who needed Rachel.

Just then the chirping of the back door hinges came up through the hall and kitchen behind her. She heard him pound his boots on the rug at the door, and she listened to the sound of his coat slipping from his shoulders, the creaking wood beneath the back steps. Joy and relief ran through her arms and hands and fingers.

She twisted out of the chair and went to the top of the steps, where she saw him, his back to her, unlacing his boots.

"I swear I'll never understand those sows. Something in a storm that makes them want to farrow—I'm sure of it," he said, without looking up. "You weren't worried, were you? I figured I'd better stay out and supervise."

His coat hung from its hood on the hook.

"Maybe I should have come in to tell you, but I figured after this long together you wouldn't worry anymore." He turned his face up to her at the top of the stairs. His cheeks were proud red, and his hair was tinged with sweat that ran in a band around his head. Frost and snow turned his mustache into silver brush beneath his nose. "Tell me you weren't worried, Glenda—"

She hid her smile purposely. "You don't have to know everything—"

"Glenda," he said, "you're kidding?—" He slapped his gloves together over the rug on the floor and laid them, one beside the other, on the shelf along the wall.

"Rachel's fine," she said. "Hibby's home."

He stood up and smiled, then came up the stairs in his socks and stood beside her. "I'm getting so dumb old," he said. She took him herself and held him, his arms around her like a blessing.

"I started to worry about losing power, so I got the heaters going now.

Things are popping out there, just like I told you. I went upstairs and got down some extra straw—just in case I'd need it later.'' He patted her shoulders his way, almost too hard. ''That old barn comes in handy sometimes, I guess, Glenda.''

In her fingers, the flannel shirt felt warm and moist.

''Maybe a little brandy would chase out the chill,'' she told him. ''A nightcap.''

He took her shoulders in his hands and narrowed his eyes. ''What're you offering anyway?'' he said.

* * * * *

She was still awake when the phone at the side of the bed rang. She watched it ring—three, four times—in the glaze of light from the digital clock Mark had given her for Christmas. It was two o'clock.

Finally, it woke him. ''You just going to let it ring?'' he said.

''You just go back to sleep,'' she said. ''It's none of your business—'' She put her arm over his chest and reached for the phone with the other hand.

''Glenda?—I'm so sorry,'' Rachel said. ''I just thought of it now—''

Mark's breath lengthened softly. He was already asleep.

''It's all right,'' Glenda said. ''Everything's all right.''

18

Furloughed

About the life of Lester Agnes, I know almost everything I do by second- or third-hand, which is to say, by reputation—which is to say, in Canton, I suppose, by gossip. But anyone, man or woman, whose biography accumulates the stacks of lurid stories which Agnes's has in his seventy years cannot be, in total, a victim of malicious wagging. My wife, whose first twenty years are rooted in this river town, claims Lester deserves the perverse quality of his legend; and my father-in-law, a man I respect, does little more than hrrumph whenever Lester's name rises in casual conversation. He and Lester have been members of the same church for more than a half-century.

What I know is this: Lester's wife Geneva claims the week before her husband died was his most peaceful on earth—and hers. He died on Saturday. I had been there to visit just two days before his lungs filled up again and the cancer he wrestled for three long years finally pinned him. According to the scriptures, Jacob wrestled only one night and came away with nothing but a hip pointer.

"I put this house on the market today," Mrs. Agnes told me last week when I stopped over to see them, "but I don't think Lester will ever see it sold." She put down a huge cinnamon roll on a plate in front of me, assuming, as most do here, that all men eat that much at three in the afternoon.

"He seems pretty chipper," I told her, trying to lug in the gospel of hope.

She nodded to acknowledge my propriety.

"The kids have all been here now. Wanda just left, but the two of them said it all—she and Dad—what had to be said."

Perhaps it was the sheer length of a battle whose outcome was never in doubt, but Geneva Agnes never seemed fragile about her husband dying just a room away.

"It's all okay?" I said, eating the roll so as not to offend, "I mean, between them."

"Things won't ever be hunky-dory," she said. "I long ago gave up on that kind of miracle."

Once, or so I heard, Lester invoked the prayer chain of the Canton church to ask God's help on his wayward daughter Wanda. He'd found cigarette butts in her Nova's ashtray. "They didn't fight?" I said.

"Wanda's got better sense than that," Geneva said, "even if Les doesn't." She pressed the top down on the tub of margarine once I'd taken what I needed. "But he didn't pull anything. It's about the best I could hope for." She picked herself up from the table to put the tub back in the refrigerator. "She blames him, you know, for all of her problems. That's what her psychiatrist says to do, I guess, and who am I to judge?"

"Sounds like a psychiatrist," I told her.

"It's probably true," she said.

"You think so?"

She pulled a towel out from the rack beneath the sink and wiped her hands, then came back to the table. "You do the best you can when you're doing it," she told me. "I'm not sure he ever knew any better thàn what he did. I tell Wanda, 'You spend all your time looking behind you and the day will come you'll spin yourself around completely and leave yourself looking at your shadow. That's all.' That's what I told her. And lookit here what this man did. We never had a thing, Reverend—when we were married. Nothing. And lookit here now, at this house, what kind of place it is, with a big screened-in porch. I only wish he could live here awhile yet because I think I'd be a better wife without hogs forever in my backyard."

If you live with a man like Lester for all those years, I suppose you gain an inordinate amount of strength yourself.

"He was way too strict," she said. "I know that now. But it was a different time then, and he always thought he knew what was right." When she laid her heavy hands on the table, my side rose. "Most of the time, he meant well."

Farming, some say, plants men down under long before their time. That may be so, but the dozens of widows in the Canton church argue that farming may be good for their wives. Robust, happy in her quiet way, Geneva Agnes, I assume, will now join a score of Canton widows who are never home when you call, who make every travelogue, benefit, and request program, play a little charity bingo, and just about every Saturday night walk four abreast up to one of the local restaurants. Maybe her best years are still in front of her. When Christ admonished whole cultures for not caring for widows, I don't think he had the rural Midwest in mind.

"How you going to manage without him?" I said.

She pulled the coffee cup to her lips, let it sit there for a moment in front of her glasses. "Same as always, I guess, except one less to cook for."

Maybe I shouldn't have asked her then what I did. But one place I've always failed is with my own niggardly reticence. So I asked her exactly what was on my mind. "You love him, Geneva?—did you?"

She sipped her coffee and swallowed. "More than ever, in the last three years—when he needed me," she said. "I don't really think Wanda knows that either." She looked down at her arm and rubbed her hand across her wrist. "Sometimes I think about the way Jackie stood there with her kids when Kennedy was shot. You remember that?—or you too young?"

"Sure," I said.

"I want to be like Jackie at Les's funeral," she said. "I want to stand there and not fall apart, if you know what I mean." She put down the cup and raised her hands, put her palms together, then looked up at the wall, as if what hung there were some half finished portrait. "I want to show everybody in that church that I loved him, but I want to stand in front of them looking strong as Jackie too." She'd find something within her, I thought, like an actress, something that would be there when the time came.

"You're going to do the funeral, you know," she told me. "He's got the whole thing worked out already." She grabbed the Bible from between the book ends behind the toaster and slipped out a scribbled page full of notes. "He's got it all here, what he wants, even what the choir is supposed to sing." She opened the sheet and flattened it with the back of her hand. "That's like him. He never really thinks whether it's what they want."

"He wants me to officiate?" I said.

"You been here for a lot of it."

"Nine months."

"Longer than anybody else." She pushed the sheet across the table. "He likes you. Maybe because of what you don't know."

"He told you what to write?" I said.

"He wrote it himself—last Thursday, I think. Sat up for an hour at least, him and the Bible, and that silver pen he got from the Pork Association."

The hand was more comfortably set down than I would have expected of Lester Agnes, an almost feminine grace in the l's and the g's. "Lamentations," I said, when I read the text the old man had written in. "It doesn't happen often that people choose Lamentations for funerals."

"People like my husband don't happen often," she said, almost sheepishly, smiling.

* * * * *

We've been building an elevator in Canton, twenty-four hours a day, seven days a week. We never stop pouring concrete because the whole thing is one huge tower of cement, poured in a pair of barrels the workers call Siamese twins. Whenever I worked the day shift I could stop off at the Agnes place in the afternoon, when the rest of the crew was on break.

I suppose it's the preacher in me that appreciated coffee and rolls with Geneva Agnes more than a 20-ounce Pepsi out in the heat with the guys on the site. Sometimes I wonder who's most nervous when I'm with them—me, the truck-driving preacher on furlough, or them, the wild-ass high school drop-outs who, I'm told, scuttle the dingier part of their profanity the moment my truck pulls up. I've tried like mad not to be the preacher since we've been here, but to them at least I can't shake the office. They call me Reverend, somewhat jokingly maybe, even when my beard is thick with road dust and sweat hovers in half-moons beneath my arms.

"Agnes dying yet?" Toby Maasdam asked me last Wednesday, when both of us got shifted to nights. Toby's a kid with a future as an elder. I know that. He's rebellious right now—nineteen and almost pitch black from all day in the sun pouring concrete. But he's got this peculiar, latent seriousness in him, something that coaxes itself out when the other guys, their foreheads strapped in red handkerchiefs, wouldn't say a word about anything with more weight than a six-pack of Bud Light.

"Who knows?" I said. "Maybe he'll pull it out."

"Ornery old bastard," Toby said. "He probably will."

A thick, gray river of concrete flowed down the funnel from the back of my truck. I teased it along like I'd seen the other drivers do it.

"A couple years ago Fred Willemstyn had to wrestle old Lester off his son. You ever hear that one, Reverend?" With the heel of his half-length hoe, Toby rapped a stud as the mush flowed into the forms.

"I don't always pay attention to what I hear anyway," I said.

"Fist fight," he said. "He and Sam. Actual fist fight. You believe that? A kid's whaling away at his old man, and the old man is winning. Sam's no lightweight either. You ever see him? He moved to Colorado now—had to get away."

"He was here last week," I told him. "I met him."

"I bet he could take the old man now. Lester's in no shape to punch it out anymore, I guess, is he?" He ran the blade of the hoe over the bed of concrete. At night the work goes easier. During the day sometimes, the heat gets so strong that the whole mess sets up faster than it should.

"What's he look like, dying?" Toby said.

There's always a serving of seriousness in what he says.

"Something like what you're going to look like yourself someday, I suppose," I told him.

He laughed, then he dragged his hand through his underarm and wiped it off on his pants. "You always had that kind of preachiness in you, or is it something you learn in seminary?" he said.

"It's something I try like mad to avoid," I said, "like dying."

He smiled again. "That's what I like about you, Reverend," Toby said. "It's like Sunday School everyday."

"You were saying—about the fight—"

"Fred Willemstyn said it. He was there. It ain't gossip." He pulled a flattened cigarette from the pack in his hip pocket. "He said he got old man Agnes in a hammerlock just to keep him off. They weren't even wrestling, mind you—we're talking fisticuffs here." He stuck the cigarette in his mouth and took up the pose, waving his fists at me.

"Spare the rod and spoil the child," I told him.

"You met Sam. He strike you as a bad-ass?"

To me, Sam Agnes looked, spoke, and acted like an accountant, not a boxer.

"Old man Agnes going to hell, is he, Reverend?" Toby said.

"It's lucky for him you aren't the judge," I told him.

Someday—and probably not all that long from now—Toby will marry and father a child, and when he does he's going to think seriously, maybe for the first time in his life, about how he wants that baby to grow up. That's the day he'll be elder material. Just wait.

* * * * *

Lamentations 3:21-33:

"Yet this I call to mind and therefore I have hope: Because of the Lord's great love we are not consumed, for his compassions never fail. They are new every morning; great is your faithfulness. I say to myself, 'The Lord is my portion; therefore I will wait for him.'

"The Lord is good to those whose hope is in him, to the one who seeks him; it is good to wait quietly for the salvation of the Lord. It is good for a man to bear the yoke while he is young. Let him sit alone in silence, for the Lord has laid it on him. Let him bury his face in the dust—there may yet be hope. Let him offer his cheek to one who would strike him, and let him be filled with disgrace.

"For men are not cast off by the Lord forever. Though he brings grief, he will show compassion, so great is his unfailing love. For he does not willingly bring affliction or grief to the children of men."

I don't mind saying that within the context of Lester's life that passage makes entirely no sense, but that's the passage he wanted me to preach on at his funeral—me, the furloughed preacher, the truck-driving Reverend who visited the sick only because Canton church had no preacher just then, because I was the nearest facsimile.

So what does his choice of the words of the prophet say about the legendary Lester Agnes?

I risk understatement when I say that a man like Lester Agnes was of the old school. He's moved to town now, but years ago he must have stood in that rented acreage where his family lived in the same power- ful, almost eternal way this new elevator is going to stand above town, impervious to tornadoes, even the monsters that swallow village blocks whole and disgorge jagged pieces of people's lives hither and yon over knee-high corn. Twenty-four hours a day we're building a Babel here, a storage barn for mammon, but this elevator is really a kind of Lester Agnes, who was a monster himself, unyielding, dogmatic, cock-sure of his own strength.

His own wife told me once how he hated syrupy fundamentalism, especially the spiritual goo of religious broadcasting. She'd have it on the radio, she said, when she knew he was out at the chores. He'd warned her often enough about it, she said, how it was a drug not to be toyed with, how it was crap, how it made a county-fair teddybear out of God Almighty. So one day he came in and surprised her, caught her off guard. She was washing her hair in the kitchen sink, and she couldn't get to the radio. They'd been fighting earlier, she said, and Lester had been angry.

"I thought I told you not to play this junk anymore," he said. "I thought I told you I wouldn't have it in my house."

"It happened to be on," she said. "I was washing my hair and I wasn't even thinking."

"You're lying to me," he said. "I know dang well you're lying, Gen—"

"I wasn't even listening," she said.

He didn't think at all, she said. He just pulled a hammer out of the utility closet beside the door, walked coldly over to the counter top where the radio sat, then smashed the radio to pieces with three arm-length blows. It was a portable she'd bought herself at Coast-to-Coast, on sale, she said, not worth more than ten dollars.

Then, she said, he replaced the hammer on the shelf, pulled out the wisk broom and dust pan, and swept the pieces off the floor, as if to say, I suppose, that he hadn't meant to make his point with untoward malice.

On the basis of the funeral text he chose for his own funeral, I must somehow believe that man took comfort from the words of the prophet of Lamentations. "Let him sit alone in silence, for the Lord has laid it on him. Let him bury his face in the dust—there may yet be hope. Let him offer his cheek to one who would strike him, and let him be filled with disgrace."

If I had a nickel for every time I've heard people say that the Lord works in mysterious ways, I could retire, buy a big house in town with a screened-in porch. But when you look at Lester Agnes's last wish, a passage on humility from Lamentations, you can't help think that it's not God's ways that mark themselves with mystery, it's also man's, his image-bearers.

Lamentations for Lester.

* * * * *

Why am I here?

Everyone, I think, has a right to his or her own mid-life crisis. Call it that, if you want, but I think it was honesty, finally, that pushed me to put my profession on hold, no matter what Canton people might say about a preacher driving a gravel truck. I resigned my pastorate partly because of the sorry look on the faces of some of my colleagues, preachers whose eyes have long ago lost whatever enthusiasm once burned in their souls. I didn't want to be one of them.

I'm driving a truck in my wife's hometown because I want to know I should continue preaching. I want to see God's hand scribble something in scattered gravel or write Latin on the side of a wall of perfect concrete. I want to know for sure that the profession I chose once, years ago, is where I'm meant to stay. I don't want the office to strangle me, like it has some of my colleagues who feel bound now by a choice we all made in some faded enthusiasm generated so many years ago that the person who made it then, now seems less myself than my high school graduation picture.

I took two years off to decide my future, even though I'm forty; and I don't care if all of Canton thinks I'm a failure because I've boxed up four years of education and parked it all up in the attic of the house we've rented, then jumped into a cement truck.

"What you doing hauling cement?" Toby said to me one day already last fall when we were pouring a driveway.

"I needed a break," I told him.

"So do I," he said. "Maybe I ought to preach."

Lester Agnes asked me about it one of the first times I went over to visit him, sent there by the church because he knew none of the elders were capable of telling him anything about faith he didn't already know. He was probably right.

"You running away from something?" he asked me.

"I don't think I'm running away," I told him. "I just got a late start on deciding what I am going to do with my life."

Lester probably never had an appreciation for irony. He didn't smile. "I'm not hearing you straight," he said.

"I'm just on leave," I told him. "It's not like I've quit."

"You doubt God?" he said. "You lose your faith somewhere?"

"It's not that," I said. "I doubt myself."

If a cartoonist were to draw Lester Agnes, he'd feature that gray-black bush of eyebrow that flexes into a thicket of seriousness no smile can deny. "Takes a man to say that," he told me. "Took me almost a lifetime." For a minute there I wondered who was bringing whom the comfort.

"You aren't quitting then?" my father-in-law asked when I told him I wanted a job for a year or two.

I told him I wasn't necessarily going to quit preaching, just check out my options.

He had his fist up in front of his mouth, as if he were going to cough. Then he flipped off his cap and brushed his hair back with his forearm, looking at his daughter. "I can't pay what you're getting in the ministry," he said.

"We know that," Mindy said.

Then he chuckled, pulled his chair forward, and spread his arms across the desk in front of him. "What on earth you know about cement?" he said.

What I hated most was telling my consistory because I knew it meant facing up to something I didn't want to know. They were the only people who didn't question my decision.

"If it's what you want," my vice-president said. That's all. Maybe I'm wrong, but the night I told them I wanted a leave—no strings attached—was one of the best meetings we'd had in the eight years I'd served that church.

The only person who encouraged me was my wife, who claimed she sometimes wondered whether twenty years ago, when we fell in love, she could ever have guessed I might become the man the ministry had turned me into.

"It will be a furlough for me too," she said that night. "You understand that, don't you?"

I suppose I'm not the first man to have wondered at a time like that whether I'd really ever thought much of my own wife in all those years already behind us.

* * * * *

Back in Forest City, my last congregation, I gave one night a week to the local hospital, on call like an ambulance driver—the man who parlayed the gospel of comfort wherever distress had no outlet. Strangely enough, one of the best lessons one learns in the ministry is not how to preach but how to listen, and the hospital is a great classroom for slow learners like me.

The only old-fashioned neon sign I remember in the whole city was the one at the hospital's back door, the one that said EMERGENCY. By habit, I suppose, I walked in that door on the last night I served as volunteer chaplain, because as often as I'd get called, I'd end up there, holding hands with some distraught mother or listening to the frantic prayers of a Geneva Agnes, sometimes futile prayers for a lifelong husband hooked up to a monitor whose flattened line already spoke God's own truth.

This time it wasn't emergency.

"They're up in 434," the nurse said when I identified myself at the desk.

"Who?" I said.

"The couple—they wanted to see a priest," she said.

I didn't bother telling her I wasn't a Catholic.

"They lost a baby?" I asked.

She flipped the steel clipboard shut and stuck her pencil in a mug above the computer list of patients. "I really don't have much information," she said. "Didn't they tell you anything?"

Four years I'd spent as emergency chaplain. Fourteen years in the
ministry. Somewhere along the line you lose the ability to be surprised
by anything. Whatever the nurse had told me over the phone, I'd forgotten
by the time I got to the hospital.

"They aren't too good with English, I guess," she told me. "All I
know is that they wanted to see a priest."

"What are they?" I said.

She shrugged her shoulders. "Some kind of Orientals," she said. "Lao
maybe?—Chinese?"

The hospital had laid carpet down the corridors just a year before,
probably to break the image of the halls looking so much like tubes of
off-white tile. Even with leather soles you could walk as quietly as a
nurse.

"434?" I said to the nurse at the station upstairs. I knew where the
room was, but I needed information.

"You are?—" she said.

I pulled out the tag I'd forgotten to clip to my coat pocket.

"I'm sorry." She looked at me with the kind of deference one comes
to expect from people who suddenly realize they're in the presence of
saints.

"All I know is they're Orientals," I said. "Clue me in."

The way she fussed with her dangling earring told me she wasn't more
than twenty-two. "Mrs. Ling had an abortion," the nurse said. "No
problems really. She's a stage III Hodgkins, and Dr. Lambert advised
it because of the chemo and everything, not to mention radiation." She
pulled the stem out of her ear lobe and looked at it closely. "You may
go in. He's there—her husband. He's a student. They're really young."

I knocked first. The door opened slowly, a man's face and shoulder
edging out from behind it as if inside they were storing a secret. "You
are Reverend?" he said, and I knew immediately that he was Chinese
or Taiwanese because he had to have been raised Presbyterian.

"I'm the chaplain," I said.

He stood straight quickly, opened the door, and greeted me politely.
"How can I help you?"

Whatever emotional strength the man tried to manifest was undermined
by fear and the cold shock in his wife's dark eyes. Her hair, parted down
the side, fell around her face as if he'd laid it out perfectly for her, ex-

pecting distinguished company. Tightly drawn blankets sheathed her
body, and both her arms lay motionless at her side.

"We need baptism," the man said. "We are both Christians. My father
is a preacher in Hong Kong."

"For you?" I said.

His eyes twitched slightly, as if I'd spoken a foreign tongue.

"I mean, you two need baptism?" I said.

He pointed at his wife, then at himself, his eyes quizzical. "I'm sorry,"
he said again. "No, no." He drew a wide, but very polite smile. "No,
no. The baby." And he produced from nowhere a very shiny, stainless
steel, barrel-like receptacle. "You baptize baby," he said. "Please. My
wife is Christian too."

The fetus was dead, of course. My very first thought was how this
man and his wife had talked the doctor into allowing him to keep it there
in the room, even if it was only for an hour.

I could have launched in, right then and there, with a treatise on the
efficacy of the sacraments. I could have argued that sprinkling the water
of Christ's redemption over the sacrificed body of a infant who'd never
really seen the outlines of God's world was nothing less than silly, even
if the church I came from never promised that the water I shook over
him was holy. I know men who would say it was profane, even to con-
sider it. But I could just as well have countered my own argument by
saying that if these grieving parents had had a choice, most certainly
they would have carried the child into real life, that in all likelihood even
now they looked upon one pound of organic waste that lay in that receptacle as their own baby, taken from them, not by the doctor's hand, but
by God's. Would the Lord Himself have done any less than satisfy their
need for blessing? Would Jesus Christ have flatly laid out for them the
theological absurdity of what they were asking?

My seminary friends and I could have labored late into the night outlin-
ing the central dogmas, testing our own best queries, and looking to the
Bible, the creeds, and the church fathers. It would have made a great
exercise, a simulation worthy of young men and women slavishly preparing for service in God's kingdom.

But I said nothing. I acted.

I took the container from the man's hands and walked toward the basin
beside his wife's bed. I ran the water from the long spout and, without

putting down the precious fetus, washed my hands one at a time, because even in my mind I thought I was about to do something sacred. When both hands were wet, I took that receptacle over to the bed, nodded toward Mr. Ling, and stood beside his wife.

Water dripped down over the pale gray blanket spread tightly around her. I reached for her hand and held it in my left, and then, simply by the movement of my hand, I baptized that dead baby. "In the name of the Father, and the Son, and Holy Ghost," I said, "I baptize you into God's kingdom of love."

I let go of her hand and took the father's with my right, then brought it with mine to the container.

"What is its name?" I said.

"Chun Li," he said.

"Chun Li," I repeated. "God's child."

"Yes," he said. "Yes, Chun Li God's child."

And then I prayed. Both his hands were on mine.

Some say war cripples men by pushing them into action so fraught with heroism and horror that the temper of their lives ever after will pale in the contrast. I've never been to war, but I know what it is like to walk out of a hospital room like the one I had been standing in that night, and wonder, in the crystal clear air of cold January, whether you really can go home to kids whose greatest concern is trying to avoid piano practice.

That night I stopped at a fast-food place and had a shake because I didn't want to go home. The man who served it was my age, maybe older, and he wore the rust-colored hat of the manager. All he asked me for was my order, and all he gave me was a chocolate shake and thirteen cents change from my dollar bill. He never really saw anyone there in front of him but someone identified as the customer.

It wasn't any theological crisis I faced in baptizing a dead fetus that sent me on furlough, that made me question whether or not I wanted this office of comfort-bringer for the rest of my life. It was that man in a red tie and a rust-colored hat who made a living for himself and his family simply by asking people what kind of hamburgers they wanted.

I sat down with a crumpled newspaper, the cold shake making me shiver, even though the place was warm. And I knew I couldn't go on in a role where the whole world looks at you as God's own hands. I

sat there at a swinging seat, leaning over a formica table, and I wondered
whether I wanted to spend the rest of my life in a job no more complex
than that man—mixing shakes and making change from a register whose
keys are menu items.

That night I decided to quit the ministry for two years.

* * * * *

From a hundred feet up, the river winds like a thick black snake through
the quilt of straight-edge street lights mapping the city at night. If you're
not moving around up on top, you need a jacket because soon after midnight, cold descends from the clear sky even in July, and the charge
of heat the late afternoon sun buries in town won't reach high enough
to relieve the chill. But there's an odd kind of honor I sometimes feel
in standing up on top of the slowly rising elevator in the middle of the
night, the whole town asleep in trust beneath me—a watchman's honor,
I suppose, an odd sense of responsibility that sometimes makes me want
to mark the hours and yell out all's well to a snuggled community of
bedrooms.

Last night I took my break up on top of the platform where the concrete's being poured. Toby came walking over as if he wanted to talk.
It was clear to me that sometime in the very recent past he'd had a drink,
so I offered him some of my coffee and he drank it out of a pop can.

"You going back?" he said.

"To what?"

"To the ministry?" By habit, I suppose, he took out his cigarettes.

"Actually, I'm thinking of making a career of hauling gravel. That's
a career with a future."

He didn't seem to catch my angle.

"Some people are just made to be preachers, you know? This kid,
Ben Vellinga, he's going to be a preacher. When we were in sixth grade
he got this brand new 10-speed. I wanted to ride it, see? So I did. At
school. And later that night his old man calls my folks and lets them
have it for me riding Benny's brand new Huffy. Shit. That kid's going
to be a preacher because preacher's have this kind of wall around them
that somebody's put up for them—you know what I mean?"

"I got a wall, you're saying?" I said.

"You come around the site and things change just like that." He snapped his fingers. "Even the bosses. You don't ever hear what I hear. You got this aura."

"What color is it?" I said.

Steam rose in a rounded triangle from the top of the can.

"It's whatever color heavenly auras are," he said.

I've never been much for a youth pastor. In the two churches I've served, I really wasn't all that successful at relating. Maybe it was because I was never young myself.

"I tell you what, Toby," I said. "Maybe I'm tired of lugging around my aura. Maybe I want to be Toby Maasdam and see the real world."

He laughed at me—this kid, nineteen years old, laughed at me as if I were the child. "No, you don't," he said. I hadn't said anything at all, but he put back his cigarettes without lighting up. "You ought to go back—really," he told me.

I've been trying hard to be more direct because it's struck me that no one in the Bible, not even Jesus Christ, was the kind of sweet guy I thought I was supposed to be. Today, smiley TV preachers set the standard, not the Lord. I was trying to be more honest, so I said to Tony, "What you got on your mind, anyway?"

And he pulls out this junk from his hip pocket. He's got a ring, and some kind of necklace, ticket stubs, and a couple of pictures, wallet-sized, all of it in a clear, sandwich bag. He holds it out in front of him as I'm supposed to understand the entire dilemma.

"I got this aura, remember?" I said. "Nothing sinful gets through it. You're going to have to spell it all out because I don't understand a thing."

It wasn't until that point, I guess, that I really began to understand that whatever troubled him was something worse than he'd ever felt in his life. He really couldn't say anything at all. He stood there and bounced the junk in his hand, as if he were about to drop it off the side of the elevator.

"Let me guess," I said. "It's a woman. He shook his head. "It's a woman and she's dumped you. You got the shaft."

He just kept bouncing this bag of stuff.

"Wait a minute," I said. "I got it now. It's a woman, and you dumped her, and the problem is that you still love her," I said. I shook out the grounds from my thermos top and poured in a little more coffee. "Now you want me to tell you whether to try to get her back."

Finally, he looked at me. "You make it sound so cute," he said. "You got it mostly right, but you're just imagining. I saw it, dammit. I saw the whole thing."

"With some other guy?"

He nodded.

"What'd you see?"

"The whole business."

"Window peeking or what?"

"Doesn't matter," he said. "I don't have no aura. I saw the whole stinking business myself." He tossed the stuff back and forth between his hands like a beanbag. "I saw them in the guy's pickup, damn feet sticking right out the door."

The thing about the ministry is you're sometimes thrust into situations light years from your own experience, but always you're asked to spell out God's Word, as if four years of seminary somehow plants the truth in you like seed corn. This time I said the first thing that came to my mind. "Dump her," I said. "Go ahead."

He looked up at me as if he were angry.

"I been trying for the last week," he told me. "I been wanting to drop it in the mush here, in the elevator, make this whole thing like a huge gravestone—big sucker."

"Why don't you?" I said.

He swallowed hard. "Because I'm no saint either," he said. He brought his chalky hands up to his face and scratched his forehead with the back of his wrist. "I don't know what I'm getting so righteous about."

He didn't dare look directly at me. He took a drink of his coffee. "I want to know from you if people just have to be what they are—or if they don't have to be that, not exactly. If they can be something else, you know, something better? You know what I'm saying?—I mean, I want to know if it's in her to do this again, you know?—I mean over and over?"

"I don't know the girl," I told him.

"But you know people," he said.

"I got this aura, remember?" I told him.

"But inside. I mean, you know people inside. That's different than what's outside. I know them outside.''

He stood there wielding that sandwich bag full of stuff, and I refused to think too hard and long. I went on honesty, hoping it was God himself pushing me the right direction.

"Throw it,'' I said.

I don't think it was the answer he expected.

"Go ahead,'' I told him. "Bury it.''

"Forget her?'' ɯe said.

"Bury the memory. Bury the hate. Don't bury her,'' I said.

He looked at me as if he couldn't believe what I was saying, and for the first time I saw a kid in him, a child edging on tears. But he couldn't do it.

So I took the bag out of his hands and threw it down between the forms myself, dropped it on the bed of concrete, still soft and wet. I grabbed a hoe from where it stood against the side and pushed the bundle under the mush.

"No matter what happens, you got to try to forgive. No matter what,'' I said. "Even if you dump her. Even if she's history. You can't live with hate.''

His eyes looked more scared than I'd ever seen him, this big dark-skinned kid with arms thick as bridge cable.

"I'll always know it's in here, in these walls,'' he said.

"I'll buy that,'' I told him. "But you can't get it back out and carry it around in your hands.''

He turned toward the forms and hammered the wood with both hands, cussing out the town below like a madman. He put his elbows up slowly and leaned forward to rub his temples. His face went down.

"You still want her, is that it?'' I said.

He hunched his shoulders, looking down at the street. "So you think it's going to happen again?'' he said. "You still didn't answer my question.''

"I got no crystal ball, Toby,'' I told him, "and I don't know her. But whether or not you ever marry, you got to believe that she could love you for the rest of her life.''

"Why?'' he said.

"Because she's just like the rest of us. Somewhere in her she's got the image of God, and she can be something even she doesn't think she can."

"You didn't see her in that truck," he said.

"I didn't," I told him. "But that doesn't change what you got to do. It only makes it tougher."

The ring of the chains said once again we were underway.

* * * * *

Honesty notwithstanding, there are things I can't say at Lester Agnes's funeral. One night Toby told me how Lester and his son Sam went to war on a gravel road just south of the place they rented. Combat was in the air already, of course, but the two of them supposedly saw each other coming, Lester in his pickup, Sam on the tractor pulling a field disc. Toby says that once they saw each other, each of them decided he wouldn't budge. So they didn't, and the disc ripped right through the side of Lester's GMC, curling back the whole fender like a piece of sod, he said.

"Yet this I call to mind and therefore I have hope," Lester's text says, "Because of the Lord's great love we are not consumed, for his compassions never fail."

I'm making my last trip to the elevator this morning. It's dawn, and I'm four miles east of town. The sun is breaking up a long thin line of clouds I see behind me in the mirror. Out in front of me, God himself has hung purple curtains in the wide sky west of town. It's the morning of the funeral. I'll shower when I get home, run over my notes, and meet Sam and Wanda and Geneva, plus a score of estranged relatives in the back of the church a half hour before the service. And then we'll put Lester down.

A flattened swath of sunlight sneaks west over the landscape beneath the thick clouds that later this morning will bury the cemetery in a dark, windless overcast. But right now, just for a half hour at most, the sun is here, stretching the shadows of the cottonwoods out over the river like giant hands, gilding the corn that's already tasseling, turning Canton's brand new grain elevator into a pillar of alabaster, like an outdoor movie screen lit, shining against the darkness west.

It's a Tower of Babel, I suppose, the farmers' own peculiar attempt to reach toward the sky. And I might call it the biggest of the barns built

to store up wealth against the future. It's a symbol of riches for sure.
But it shines like something divine this morning, standing up against
the purple curtains of a storm. It's lit into eternal whiteness, as if all
the care we've put into it, the weeks of twenty-four shifts we've put in
to keep it perfectly seamless, the hot days, the cold nights, have not been
in vain.

But I was up there last night, and I know that somewhere in the mush
lies a packet of pictures and jewelry in a sandwich bag. Twenty years
from now some co-op worker may well find a crack in its flawless edge
and wonder what kind of workmanship really went into that wonder.
I know that elevator is not as pure as it looks this morning, a pure mar-
ble wall against the clouds.

How am I to believe that an ornery bastard like Lester Agnes can take
comfort from Lamentations, from waiting on the Lord? And how am
I to believe that Toby's girl—and Toby himself—can be what he hopes
they can be as long as they both shall live? How am I to know that God
is calling me back to the ministry?

That new elevator stands as a symbol, flawed but radiantly white against
the darkness.

I may not know men outside, like Toby says, but I feel this morning
as if I do know what's inside. And what I see in all of us—in Toby and
Lester and Geneva and a couple of Chinese Christians in horrid human
pain—is mystery, something more than what we are, mystery that in
its own way images the God who made man, a God who is there, like
the prophet says, and who I will praise, not because I understand him
fully, but because I can't.

What the prophet says in Lamentations is that this mystery loves us
for his own silly reasons, and what Lester Agnes and I both know is
that he does, oddly enough, even when we don't love ourselves.

And that is the gospel of comfort I need to preach, if only to myself,
today at the funeral, and tomorrow again, and again, and again, and
again.

Learning to Speak

"It's a funny thing that I never heard about all those people being killed," Vernon said. He was reading the newspaper while his daughter picked up the sandwich plates and stacked the tumblers according to the arrangement: whenever her mother was out somewhere, one of them made supper and the other cleaned up the dishes.

"Twenty-five people killed right in this county in 1895, and I never heard a word about it. You read this, Karin?"

"It's not funny," she said.

"I don't mean it's funny—I mean it's odd. I was born right here in Sioux County." He flopped the paper in half and put a finger in the crease. "Somewhere along the line I should have heard the story. I don't care how long ago it happened." Karin pulled a dish towel from beneath the sink and flipped it over her shoulder. "Things just get forgotten eventually. That's the way it should be. Finally they just get buried."

Karin enjoyed stopping conversation like that, he thought, but he let it pass. "You'd think there'd be a monument around here somewhere. Something. My goodness—twenty-five people." He put down the paper and blew on his coffee.

"You were never in a tornado, were you?" she said.

From behind, he saw her shoulders tighten when she scrubbed the frying pan Angie had left unwashed after breakfast. "I've seen what kind of damage they've done," he said. "I've been around within hours—"

"I mean really in one?" She straightened her shoulders and stood still, her back to him.

"Not really in one," he said, "not like Dorothy and Toto—"

"I'd like to see one once." She was staring out at the horizon, looking out the window over the sink.

They had bought the house for the window to the west, because Angie had said she had to have a view when she washed dishes. She liked the finished basement and the cedar-lined closet in the extra bedroom, but it was the big window above the sink that had sold her, the window and the view of the prairie stretching westward to the sunset.

"I think it would be neat to have one blow the roof right off our house," Karin said. "They do that."

"Oh, really?"

"And I'd like mother to be gone. I'd like our whole roof picked right up and flung out into the street." She kept her hands beneath her in the dishwater. "Turn the whole place into a doll's house. No roof. And then mother comes home and finds us there—you and me—kicking through all the junk."

Vernon dropped the paper on the unwiped table and stood. "Anybody ever tell you you've got strange dreams?" he said. He walked to the dining room window and looked west over the back yard, where Karin was staring. A roll of thunderheads, thick as mushroom clouds standing shoulder to shoulder, rose from the horizon. Big birds, hawks probably, hung in the air, facing the stiff east wind like kites. "Keep your hat on Missie," he said. "It's that time of year, all right."

"I'm only kidding," she said. "You know I'm kidding, Dad."

Karin was little when they bought the house, little enough to fit in the bathroom sink. Somewhere he had a picture of that, her fat little body, perfectly right-angled, legs flat-out in front of her, tucked in the bathroom sink. Lisa was older, maybe three or four years old. Lisa had been the oldest, sixteen when she'd been killed. Sweet sixteen is the way he always thought about it. That was two years ago already, he remembered, two years that had just blown by. Karin was fourteen when it happened—just old enough to understand it all too well, it seemed. Her only sister's death had aged Karin; there was no doubt about that. Even her teachers had said that part of Karin's problem was lack of friends. "She's just so mature," her English teacher had told him once in the teacher's lounge, as if it were, for her father, a fact to be proud of.

"So where is Mom speaking tonight anyway?" Karin said.

His hands hugged the cup. "Those clouds put the fear of the Lord in me, you know that, honey?" He knew she was still looking outside, like her mother would have.

"We got alarms at school. It's tornado awareness week, you know?—

you know that, don't you?'' She turned the plug on the drain stopper and shook the water from her hands into the sink. ''You run the school. You're supposed to know things like that.''

She liked being aggressive with him, and it was at least partially due to her age, he knew. He'd seen enough high school kids in twenty years of education to know the earmarks: a kind of eternal brooding that often hatched razor-sharp sarcastic outbursts—as it often did when she was alone with him—or defiant silence—as it usually did when her mother was around.

Part of Karin's way was nothing more than the cancer of adolescence. That was part of it, all right. After all, he thought, it had been two long years already since Lisa was gone.

''We ought to have devotions,'' he said, as lightly as he could. ''I just plain forgot about it—''

''That's because Mom's gone again. We never do when she's gone.''

He allowed her that one too, letting her speak. ''When I was a kid we read the Bible three times a day—after every meal.'' Once he had said it, the grandfatherly condescension in his voice embarrassed him, like the old lines about walking eight miles in ten foot snowdrifts just to get to school. ''You pray later on by yourself, will you? It'll help my conscience along.''

There weren't many dishes because it hadn't been that much of a supper, something of a bachelor's delight—ham and cheese and a pickle. Karin ate a hot dog he had stuck in the microwave. There was a couple of potato chips apiece and some cole slaw that Angie had thrown together when she knew she would be out speaking again.

''You ever hear the story of the chicken that went up in a tornado and came down fully plucked?'' he said.

''Sounds like a cartoon,'' she said.

''True story.''

Karin looked at him and smiled as if he were spinning a tall one. ''They ought to have that chicken in a museum—have him stuffed so everybody would know it really happened.''

''Doubting Thomas,'' he said. Sometimes he felt as if he said things just right he could get through all the tough stuff and find real softness underneath somewhere.

When Karin was little she loved the piano; by the time she got into

junior high, she hated it. Now, it wasn't much more than habit that kept
her practicing. He had taken lessons himself when he was a boy, because
it was the aim of every mother in town to have a son who could play
the church organ. Once he'd even done well at some recital in a college
classroom, but just about then puberty set in and the piano lost. He and
Angie never had a son, but he figured it was much easier to keep girls
on the bench anyway. Karin had played the church organ for a year
already. It made Angie very proud, because Lisa, their oldest daughter,
was just as good a pianist before she was killed. Angie liked seeing Karin
up there in front, her legs swaying over the pedals, like Lisa's had.

"How come somebody pretty as you doesn't have a date?" he asked
her. She was paging through the hymnal, then playing whatever came
up in front of her.

"I try to keep my weekends free to be with mom and dad," she said.
"Something I picked up in Marriage and Family class—just my way of
keeping the family together."

"How very thoughtful of you," he said, with something of her own
medicine.

Karin was a beautiful girl, but nothing at all like Lisa. Her hair was
straight and blonde, like his own, and her eyes were pale, almost colorless. Lisa was dark and slightly chunky, not pretty really, but full of
spunk that kept the boys around, as many as she wanted. Lisa was her
mother's girl, from her high instep and her stubby toes to her hard teeth.
Always joyous and talkative, she was a cheerleader from the time she
was in seventh grade.

Karin was his daughter, an excellent student who took very little pride
in her work, even though what she accomplished was noteworthy. For
her, doing schoolwork was a matter of accepting one's personal responsibility; getting good grades was simply expected. Her deepest emotion
showed only in her silence. She was like a farm girl that way, tight and
stern, all the zeal of old Presbyterian.

Lisa was tops in school too, but she had a thousand interests other
than homework. Now, two years after her death, he remembered her
verve fondly; then, her behavior had often been a headache. He once
told the school psychologist, jokingly, that it would be good for Karin
to get rip-roaring drunk sometime. It would loosen her up, he said, even
if it was something a father shouldn't see—or even say, for that matter.

Lisa had always needed someone to put on the brakes. In the last few months, he often wanted to kick Karin out of the house.

"Don't play that one again," he told her. "It reminds me of the Titanic—"

"Of what?" She stopped in the middle of a line.

"The Titanic. Years ago I saw a movie about the Titanic. When it was going down, all those still on board sang 'Nearer, My God to Thee.' " He raised his forearm like the prow of a ship and let it slip down slowly. "I hear that song and I remember the movie."

"It ought to be an inspiration," she said.

If he wasn't sure she loved him, her sharpness would have angered him. Her mother hated it when Karin talked that way to him; Angie called it disrespect.

The sound of the wind through the storm windows reminded him of his inability to fix anything. After five years of graduate school and twenty years administrating in three school systems, he couldn't stop a window from chattering in a stiff breeze. Karin didn't stop playing because she never heard the wind rise; it was as much a part of her environment as the rumbling of the trains that ran no more than a half mile west of the house. He heard the shrieking because he was trying to read an article on evaluation of instruction in a journal he read to stay on top of things. Maybe the wind made it a good night to be home, he thought.

"Karin, you're home because you knew she was going to be gone, aren't you?" he said. "That's really why, isn't it?"

She put both hands down beside her on the bench and stared up at the family tree hung above the piano. "I know it's good—what she does. I know it is. Shoot, people say it all the time: 'Boy, Karin, your mom sure had me crying.' " She laid her hands on her thighs. "I know it's so helpful, but I don't always like it."

"She's your mom," he said.

She took the hymnal from the rack with both hands and closed it reverently. "Some facts go right through me, in one ear and out the other."

"You don't like her talking about it, do you?" he said.

Karin turned towards him on the bench, the hymnal still there in her hand. "I'm glad I can talk to you, Dad. I just can't say anything to her anymore without it coming out like fire or something."

"What is it?—"

"It's the way she broadcasts all that stuff—all that stuff that belongs to us. It's like she's on a mission or something. She thinks everybody's got to hear how she's strong enough to handle the grief. It makes me sick." She pulled at the buttons in the vinyl top of the piano bench. "It's just that I got a right to my dark side, don't I?" She twisted herself toward him, but didn't face him. "Besides, it's over. It's all two years ago already now." She tapped an even cadence with her fingers. "So where is she tonight?—some church somewhere?—some PTA? 'Feature speaker, Angeline Fields will talk about dealing with grief—please bring plenty of Kleenex. She'll be discussing every detail of her dear, sweet daughter's death.'"

How could he tell her that it made him nervous to think about her up front of some church group telling it all—all the last things: how they lined up patients for Lisa's organs—retinas, bone marrow, kidneys, everything shopped out like rummage? How could he say he knew exactly what she was feeling? There were things he didn't need to hear replayed again and again and again.

"I'm sorry," Karin said.

He remembered how he'd left some enrollment data at the office, something he planned on looking at over the weekend. He thought about leaving to pick it up, about the track meet going on at the athletic field and how he used to attend those things, every single function at school.

"Next thing you know she'll be writing a book," Karin said, "and there we'll be—both of us—in her television show."

"Look at the dozens she's helped," he told her.

"I'm sick of hearing that," she said. "It's a trade-off—Lisa's life and death and our grief and our own feelings—all of it swapped for 'the dozens she's helped.' I keep losing on that one."

Out the front window he watched the branches of the big maples sway like long stalks when the wind caught in the thick buds just ready to leaf.

"Lisa's death is the best thing that's ever happened to Mom, isn't it?— it's made her a celebrity."

He shrugged his shoulders, waiting for his daughter's tears.

"Tell me I'm wrong, Dad," she said, standing. "I really want you to tell me I'm wrong."

She didn't cry.

What was happening outside worried him. Tornado days were thick and windless and unusually warm in the morning when he'd leave for school. Humidity veiled the sun's sparkle and cast the school buildings in a haze that glowed, as if somewhere down the road one could find a lake steaming in a section of prairie farmland. Some springs, every single afternoon sky would telegraph an evening storm; each morning's stillness threatened, as if dawn were a cease-fire in the very eye of the hurricane.

Things would build all day long until dusk, when the gray-green thunderheads out west would mass like a mountain range mirage and rise slowly in the sky, rolling upward into huge raised fists. Then it was just a matter of when and where and how violent.

The only way to live with tornadoes, he knew, was to respect them from the moment they hinted they could be somewhere up there in the swirl of angry clouds. "Ain't a thing you can do about it anyway," his father had told him years ago, "because the Lord'll have his way with that wind." It was something he had never told his family, not even on those windy nights when they sat together in their own storm cellar.

The first time it happened—the very first time after they had moved to the country from the suburbs—Angie had been frantic beneath the fake composure she wore to stifle the kids' fears. Plenty of rain had fallen that spring, and the new house sprung a leak—water a couple of inches deep in the fruit cellar some builder had dug a foot lower than the basement floor. There they sat—Angie, with her robe rolled up above her knees, holding Lisa who slept right through it; himself holding still speechless Karin, her eyes like pocketwatches in the dim glare of a naked forty-watt bulb set in the concrete wall. His pants legs were rolled up above his calves like peddle-pushers, and they sat there barefooted, ankle-deep in rain water while outside the wind swept over them like a passover plague.

"Look, honey," he'd said, pulling his foot back and forth through the water as if all of it were an afternoon's cool game in a wading pool. He lifted Karin from his knee once, and dipped her toes in the cold. Her little body stiffened as she scrambled back to his lap.

There was no tornado that night; they heard later that somewhere out on a farm a grain bin had been flattened. But for three weeks after, Karin woke up crying at night. Angie claimed it was the shock in her wordless memory.

Lisa was killed in fog, a January freakish thaw, a whole week of forty degree temperatures that melted the snow during the day and raised white curtains through the night. A simple case of not seeing the car in front of them. Jerry was driving, one of the boys she was going with. The fog banks sat in scattered clumps over the land: you're driving along and you're in one end, out the other, very suddenly. Jerry didn't see the other guy until it was too late. He swerved and the car twisted, then rolled, Lisa springing out—almost missile-like, the way it seemed when Vernon saw it happen in his mind. She broke her neck. No one else was hurt. Jerry wasn't going that fast.

The phone rang late. DOA, they said.

"We shouldn't have let her go out," Angie said. "We should never have let them go."

Angie was the kind who always relied on him for good sense. "The girls want a puppy," she told him once, not long after they moved into their new house, "one of those little ones with floppy ears and big, clumsy feet." Angie knew better; she didn't want dog hairs in her carpet, but she'd say those things, bartering her own fancy against his common sense and her own better judgement. She relied on him that way, and she had the Bible to back her up—wives and husbands, the way Paul spoke of them. That's the way Angie was; she always wanted him to apply the brakes. He was the head.

For awhile it was all she could say: "We really should never have let her go." She'd sit there in the easy chair with her legs folded up beneath her, while he'd be alone on the couch, in the corner adjacent to her. He knew what she meant—he shouldn't have let them go out in that fog.

Then she started speaking, six months later maybe—not more: "Dealing with Grief." Twice he had sat through his wife's presentation— months ago already. Once he had heard it in his own school, in Karin's class, Marriage and Family. The class had been spellbound through Angie's long and detailed narrative of Lisa's death; and Angie had kept right on talking, right through the bell. Karin sat in a row at the side of the classroom, three seats from the back, with her jacket on. That very afternoon Karin had told him how all her classmates had said how her mom's speech was so moving. Some had even cried, she said. All of them had told her again how bad Lisa's death had made them feel, and how badly she, her younger sister, must still feel about the loss. They all told her how sorry they were for her, again, just as if it had happened yesterday. It was as if the whole business had happened all over again, she told him.

"I felt like some kind of freak," she said, sitting right there in his office, tangling the strings on the hood of her coat. "I don't know why, but I just felt like I was on display and the whole dumb world was gawking at me."

Karin didn't come into his office often, because she didn't like to be known as the principal's daughter. Only once before had she come in. That was a Monday in November, a day after the preacher had prayed aloud for the Fields' family. "Sometimes we forget that some old hurts never really heal, Lord," he had said, even though Lisa had been killed more than a year before. "Bless Vernon and Angie; and bless Karin, Lord, keep her strong—" The prayer had gone something like that.

Karin had wanted to know if her mother had requested the preacher pray just for them. "Mom put him up to it, didn't she?"

She did, he told her.

"They put a W up in the corner of the screen," Karin said from the family room.

He figured it was silly for him to pretend he was sitting there reading a stupid article that really didn't interest him. "Did it say anything else?" he said, stacking the papers.

"Here it comes now. 'The—National—Weather—Service. . .' " She read it as the words marched across the bottom of the screen. ". . .for-all-of-northwest-Iowa,-southeast-South-Dakota,. . ." He picked up his coffee and headed toward the family room.

"Where is Mom speaking?" she said.

"A church in Sheldon," he told her.

"They're in it too." She sat there in her robe, as if she were a housewife. "What's she got this time?"

"The calendar says it's a Mother and Daughter banquet."

"Perfect," Karin said, "just perfect."

He watched the flow of letters repeated across the base of the screen. "You read that article that says you can see if there's a tornado around, right on the screen of your TV?" He picked up the paper from beneath the lamp on the corner table. "Here, listen—it's named after some guy in Des Moines—'The Weller method involves darkening the screen of a television set turned to channel 13.'" He glanced up at the dial. "'The TV is then turned to channel 2. A tornado within 10 to 15 miles should cause the screen to light up continuously.' Isn't that something?"

"Hocus pocus," she said.

"Last of the teenage skeptics, aren't you?" he said.

"It's not like seeing one anyway. It's not like actually standing outside and seeing one there in the sky, being right in there inside."

It was almost eight. By now the track meet should be over, he assumed, unless some cocky pole-vaulter were still going at it. He thought he might drive over quickly, tell the crowd about the warnings. Of course, they could see the storm in the sky, smell it in the air. You could feel tornadoes in sudden surges of temperature, in the deadly stillness one moment, the power of the strong winds the next. In the country, people knew hot spring mornings, no matter how pretty, were as much a false promise as the harlot in Proverbs.

"I'm going upstairs," he said. "I got to see if the lights at the field are still on."

In the upstairs stillness, the wind sounded more like an enemy, shaking rattles from the storm windows. If the kids were little now, it would be impossible to get them to sleep in the noise. From Lisa's bedroom you really couldn't see the field, but you could see the domed glow of the mercury lights maybe a mile away on the opposite edge of town. Angie always kept the shades up in Lisa's room—and it still was Lisa's room, everything about it. He wasn't unaware of the kind of stubborn grief that could turn a dead child's bedroom into a monument. He'd heard those stories often enough, even before Lisa was killed. But it wasn't that way with them. Lisa's room was Lisa's room because they had no other use for it. Angie didn't own a sewing machine; he had an office in the basement. Besides, Angie claimed that Karin might want some of her sister's clothes someday. To Angie, it just wasn't all that long ago yet.

He stood at the window and watched the branches of the maples out front shake in the wind. Miles away, back to the west, lightning ripped open the sky, and white houses across the street lit up in the sudden flashes, as if somewhere above the town some giant photographer was studying their lives with his candid photos.

It was the first thing she did when he put down the phone that night. She got out of their bed and walked directly to Lisa's room, as if to make sure that some cop hadn't made a false identification, as if she would find Lisa there asleep as she had been for so many times before, her rhythmic breathing steady as the pulse of their own sixteen years together. It was something neither of them could ever imagine, not in their sharpest nightmares—how it might be without one of the girls. And that's where she cried first, where they both sat and cried that night, there in Lisa's room.

He pulled down the blinds.

From their own room he could see the western sky, the thick clouds running overhead in what seemed confused directions. At night storms were so much more scary because you couldn't see clearly what was coming, not even in the intermittant flashes of lightning. He sat on their bed, his hands up on either side of the sill. He often thought it was odd, Karin sleeping right next to their bedroom now, with Lisa's room empty on the other end of the upstairs. Sometimes he thought of the arrangements of their bedrooms like the front seat of a car, the three of them—Karin, Angie and himself—tucked close together with no one on the passenger's side. He would have liked Karin to take Lisa's room, put a buffer between them so the sound of their love-making wouldn't seep through the walls so easily. But it was something he never would have said, not to Karin. He'd never said it to Angie either.

Long ago, before they were married, she had told him she wanted eleventy-seven kids, but somehow that had changed after Karin. Two had been enough. Maybe if they had had more.

He couldn't forget Karin's blackness the night when he invited the new teachers over for a little Christmas cheer. Angie had taken out the book, the scrapbook of Lisa's bracelets and school awards, the trinkets Angie had assembled so meticulously in the months after Lisa's death, as if their memories of their oldest daughter would be lost otherwise.

"I want you all to see this," she told them. "None of you ever knew our Lisa." Angie grabbed the plate of crackers and cheese, then set the scrapbook, cover open, on the coffee table. She expected them all to watch her turn the pages. She handed the plate to Karin. "Be a sweet and take this out of our way, will you, Kar?" she said. "It's such a

shame none of you ever knew her. Here, look at this—this is what her
first grade teacher wrote on her evaluation. We were in Delafield then.''
  Karin put the plate down on the piano bench and left, walked right
out of the house. Angie never knew. She never even guessed about
Karin's way of taking all of it. Angie forgot Karin.
  "Did I mention how she would play the organ?" Angie asked them,
her teeth out over her bottom lip as if to keep it from twisting.
  Vernon looked at the prairie fields, flat and colorless in the bursts of
sharp light. Storms were different on the prairie than they had been in
the suburbs. In the city there were so many people that you didn't worry
as much; it was as if the odds were thin when everywhere you looked
there were people. Out here the whole town seemed to sit on the land
like something unnatural, a mistake, like the clapboard towns in old TV
westerns, no trees to hide behind, no hills to ward off the danger.
Thunderheads came in like regular visitors; storms had minds and
tempers.
  He'd come back to his home town, to the plains, because on the prairie,
people were closer to God somehow. That's what he told himself.
  He heard the siren behind him, from the center of town, its flat-pitched
moan holding steady in warning. Still seated, he looked out once more,
as if there were something to see in the bitter sky.
  "Karin," he said, but he heard no one answer. He waited momentarily. It would be strange, the two of them in that fruit cellar alone,
because it wasn't like the old days anymore. It wasn't as if she needed
protection, needed a father to hold her on his lap.
  He went downstairs slowly, one hand up on the wall in the semi-
darkness. He called her again, almost quietly, but heard no voice. The
dining room was dark, and he heard no television voices from the den.
  "Karin?" he said, but she was gone.
  He walked back to the kitchen, but no one was there. Downstairs,
the warning siren was louder and more shrill. He looked down the basement stairwell to see if there were any lights, but there were none. She
had to be outside.
  He circled up through the kitchen and left out the front door. The wind
softened into a calm that barely disturbed the maples. A few light breezes
like cold slaps, quick and short, brushed by him, the only motion in the
air. The streets were deserted now. He ran to the curb and looked one

way, then the other, but the only thing moving was the police car a block east and south, its lights flashing steady red echoes off the white sides of houses that stood in the gaps between their place and Main Street. He remembered that she wouldn't be out front, out to the east. She would be in the backyard watching the sky. He ran up the sidewalk that curled around the north edge of the house and stopped at the far corner, looking for a pillar of darkness against the strange green air.

"Karin," he said, louder.

He had talked to Benson, the school psychologist, about all of it once himself. "There are professionals who say you've got to give grieving parents five whole years to unscramble their lives," Benson had said. "I've heard that said. You shouldn't try to say anything to them for at least five years."

He hadn't asked him about siblings.

Somewhere it was written, he remembered, "Faith," or so it echoed in his head, "is the assurance of things hoped for, the conviction of things not seen." New Testament, he said to himself, New Testament.

He found her sitting in the back yard grass, her legs bent beneath her, her robe laid smoothly over her lap, watching the sky, as if there were stunt pilots moving playfully back and forth before her.

"Karin, it's dark, for pity sake. Even if one comes, you're not going to be able to see it at night." He put one knee down next to her and watched the sky.

"Maybe you're right," she said.

Lightning played behind the clouds like July sparklers.

"It's something, isn't it—how calm it got all of a sudden?" She never took her eyes off the storm.

"Perfect weather for it," he said.

"Sometimes it takes two-by-fours and runs them like long spears through metal barrels. You believe that?"

"It's happened." He put down the other knee and sat on his legs beside her. "You know we ought to be in the basement. I'm not particularly interested in some wild trip to Oz."

"I've never seen a tornado," she said. "I can get down there if I have to."

The sky turned a dim rust color; layers of clouds, black against gray, rushed as if driven along above them, but the open backyard seemed somehow protected by a odd, quilted calm.

"Your mother would be wild, you know that?—both of us hanging around out here?" he said. "Your mother'd chew me out but good for such foolishness."

But she sat there gazing into the night sky.

"This is almost suicidal, Karin," he said. "We could get arrested."

"I want to sit right here till it comes," she said. "I want to see it coming—this big black funnel. I want to stand here and watch it come—"

"It's nothing to play with, honey," he said. "We better get inside—"

Lights burned in the neighbor's house, but the world seemed almost dead otherwise.

"You're sick of it too, aren't you?" Karin said. "You're mad at her just like I am for always having to talk about it. That's why we're not in the basement. That's why you never yell at me. You don't like it either—how she talks." She looked at him without turning to face him.

He pulled himself down to her completely, felt the cool grass beneath his fingers. "She's my wife, Karin. I love her." He covered her open hand with his.

"But you hate it too—the way she's got to talk about it all the time— on and on, over and over. You do, don't you?" Her face looked sturdy, her eyes aggressive. She was fighting him for an answer.

"I don't know what I think," he said. "Your mother's got her way of dealing with it. We all got to find our ways, all of us."

Karin combed through her hair with her fingers and bit back the tears. When it finally came, it was emphatic and unforgiving, her lips drawn like a line fence across her face. "I think she's shit, Dad. I think what my mother does is pure shit. I hate her."

He waited in the eerie darkness, waited in silence, and finally, he let it pass. His father would have slapped him silly for saying that about his mother, but his father never lost a child, never had to look into Karin's eyes.

She sat up, turned so her knees were beneath her, her thighs slightly apart, her hands down in her lap, trying to be strong, trying, he knew, to fight back tears.

Thunder started in a sly crackle, then slammed into the silence, but she sat there sternly, stiff as a tree, until slowly her hands rose and stretched over her eyes. Angie would have asked to be held at such a time, but Karin didn't want to be touched. He could feel her own strength rise in the way his own heart was rushing.

In his fingers he felt the ground itself through the stubble grass. "Come on," he said, "it's all over now." He tried to take her arm as he pulled up slowly from the ground.

But she pulled away from him. "Aren't you going to say anything?" she said. "You heard what I said."

"It's over," he told her. He put one hand up behind her neck. "You're not going to see your tornado. Listen—" The sound of rain swept towards them, a battalion of tiny foot soldiers. The wind lifted her hair back from her face. "It's over. Let's go in."

He saw rain coming like a sheet suddenly unveiled from the sky over the prairie fields west; in the flashes of lightning, he saw it blowing toward them steadily, easily, hanging in the sky.

"Your grandfather used to say that once the rains come, the tornado's past. It's like an 'all clear.' "

The wind returned as if suddenly unleashed.

The tears ran out finally and fully from her twisted face. She used the back of her fists to rub through her eyes. "I'm sorry, Dad," she said. "I don't know how to feel."

Her shoulders felt so broad when he squeezed her, too broad for his youngest daughter. "It's over," he said. "There'll be another time. Come on, your mother would kill us."

They rushed through the opening volleys of a downpour his father would have called a gully-washer, a shower that came so fast that at the back door both of them felt the water down their cheeks and through their hair.

"I'll talk to her, Karin," her father said when they both stood wiping their feet in the back hall. "She should hear what we have to say."

Later, together on the couch in dry clothes, they heard the news that a tornado had leveled a barn and a grain bin not more than thirty miles west, straight west, nowhere near Sheldon.

They were sitting there together when Angie came home.

"I'm sorry I was gone," she said. "You don't know how scared I was away from you two. Is everything okay here?"

He took his wife's hand when she stood there next to them, just took her hand, first, and let the silence fill in around them.

Pirouettes

Kate's father had been a drinker too, but he had never had any faith at all to speak of, and neither did her mother. She remembered those late nights when she was very young, when the sound of his rage would explode out of the kitchen down the hall to the bedroom, where the girls would hear every last word, three girls trying to pretend—even to each other—that they were asleep and oblivious to the hurt in their mother's crying and his ugly swearing. Kate knew every cuss word long before they came up on the playground.

When she was eight, her mother packed up the girls and left him, moved to an old farm place north of Easton.

But Frank wasn't the same kind of drinker her father was. When Frank had too much it simply exaggerated all his faults; it didn't turn him into something he wasn't otherwise. Besides, Frank was a believer, even if he was struggling. So was she.

During the worst times, she often felt that it was her faith that made living with him more difficult. She couldn't just get up and leave like her mother, because faith kept her there with him, gave her commitment. She wouldn't have dared to say those things to her friends, because they had been Christians their whole lives. They knew so very much more about it than she did.

"How come you never say anything good about me?" Frank said one night when he came home late again. His back to her, he unbuttoned his shirt in the slanting light of the closet.

She wanted to act as if she were sleeping, but she knew that even if she would, he would shake her awake because he expected his wife to be there when he came home, to listen to him, bring her into the same conversation. "I do, Frank," she said. "I really do."

"When?"

"You should hear me sometimes," she said. She often thought it might be better if he would just yell like her father used to, get it all out of his system once in awhile, rather than stay in the same rut. "I know that if you could just write a couple of policies everything would be okay. I know that—"

He stood before the open door, his body blocking most of the light from the closet bulb. She closed her eyes when he slipped on his pajamas. "I work hard at it," he said. "You understand that, don't you?"

"Of course, I know it's just a matter of time."

"Only time an insurance man can work is at night." He pulled the string, and the room fell back into darkness. She felt his knee nudge the side of the bed, heard his hands flip back the covers and smooth the sheet. Slowly, he backed himself in, the bed leaning in his direction as finally his weight came to rest. "Rotten economy," he said.

She turned onto her stomach and watched him stare up at the ceiling, his touseled hair pointing up and out from his forehead.

"Fact is, nobody's got any money, not for insurance, not for new cars, not for anything. Lunkheads," he said.

She knew what she was supposed to do. Submission, the Bible said. But it never came easily. "We've got to be there for our husbands," the other women said, the ones who had always been Christians.

Her mother had it easier, just running away the way she did, raising a family without him.

Sometimes she wondered how many of the other women in the neighborhood—so many of them model wives, model mothers, always baking, cooking, and canning beans—she wondered how many of them really knew how hard it was to do something which they all so sweetly confessed had to be done. It's one thing to say it, she thought. It's one thing to talk about it after reading the Bible and praying together, becoming emotional, but it's quite another to lie there and smell him beside you, listen to him go over the story you've heard so often before.

Submission, the Bible said. She reached over and put her hand on his arm—kept it there, kept it there.

"You tell people, you know?—you tell them—here's the facts: 'You die tomorrow and this is how much your wife is going to need just to stick you in the ground.' That's what you tell them. Cold, hard facts. But they don't want to think about it—nope. Shortsighted really, you know? It's the stinking economy, too—''

She could feel the tension in his upper arm, his muscles twitching with each syllable.

"Lord knows I wish I could make things better for us. You know I'm trying, don't you?''

She pinched his arm to tell him she knew.

"It's you I'm working for, you know. You and Shirleen and Donny. Shoot, by myself I could make it, but I know what's right. I got to provide. I know that—''

In the darkness she could see his eyes glaring up at the ceiling.

"Thing is, sometimes I need to hear that you appreciate me, you know? It's just that sometimes you take me for granted.''

"No,'' she said quickly.

"You need me?'' he said.

"Yes, of course—''

"I got to hear you say it. A man's got to hear his wife say that every once in a while. And you mean it, don't you? You aren't just saying it now?'' He turned toward her to be sure that she was nodding.

She needed him, of course. Once she'd loved him; she still did somehow, even though it was different now. They were different together. But before God they'd promised, before God and whole church full of people, most of them church people, friends of Frank's folks.

"You crying?'' he said.

"No.''

"Jeez, you cry and it just makes me feel horrible. Try to stop, will you?''

"I'm not crying—really,'' she said.

"You got to be strong, Kate. I need somebody strong. Takes an insurance man some before he can sit back and let it roll in. You don't make it overnight in this business.''

He had been at it for fifteen years. She remembered the first week as if it were just last month. "I know that,'' she said. "I'm behind you.''

He reached over and laid his arm across her stomach, squeezed her at the ribs, light and quick like a handshake.

Her breath came easier now, because she knew that the whole conversation was over. He squeezed her again, then turned away from her, rolling on his side the way he always did, knees in, arms up over his chest, jerking the sheet close around his neck.

She turned on her side to face his back and laid her arm across his chest. It was what she had to do, even on nights when he came home the way he did. She was a believer now, not an outsider anymore, and she knew what God had said in His Word.

When she heard his breaths turn slow and noisy, she turned back away from him. She remembered that somewhere the apostle Paul had written about fighting the good fight of faith.

* * * * *

Kate Baker knew the day was coming when she would lose the typing job she had worked at in her own home for close to eight years, ever since the kids were old enough not to demand so much attention. The woman at the agency had explained more than a year ago that it was only a matter of time until the county courts went to computers. There would be no need for any typing; all the court transcripts spun out in errorless copy. "You wouldn't believe what that machine will do," the lady had said, as if it were some wonderful, miraculous thing.

The money would be missed, of course. Frank didn't want her employed outside the home. "How often don't you hear of families having problems once the wife starts working?" he had said several times in the presence of friends. At home he'd tell her that her working would reflect on him somehow. It had taken almost a year for her to get him to accept the typing job, even though she could do it right there in the family room.

But the transcripts had strengthened her faith, even helped her with Frank. When she typed them up—divorce court, juvenile hearings, felonies—she saw her own husband in perspective. Maybe he was worse than some Easton men, if you believed their wives; but she knew there were other women who suffered worse than she did.

Sometimes the cases involved people giving up far too easily. "Go on back," she would tell the transcript, earphones spinning out the details of some silly divorce proceedings. "Go on back to your wife. It's not so bad really. It's nothing worse than others go through."

Sometimes they seemed too ready to quit, directionless.

She told her friends that typing up court records was like listening to soap operas, and they thought that was great.

* * * * *

In the afternoon Kate walked out to the ice pond, as she did whenever she could during the winter months. Some of her friends walked around town early in the morning for exercise. Some, more ambitious, jogged. But she had always loved to skate.

During the day no one used the community ice rink that one of the city employees created with a fire hose out back of the village shed, two blocks from the frame house where they lived. On the ice, she knew she was alone.

After school, kids were out there, slipping around like circus clowns, playing slapstick hockey with tree branches and balled-up aluminum foil from school lunches, just as they always had, even when she was a girl. At night the junior high showed up in gangs of rambunctious boys and giggling girls, mixing it up a bit in the darkness, throwing snowballs and pushing each other around like bear cubs, the boys showing off with their roughhousing, letting out a dirty word once in a while, until just about ten when they left, sometimes with a kiss or two on cold, chapped lips, as she remembered, kisses full of tension and strange power.

Just after lunch she walked out to the pond, her skates tied over her shoulder, sat on the bench and jerked the laces tightly over her ankles, slapping the red strings into the six top hooks nearly half-way up to her knees. All morning she typed; by afternoon she needed to be out in the crisp air.

Skates on, she walked through the snowy apron and pushed herself onto the pond, evenly and smoothly, as if it were some glossy stage. Every other morning a city worker would haul out the hose and spray the surface into glass, so that by just after lunch the ice was always perfect, the sun warm, the air crisp. There was something lovely about being first to cut marks on the new ice, she thought.

She rolled her fingers into fists inside her mittens and pushed her hands into her coat pockets so that only her long legs moved as she floated over the ice in even strokes, backwards, then forwards, still warming up.

She remembered learning to skate on the Easton pond; her older sisters had seen to it she learned. The Seward girls always skated alone on Sunday mornings, like the outsiders they were, while the rest of the Easton kids would be safely tucked away into one of the churches in town.

At first her sisters had stood beside her, holding her up while her little feet squirted out clumsily, even when she wore those first double runners. Eventually she refused their help, plunging out on her own in uneven steps over the surface.

She had never really understood she was an outsider until junior high. By then she could handle herself well on skates, her skinny legs churning out more speed than most boys could. They chased her just as regularly as they did any other seventh grade girl, but she realized she wasn't really one of them when she understoood that she was the only one who didn't go to Sunday School. There were parts of their conversations that she simply didn't catch, as if she were hard of hearing or something. And she didn't laugh at the stupid jokes the others laughed at, covering their giggles with their hands, jokes laced with words she remembered too well from her father.

Skating reminded her of all that, all of the emotions. On the ice Frank Baker had asked her to the Snowball Party when she was just a freshman, one of just a few ninth-grade girls lucky enough to go. Her sisters were excited—Kate could go to four Snowballs in high school, they said, just think of it! And Frank Baker, after all, was Tony's brother—Tony Baker, the football star, son of Clarence, from such a good Easton family, and they were only the Sewards.

Everyone knew he was going to ask her out, but when he finally did, his hands jammed in the pockets of his letter jacket, she was still nervous as anything. She said yes, of course. She always did say yes to Frank.

The morning after that first date, her sisters quizzed her. "Did he kiss you?" they said. "I bet he did."

She wouldn't say anything more than what her smile told them, but she never forgot that first night's kiss, the two of them standing just inside the doorway, Frank's hands suddenly on her waist, his gentle awkwardness meeting her own anticipation.

Her body slowly warming, her legs loose beneath her, she turned backwards and floated over the ice, long arms extended, her body bent just a bit at the waist and her knees in a slight crouch, the teeth of her figure skates cutting perfectly patterned x's into the the surface at the edge of the pond. Round and round she moved, skating the same cross-over stroke—cut and glide, cut and glide—glancing back over her left shoulder occasionally to follow the edge of the ice, or beside her, where her shadow revealed her slenderness, even at forty.

Breathing hard, she felt the warmth rise in her, come up like a cloud into her cheeks and spread down into her toes and out into the very tips of her fingers, until the cold became a comfort.

She thought of it as a dance, sometimes trying pirouettes in the middle where the ice was glass, first stretching her arms out to balance her weight evenly, then spinning through turn after turn, as she had when she was girl, like the skaters on TV, until she stopped, winded, to look down at the pattern of concentric circles she had drawn beneath her.

* * * * *

On her way home she stopped at the post office. Her two children were faithful writers, Shirleen a bit more than Donny. Both were in college. No Seward had ever gone to college, but Frank was the only Baker who hadn't graduated. She knew she had to thank Frank for the children's ability in school. They both did very well, way out there in Kansas, so terribly far from home. But it was better that way, she thought, hundreds of miles from Easton, both of them removed from problems.

Shirleen had made it very clear that she wanted to stay in town and go to junior college, to be there with her mother, but Kate had insisted, never once stating the reason both of them thoroughly understood to be primary. Frank had complained about the high tuition, but Kate had made up her mind that Shirleen should go. Both kids had been good enough in school to pick up some scholarship money anyway. Most of what was left, Grandpa Baker picked up, happy that his grandchildren were going to a Christian college.

She pulled Shirleen's letter from the box and opened it immediately, sliding her finger beneath the flap.

"My teeth have been killing me," she wrote, "but I'm hoping to be able to postpone oral surgery. Yipes, toothaches hurt!"

It wasn't like Shirleen to complain.

"If I can just last till September, I can pay for it myself—if I can get a teaching job, of course."

She had to laugh to think about Shirleen not getting a job. It wouldn't be any kind of problem for a bright student like she was.

When she came out of the post office, she read the letter again while she waited for a hundred or so empty coal cars lumbering back to Chicago via the tracks right through the center of town, her skates hanging over her shoulder. When she read it through again, she understood what was being said. That little paragraph, full of exclamation points, was an unspoken request for money. There was no way her daughter could hold out until September.

When Shirleen was only five, the dentist found a half-dozen cavities. She had sat there curled up in the big leather chair, perfectly quiet, her mouth gaping, a little crossways wrinkle in her chin. And when it was finished, the dentist had lectured her on candy, not being sermony or pushy; but Shirleen hadn't liked what he said, because she knew it meant a limit on suckers and chocolate stars. Besides, her little brother Donny, two years younger, didn't have a speck of cavities.

"I wish I could just forget about those dumb cavities," Shirleen had said that night after supper. It wasn't unusual for Shirleen to say odd things when she was a child, and at first Kate had laughed a little, thinking of her daughter haunted by the dentist chair. But the words stayed with her for several days because the idea seemed bigger than the cavities—for Shirleen, the dentist's news and his little sermon meant the end of candy and everything sweet. Kate thought her daughter was too young to have to learn about nothing more or less than sin itself.

By the time she got home from the pond and the post office and had a cup of coffee before her on the table, she knew she would have to approach Frank about the teeth thing. The thought of Shirleen in pain so far away was reason enough to bring it up, no matter how she hated to think about the inevitable conversation.

* * * * *

Just before three, Wanda Detweilen called. "It's been just ages since we've had a good talk," she said, asking herself over. Kate had nothing but store-bought cookies in the cupboard, but Wanda insisted she'd just be in and out. "Don't even put on the coffee," she said. She claimed she had a big night planned, something with her husband and the kids again.

"You won't believe it," she said, after a few minutes' conversation. "Someone told Eric Jansen—right in church—that deacons shouldn't be wearing sweaters when they take offertory." She rolled her eyes and took another sip of coffee. "Maybe not outright just like that," Wanda said, "but that's what was meant."

"What exactly was said?" Kate asked.

"Someone came up to him after the service and told him that if he couldn't afford a suit, whoever-said-it would help buy one for him." She nodded when Kate handed over the plastic cream server she had taken from the kitchen cupboard. "That's just about sinful, isn't it? Can you imagine the gall? Some people are so trivial."

Kate smiled.

"I mean—my goodness, what do clothes have to do with being a Christian? Sometimes I think people in our church haven't changed at all in fifty years. Really!"

It had been more than a year since Kate wore a new summer dress to church. "Maybe somebody was trying to be nice," she said.

Wanda looked incredulous. "You don't know these people, Kate. Some of them get all excited about irrelevant things like that. You have to have lived here for a while to know what something like that means."

Thirty years already she had lived in Easton.

Wanda was just overweight enough to look like a good wife, Kate thought. She dressed well, brushed her long blond hair back into a bun, and wore sufficient make-up to tease her complexion into a perfect blush so that she looked like she did when she was a popular high school girl on the prom court.

"So anyway—" Wanda said. She was the type who had to fill every silent space in a conversation.

Kate smiled.

"How are things between you and Frank?"

From the moment she had put down the phone, Kate knew that particular question had prompted Wanda's visit. The only mystery would be discovering when it would poke its way into the conversation.

"We're fine as always," she said.

"Praise the Lord," Wanda said.

"Yes," Kate answered.

"You know, I'll never forget the day you were baptized, Kate." Wanda shook her head back and forth, always smiling, as if the memory recreated a miracle. "What was it now—fifteen years ago?"

"Twenty-one," Kate said. She hated the feeling of being thrust suddenly on stage.

"I don't think anyone could forget how you looked up there. You were so beautiful."

"I was happy," Kate said. "I really was."

"You were so pretty—pregnant and everything," Wanda said. "It was so nice." She smiled very sincerely. "You know, I don't think of you anymore as an outsider."

Kate smiled at the compliment.

* * * * *

"Seems to me sometimes my life is one long list of debits," Frank told her later that night. He wasn't drunk really, but then he never got drunk, at least that's what he always said. "It's just too bad that Shirleen can't hold out for a couple months till she gets out of school. She could pay that bill herself."

"She mentioned that," Kate said, "but if she really could, she wouldn't have said anything at all." They lay together and spoke as if they were addressing the ceiling.

"What do you mean?"

"Shirleen didn't ask for money really, not outright. Did you read it? I left it downstairs, right by the light switch. You couldn't miss it."

"I'll get it in the morning."

For a moment she felt hate reaching out of her. She couldn't believe that he could purposely neglect reading a letter from his daughter. But she held back, trying to remember those computer printouts of the kids' grades. Besides, there was still more to be said.

"If she didn't ask, what makes you think she needs it right now?" he said.

There were times when it could be so painful even to talk to him. How could she explain to him that she knew what her daughter was thinking, even though Shirleen didn't print it out in black and white?

"If she didn't need it, she wouldn't have even brought up the subject,'' she said.

Frank turned towards her and laughed. ''I don't get why people don't dare to say what's on their minds. Why doesn't she just come out and say it—if that's what she needs?''

She lay motionless, as if her body were enclosed in cement. ''Maybe she's afraid of asking,'' she said.

''She's scared of her own parents?''

Kate reached down her leg and took a handful of her nightgown in her fingers. She felt pulled into something dark and bottomless that she'd always found easier simply to avoid, something right there at the core of his own character, something shrouded by the haze of liquor. He wanted the truth, but the truth would hurt him.

''Maybe she's afraid that we might say no to her.''

She felt the way he was looking at her now, his smelly breath in a great pool.

''No is an honest answer,'' he said. ''She can't kick about the truth. I guess I just don't understand this whole female thing you got—not saying things that you mean and all that. She doesn't dare ask a simple question because she's afraid of the truth?—is that it?'' He inhaled heavily through his nose. ''Geez, Kate, sometimes I wonder about Shirleen—you got to have more guts than that to make it in the world.'' He propped himself up with his elbow, and laughed again.

''We've got to help her,'' she said.

''Afraid of our saying no—is that it? Why should she be afraid?''

She waited, as if he were going to answer the question himself. But the silence sat there in the open space between them.

''Do you have any idea why she'd be scared, Frank?'' she said.

Immediately she felt his eyes penetrate, and she wished that like her father he would strike her so she could feel one tangible sting across her face—visible, verifiable pain, an ugly blue bruise. But he wouldn't do that, she knew. He wasn't like her father. He wouldn't beat her. He was far too much a believer to beat her.

''You aren't trying to make me feel guilty again, are you?'' he said, and then he lay flat on his back, his arms above his shoulders, resting over his forehead. ''I know I'm not rich. You take some kind of joy in laying out my shortcomings, or what?''

''No, Frank, no—really—''

It took every bit of her strength for her to turn on her side and face him once again. It took the memory of love itself, of stolen kisses in high school hallways, the pleasure of giving herself to him so long ago, the sharp memory of cold water running down her cheeks at her own baptism and the graceful fragrance of flowers at the font, the horrible pain and immense joy commingled at the birth of two beautifully pink newborns. All of that it took for her to reach for him again, as if she were starting over once more, trying to start out new again.

And it took even more, she knew, now that she was a believer. It took faith for her to touch his arm, to run her fingers over his chest and keep her hand there on him, as if her own touch, or God's through her, could still the waves. She held him there, she knew, not because she was convinced that holding him would make tomorrow any different from today, but because she stood so painfully convinced that what she was doing was absolutely and finally right in her new world.

And yet her fingers were burning, as if she had just come in from an icy January morning.

"Our daughter needs her teeth fixed," she said. "That's the honest truth, honey—" She felt her voice shake with the edge of tears in her eyes. She turned her face into her pillow, so there was nothing but her one arm awkwardly reaching through the cold space of a whole world between them.

The bed rolled slightly beneath her when he turned to his side.

"We'll have to do it then," he said. "We don't have the money, but we'll have to do it. We'll find some way."

She felt his hand reach for her, felt it on her own arm, his palm and cold fingers taking her wrist, holding it for a moment, then turning over against her skin, the back of his hand lying motionless on her, then waving softly, back and forth, up to her shoulder, his touch awkward and gentle as a first kiss.

So Far From Home

Beyond the front canopy, the sun's heat took the edge off the brisk desert morning as if that ball of burning gases hung just over the heads of those who stepped outside after the Palm Sunday service, the organ music behind them. April heat was Arizona's finest, Neil thought, bone dry, efficient, never killing the way a July day could turn the whole city to bacon. "Back home now it's spring," he said to Orv Klassen, a snowbird from his own hometown. "Streets are full of puddles. The snow is melting. I miss that. There's no spring in the desert."

The old man wet his lips with his tongue. "Freeport snow this time of year is pea gravel. If it wouldn't be for Ma, I'd stay down here all year round." Klassen pulled a cigar out of his pocket and peeled it out of the cellophane, looking around at the same time to see who might be watching.

"I don't care," Neil said. "I wish I were heading back north with you." He looked up over the long white ceiling panels that he and Helene and Mary Beth had finished just before dark last night in their shirtsleeves. "I still miss the Midwest."

"You want to go?" Klassen said. "You drive Ma and I'll stay down here with Helene. I can paint, you know. That don't take no smarts. I can still cut an edge." He drew a slow, straight line down in front of him, his hand shaped around an imaginary brush.

"I miss this time of year up there," Neil told him. "The desert's no place for Easter. Nothing's coming out of the ground."

Klassen stuck the cigar into the corner of his mouth, unlit. "Never fails either. We go back up north and we get dumped on. Big blizzard. You start thinking winter's gone, she takes another swing." He took the cigar back out of his mouth and turned it in his fingers. "I told Ma we ought to wait 'til May, but Ma's got to be home Easter, she says.

It's a holiday. Shoot, last year we got stuck in the house for two-three days. Accidents all over the city. In fact, this woman got killed—woman and the guy she was with. That's how bad a storm—two people got killed yet, late April.'' He pulled a long wooden match out of his side pocket. ''You knew her too, Neil. You was still living in Freeport when she come to church, I bet—what's her name again? Oh, shoot, Ma would know. Let me think—'' He stood there staring at the cigar.

''I knew her?'' Neil said.

''Sure. She got killed in that snowstorm that come up yet after we got back. She and this guy.'' He reached down and the match popped into flame when he slapped it off the sole of his shoe. ''Bad deal too. People didn't know about her either, you know? I mean it wasn't like the old days anymore when the old Dutchmen just stuck her in hell right away, but it was a bad deal. The match kept burning right in front of his face. ''Ach, what was that name?'' he said. ''You'd know her— Helene would.''

Neil looked up at the canopy trim, where his own daughter's work seemed nearly as good as his own. She was only a kid.

''Re'-something—Rieks, Rem—I can't remember. Wait a minute— Remkes, that's it. Remkes.'' He stuck the match to the end, and the cigar popped into flame. ''Remkes, sure—''

The name froze him. ''What are you saying?'' Neil said.

''She got killed last year in a wreck—in that storm—''

''Dead?''

''Yeah. She and that man she was with—and everything wasn't on the up and up there either, you know—they was both killed when they shouldn't have been out and she with those kids and all. You had to know her, I bet. About your age. Pretty girl, but she always had a painted face—''

Karen Remkes.

''She used to go to our church. Karen, her name was. You know who I'm talking about?''

''I don't remember,'' he said.

''It's not for us to judge either—it ain't for any of us—but you can't help it when a woman like that let her own kids home alone and was out with this guy she wasn't married to. You never knew her, you say?''

He shook his head.

"A bad one. People in church felt awful about that whole business for months. Everybody tried to figure out what they didn't do right—how we could have done better with her. You must remember her. She was a hard looking woman, but inside Ma said real sweet. Wore makeup, lots of it. You remember?—"

Karen Remkes.

He didn't tell Helene that Karen was dead, even though Helene and Pastor Feringa were the only other people in the world who knew the whole story. Feringa was long gone from Freeport now, in New Jersey somewhere, at some inner-city church.

But he didn't tell Helene about Karen Remkes. All afternoon, he let it go, the kids out back in the swimming pool on the first hot Sunday of the year, Palm Sunday. Helene took a nap, but he didn't join her; and he never mentioned it all day, even though the whole story stayed floating in him like something not even swallowed.

Karen Remkes.

That was twelve years ago, at a time when the world wore a whole different face. He laid on the couch in a daze of memories, the splashing of the kids playing behind him like strange music.

It had happened five years after he'd married Helene, who'd dated him through two shoddy years in college, then waited like a saint for two more long years while he was in the service doing nothing worth remembering at some backwater arsenal in South Carolina. It had happened five whole years after he'd married her, the woman who kept waiting for him to x-off the last day of his tour. He'd married Helene right away then, a month after the army. After all that waiting she'd done he thought her so pure that he didn't have the right to tarnish the porcelain image she had of their future together—all of it romance: three pretty children saying sweet things in some perfect two-story house with a front porch so wide that people begged to visit—those kind of dreams Helene always had for the two of them.

Karen Remkes.

All night he saw that painted face in his mind, one of those nights when you fight yourself to sleep and even when you're sleeping you're not sure that time has ever passed at all. Every last twist against the sheets woke him, set him wondering about whether he'd ever quit that conversation with Klassen. He kept seeing that cigar glow, kept hearing the

accusation in the old man's guileless words. "You had to know her,"
Klassen had said, pushing it into his soul like something barbed.

Sometimes Helene would turn to him in her sleep and lay her arm
over his side, strum her fingers against his stomach, as if by some instinct to please him.

He couldn't forget. Karen Remkes.

* * * * *

Rosa Benjamin wore a painted face, her eyelids swept with silver, her
dark, perfectly sculpted cheeks already tinted in amber when he had arrived, so early that he had thought she wouldn't look as rich as she really
was at that time of day. Her husband had just joined the Suns, been traded
from Seattle, and they were moving into a mansion in Cave Creek, on
the edge of the desert. She'd wanted some interior work done, and he'd
painted for ballplayers before.

"I'll try to stay out of your way," she said, when he was dropping
the plastic around the front door. "If you want something, be sure to
ask. I got coffee on in the kitchen most all the time." Her smile was
perfectly clean.

A week before when he'd been there for estimates, he'd called her
Mrs. Benjamin, but she'd insisted he call her Rosa. And when he'd seen
a book by Charles Swindoll on her kitchen shelf, he'd been surprised.
"Are you a Christian, Mrs. Benjamin?" he'd said that day.

"My mother sure was," she'd said. "I don't know if I can help it
or not." She laughed at herself, shrugged her shoulders.

"So am I," he'd told her.

"So I was told," she said.

Right then, he'd figured his estimates weren't all that important.

But it was her make-up that stunned him the morning he started working there, the blush and the silver in the shadow, even though she was
black and didn't look at all like Karen Remkes. Her painted face.

It seemed so long ago. When he'd started seeing Karen, it had come
as a shock to him to feel it oddly possible to love two people at once,
even if he couldn't do justice to either of them. He and Helene had had
two kids then already—two kids, too fast. He'd already spent his GI bill
on a college degree that got him nothing more than a love for Nathaniel

Hawthorne. He didn't want to teach, so he'd taken a job in Freeport, making tires. He wasn't happy.

At the time, there was every reason to explain Karen Remkes. If he would have sat down then and listed all the reasons, he could have built a case for doing what they did, airtight. He remembered her too well—the way her long legs wound around each other when she sat on a stool, the freckles down her neck and the depth they brought to her skin, her long fingers, and how she constantly toyed with a strand of her long black hair when her elbows were up on a table.

Now she was dead—so many years later, out of nowhere. It was as if the credits for some long film had finally passed and he'd opened his eyes to an entire theater emptied.

After he laid the plastic over the rugs, he removed the switch covers and taped along the woodwork. How he'd ever come to painting for a living, he really didn't know. He and Helene and their two oldest left for Arizona once the dust from Karen Remkes had settled, once Helene had decided that she would fight for him, fight herself maybe—once she'd forgiven him. Feringa said a change would do them good, so they'd moved to Arizona and left the ghost somewhere back there in Freeport, a story no one else—only Feringa and Helene and Karen Remkes—had ever known. All of that was twelve years—a whole lifetime—ago.

Karen Remkes was dead, for a whole year.

He pulled out a brush and softened it against his palm.

"You a basketball fan, Mr. De Master?" Rosa said, her voice coming up as if out of a cave.

He turned towards her. She was a tall woman, taller than he was, and very slim, very beautiful. "My son won't let me finish this job without getting your husband's autograph," he said.

"I'll try to remember," she said. "They're in Boston right now—then the Knicks and Atlanta. He's hardly ever around."

She wore old jeans, even though her face was perfectly made up, as if some professional had been there to do it just this morning.

"I can get you some tickets," she said. "We got them all over this house. Maybe I can find some myself for the next time they're in town."

"You don't have to"

"Shussh now," she said. "We get tickets all the time."

Her voice had a sweet Southern smile in it.

"You go to some church in town here?" she said.

He dipped the edge of the brush in the pail, still brimming full, and brought it up to the edge of the ceiling. "We do," he said. "A little church on the east side you never heard of."

"That so?" she said. "I was brought up in a little church in Chicago. Wasn't on the east side though." She laughed as if he should know why.

"You go somewhere here?" he said.

"Not much. When Eliot's home, he's tired. Plays on Saturday nights, sometimes Sunday afternoons. And going's a bother too, usually. Ain't a lot of churches in this town with black folks tall as he is." She crossed her arms over her chest and watched him. "He's got to be signing all the time—'Gee, it's Eliot Benjamin!' You know what I mean?"

"Sure," he said. "I understand."

"Well, my Mama doesn't."

The paint brushed on smoothly—gray, just the slightest gray. "That's what mothers are for," he said.

"It ain't all in going to church anyway," she said. "'Some keep the Sabbath going to church;/I keep it staying at home,/With a boblink for a chorister,/And an orchard for a dome.'"

"I've heard that," he said.

"Emily Dickinson," she told him. "Except I haven't seen no boblinks in the desert"

"I knew I'd heard that."

He'd never learned to feel comfortable with a customer right behind him, watching him stroke on the paint.

"It's Easter week," she said.

"Pardon me?"

"I said, 'It's Easter week,' and I feel so far from home."

When he turned to her, she smiled, innocently, like a mother might have. She had need in her eyes, emptiness that's barely whispered, but determined, even desperate enough to make him turn his head finally, drop the brush to the pail when she wouldn't look away.

She'd left then, had been gone most of the day.

He worked all day, trying to decide whether or not he was going to tell Helene. The whole story was so far behind them, so deeply layered in months and years of a new life that to bring it all back up again would only strip the trust that faith, and time, had laid there. She'd forgiven him. She'd never really said it, but he was sure he was forgiven.

The two of them had sat together in a cabin high up above the Mississippi, nothing but trees and bluffs, and eagles floating on updrafts over barges moving motionless on the river down below, a place not even an hour west of Freeport, a place Feringa knew they could be alone—Helene, and himself, and the preacher—and all day long they'd talked. Helene had cried off and on, but he couldn't.

By that time he'd had enough of Karen Remkes. By that time he knew he wanted Helene and the kids. He knew he wanted her back all right. He knew what was right, knew it in his head. Knew it. Of course he was forgiven. But he couldn't cry. He'd sat there all day long and tried as best he could to make it very clear that he wanted his family back and he was sorry for what had happened, for what had happened to Helene.

"Don't say it that way, Neil," Feringa had said. "Don't say 'it's what happened.' Say you're sorry for what you did."

And he did, time and time again.

Five years before that day on the river, he had come home from service, got off the plane at Midway, and looked for Helene in the crowd. "I'll pick you up after work," she'd said. "I'll be there with bells on." And she had. She stood there at the ramp with this silly corsage of mistletoe and three silver bells, even though it was the middle of August. He'd come back from his post in South Carolina, full of boredom and anger—guilt too maybe, because so many of his friends were dodging death in Vietnam. And there she stood like the holy virgin, waiting for him with bells on. And that day in the cabin, all she could do was bite her lip and wipe her eyes and look down at the floor. That's how he'd hurt her, this woman he loved now in ways he never really could describe.

"Stay away from her now," Feringa had told him when the two of them were alone after that longest of days. "Don't you dare come around her until she says she's ready to see you."

Alone, he'd followed the river north and taken a motel in Iowa, keeping the Mississippi between them, then left the number with the preacher. She let him alone there for three days, three days he'd spent lying around, watching TV or reading, finally picking up a paperback and trying to page through Hawthorne again, as if something might be back there, something full of ideals that he'd lost making tires. But all of it seemed gloomy and full of sin, as Hawthorne always had been.

Three days later she called, told him she was on the way.

"I don't want you here," he told her over the phone. "This place isn't good enough for you."

"Don't say that," she told him. "Don't ever say anything like that again to me. Don't protect me."

So that night he sat in the Sunset Motel, room 167, Dubuque, Iowa, staring at the ice cubes floating in a glass of Coke, as he listened to her tell him that she'd try, that she didn't promise anything because she knew that she couldn't take him back alone, not in the way she'd known him. But that God Himself was building her up, and that maybe the two of them could forgive him for what he'd done to her, even if she wouldn't forget—"couldn't," she'd said. Could never.

Three months later they moved to Arizona. Feringa said it would be a good idea.

He'd never seen Karen Remkes again.

Of course he'd been forgiven.

* * * * *

"How long are you going to be over there?" Helene asked him after that first Monday he'd painted at the Benjamin's.

"They're just moving in. I got the bedrooms yet and some closets— maybe a couple days." He was taking the dishes out of the dishwasher.

"You need me?" she said.

He thought maybe he hadn't heard her correctly. "What's that?"

"I said, 'do you need me'?"

"Of course."

"I mean to paint, dummy."

When he looked up into her eyes, it struck him as strange that she could smile so easily. "Oh," he said. "I get it now. You mean do I need you to come along and help me finish up?"

She put her hand up to his forehead as if he were sick. "You're as bad as our son, you know that?—absent-minded."

"Come on," he said. "I was just thinking about paint."

The darkness was gone from her eyes now. After all those years, he thought, no veil stood between them anymore, as it had for years after

Karen Remkes. Helene looked straight into his eyes now, as if there were nothing to hide from anymore.

When he reached down and took the orange juice pitcher out, water from the top splashed over the dishes on the bottom rack. "Shoot," he said.

"Something's bothering you," she said. "I can feel it."

He wanted to tell her. He wanted very badly to tell her.

That night he sat with her in front of the television, and he remembered a Fourth-of-July late afternoon when they'd listened to a Phoenix Symphony's 1812 Overture, complete with cannons. The two of them had sat together on the grass, little Mindy between her mother's crossed legs, Mary Beth wandering around on her own, picking up pop cans. She was almost eight then. He'd held Josh, then a baby. He'd made the ham sandwiches, and they'd carted them along in an Igloo cooler, ham sandwiches and Kool-Aid, and there they'd sat, a little family picnic with the cannons going off, one family in a couple thousand people in an Arizona sun, down deep in the west, a sun that must have decided to opt, that holiday, for mercy.

They never spoke of Karen Remkes that evening, but when he thought about it now he wondered if maybe that day was the beginning of their new life. Distrust had kept smoldering in both of them, but that night he remembered looking at her in that cotton skirt pulled up over her knees like some sweet hippy girl, Mindy in the nest, and he'd decided that he would never do it again, never.

"You hear me?" Feringa had said in that river cabin. "It'll probably be as hard the second time, but chances are that you're going to find another woman somewhere. You're going to hurt Helene again—you hear me?" The preacher leaned back, his elbows on the bed behind him, as if what he was saying wasn't so terribly important. "If we go by the numbers, Neil, statistics say you'll do it again."

Helene had sat beside the desk, her chair swung away from him. She wasn't crying just then, but she wasn't looking at him.

"But numbers don't run our lives. We got choices."

Neil nodded.

"Say it," Feringa said. "We got choices, don't we?"

"Yes, we do," he had said, as if the man was his C.O.

"And it's not going to happen again, is it? Tell this woman you've married, tell her and me and God himself that it's not going to happen again.''

He swallowed hard, pulled his hand up to his face. He had wished he could cry somehow, show her that he was sure he wanted her back.

"Tell her," Feringa said.

He'd said it that day, swore to it. And on the ride back home from the Arizona holiday concert, the kids asleep in the backseat darkness, he'd told her again, flat out, when he was sure she wasn't expecting it. "It won't happen again," he'd said. "I love you, Helene. You got to believe me."

They'd said nothing else, but she knew perfectly well what he meant. That was the last time that the two of them had met at the heart of a memory that would never really die.

But he knew that now he was the one with the painted face. As long as he'd keep Karen's death inside, he wouldn't be able to look at Helene. "Tomorrow," he said, during a commercial right before the news. "I got some extra closets. I get them finished and I'm done over there." He picked up a magazine from the table beside him. "Whyn't you come along?"

She looked up at him strangely.

"I mean, at the Benjamin's—the basketball star. Help me finish up?"

"Oh," she said. "I'd love it. I need to get out again."

Karen Remkes. He'd tell Helene tomorrow. They'd be alone in the mansion. He had to. Take the veil away.

* * * * *

When the lyrics would emerge from the bumpy rhythms and the wild vocals, he figured out that what was playing in the house was actually Christian music, heavy rhythm-and-blues, a style like Aretha Franklin, someone he hadn't listened to since college days. But it played all morning long that Tuesday, background music, because Rosa stayed home. Most all of the furniture was dropclothed and plastic strips ran over the carpeting, but the woman found things to do all over. Sometimes she'd sing along—Deniece Williams, she said it was, compact disc on the Sony half-uncovered in the living room.

He put Helene to work in the bedroom closets, while he finished up with the rolling. But Rosa was in and out all morning, as if she wouldn't pull herself away, and he couldn't get himself to bring it up with someone else around. The right moment never seemed to come.

Rosa ordered out and bought them lunch—egg rolls and a half dozen white cartons of Chinese food. She'd insisted on it, even though he had planned to take Helene to this little place in the desert that served up specialty sandwiches on a toy railroad.

"I'm going to have to call someone about the washer," Rosa said, over lunch. "I can't get it to work at all. Movers said they hooked it up and it's plugged in all right, but nothing much happens when I hit the buttons." She pushed the sauce around her plate with the last bite of an egg roll. "Eliot said just to get a new set once we moved here, but I got my mother in me. You get used to something and you don't want to quit so easy—know what I'm saying?"

Helene liked Rosa. Neil could tell it by the way he seemed to disappear when they talked together. "Maybe they didn't level it," he said. "The thing's got to be leveled. Sometimes movers don't do it."

"So who do I call?" she said.

"Let me take a look," he said. "Some repairman'll cost you thirty-five bucks just to drive out." He no sooner had it out than he remembered what kind of salary Eliot must bring down playing with the Suns.

"Little things like that get me. You're alone so often, you know?" Rosa said. "I got all the money in the world, but I don't always have him around." She said it right at Helene, aimed it at her. "You got it fine, you two working together. That's so nice."

"Don't you ever go along?" Helene said.

"It's no joy to live in hotels and bump along with fourteen men who act like boys. It's no big thrill."

She kept looking at Helene, kept addressing her alone, and Neil could see something emerging from her.

"Sometimes I don't know about him," Rosa said. "Sometimes I don't know even about us. I get scared."

"I'm sure you don't have to." Helene said.

"It's being alone that does it."

He knew that just at that moment Helene was figuring out in her head whether to keep it up now and hear the whole story out, or seal it right then and there, make some move back toward the bedroom closets that would show this woman that she hadn't the desire to listen to some rich lady spill out all the pain. He watched Helene, even though he knew what she would do.

She poked at a water chestnut, brought it up to her mouth slowly, one solitary chestnut, as if time were of no matter.

"We just moved, you know?" Rosa said. "It's a job with big money, but sometimes I wish Eliot was nothing more than a janitor—you know what I'm saying?"

Neil took a fork full of food directly from a carton. "Where's that washer?" he said. "Let me have a look."

She pointed at the open door off the kitchen. "It's right there around the corner. I'll pay you for—"

"For heaven's sake," Helene said, "don't be talking like that."

Only a washer and a dryer stood in the utility room. There were no boxes, only a pile of clothes, her things, on the dryer. There were no tools around; he figured her husband didn't need any tools—who needs to repair anything with the kind of salary he brought down, he thought, a power forward who could shoot like Eliot Benjamin?

Behind him, if he wanted to, he could hear their voices plainly, but he chose to busy himself with the washer. All he clearly heard were the silences that stretched out between some slow, checkerboard conversation. He sat down on the cement and felt beneath the steel frame for the adjustable risers. Of course, he had no level with him. He knew exactly where it was back home. If he were in his own utility room now, he could reach up and pull it off the top shelf, where Josh couldn't grab it. He'd just have to eyeball the lines and hope he could get it close enough.

He tried to bend down as low as he could to see the angle of the frame against the floor. He was right—it looked off. The movers hadn't leveled the machine.

He thought that maybe he'd need a piece of wood for a little shim, so he got to his feet and looked around. Maybe Rosa would have some little piece of something. He went to the door, still open, and that's when he heard gusts in Rosa's breathing. He stopped immediately, listening, but conscious too of the fact that his silence might be conspicuous.

"He was all I ever wanted," Rosa said, her voice muffled. "It's so hard to be alone."

He couldn't shut the door and not listen. They would know that he
was deliberately closing himself off. He didn't want to hear the two of
them. He didn't want to hear the pain.

"But I feel the Lord now," Rosa said. "It's like all I got is Him.
If I don't have Eliot, at least I got Him."

There he stood like some eavesdropper, but he had to listen in because
he didn't have a shim and he didn't have a level.

"You aren't really alone," Helene said. "You never are."

"That don't mean there's no pain. But I know He's there. First time
in years."

"Neil left me once," Helene said.

He turned away. He had no part in this conversation. Two women.
He could at least try to adjust the blame washer with the levelers. The
floor wasn't way out of whack. He could balance it somehow, eyeball
it close enough so that he could turn it on and see what happened. If
it would run, it would be close enough. She wasn't likely to have a piece
of wood anywhere around. Not even an old yardstick. Not people this
rich.

He heard Helene's voice, and he didn't want to listen. He didn't want
to hear, but it came in like something wired to his soul.

"I could've quit on him. I had all the right in the world. But when
I didn't have Neil, I felt God holding me up. I remember praying and
just knowing that God was right there above my head. Like I was a kid
again."

"But it hurts—"

"You can't trust anybody," Helene said.

"Sometimes I just sit alone in the bathtub and I cry. And I don't even
know why."

Helene waited. "I stood out over a river once in Illinois, and I could
have been the only one on earth right there—"

"I'm glad you're here," Rosa said.

Neil got to his haunches, then to his hands-and-knees in front of the
washer.

"I start to hate him. He comes back and I take him, and I don't trust
him sometimes—I get almost to hate him. And I start to hate myself—"

He slipped his legs beneath him and sat there in front of the washer.
He didn't really need a shim. He could adjust the whole thing well enough

with levelers. This was no old Midwestern basement, thawed into a jigsaw puzzle of cracked concrete.

"Neil had this other woman," she said. "I know all of that."

"That man of yours?" Rosa said.

He waited in silence.

"Years ago," Helene said.

The cement was cold against his hands. For a time during that day at the cabin on the river, she and Feringa were outside on the bluff, looking out into the sky at the eagles. He watched the two of them from the window, saw the pastor hold her. And then he had looked away because he didn't want to know that someone else could hold her when he knew he couldn't. He walked into the bathroom and stared at his face in the mirror, watched his eyes and tried to cry, stared himself in the face.

"He'll never be the same in my mind," Helene said. "I can't ever go back to what he was or what I was."

"But here you are—"

"It's different now, but I love him. He loves me too. But it's all different."

It hurt him to hear her say that, even if he knew it was true. He looked at the washer. He couldn't make it square. He couldn't do it without tools. He couldn't be sure.

"So where is the other woman?"

"She's dead now," Helene said. "For a year already."

The steep percussion of the music in the background shook around him, in his head, when she said what she did so clearly. He got to his feet immediately and put both hands down over the sides of the washer. She knew. Helene knew. He couldn't believe that she'd known it already.

Without a noise, he stepped out the back door and walked into the desert alone, reaching for breath the way a runner does, his breath stuttering, as if he'd seen something fearful. She'd known. She'd known before him. And she'd never said a word.

The dingy green of pan-flat prickly pears littered the dusty desert floor, and saguaros stood with their arms raised like pipes from some abandoned organ against the roan horizon. He was alone in the hot, killing desert where there was no spring.

That she could know and not tell him. What was in her to keep it from him? How could she hold back for all those months? Was she afraid of him, some hint of grief? Afraid of his saying that it meant nothing at all to him to know that Karen Remkes was dead?—afraid of sensing even the slightest chill in his voice, a thinness she'd read betraying something she still—years later—couldn't quite disbelieve? Why hadn't she told him? Was there still this darkness between them?

Of course there was darkness. It was that simple and that true. It was sin, and it was always there. It's in us, he thought. It's what I've always known—Adam's sin. Try as they might, it would not disappear. There would be Fourth-of-July moments, but the darkness would never lift, never.

There was no Feringa to call now, and Helene had the woman in the mansion who knew exactly what she felt. He stood there alone in the brush and dirt.

Karen was dead. What had he done? She'd been out with some other man, died somewhere, her children deserted. What part of all that was his fault? The old Dutchmen would send her to hell, Klassen said. But no one can be so sure. It really was his own fault, in part at least. It had to be his fault. Not that he loved her anymore, this woman from so far out of the past—not even that he'd ever really loved her. It wasn't love that wouldn't let go of her memory now, wouldn't let her die in him. It wasn't that. Maybe what kept her there alive in him was that he'd not loved her—that he'd never loved her at all, only hurt her and used her, and that now she was gone. His pain was knowing that maybe he'd sent her to hell himself, destroyed something good in her, something in that painted face.

The rough touch of his frayed sleeve scraped across his cheeks when he tried to hold back the tears, but they came now, came fast and full from something overflowing inside him, something finally wounded for what he'd done himself.

"I'm sorry," he said, as if Karen were there beside him now, as if she weren't dead. "I'm really sorry."

But he knew he was alone, that Karen was dead and no one stood there beside him to listen, not Feringa and not even Helene. "God, I'm so sorry," he said again, wiping his cheeks with the heels of his hands. "God, I wish somebody could forgive me."

He felt the heat of the Arizona sun like some burden on his shoulders, the brightness of midday so brilliant, the perfect turquoise sky like something painted in against the dusky desert tones, the strange beauty of the desert lit by the sun, the light of the world. The light of the world. The light of the world.

And it came to him then, in one phrase repeated as if by rote, something written forever on the walls of his mind. He knew that he was not alone. He knew for the first time what his heart had never known fully, not for almost forty years—what he'd heard in Sunday Schools and around the dinner table, what he'd studied in Bible classes and grown weary of in years of Christian schools, all of that came up like something on an assembly line straight out from his soul; but this time the truth stood naked before him. He was not alone. There was the Light of the world.

He saw it in the sun-drenched beauty of a desert landscape, and he felt it in the presence of someone there with him in the wilderness: that the darkness all around has already been removed, that the veils are gone, and that once and forever, this very week, all of his sins were forgiven— what he'd done to Helene, what he'd done to Karen—what he had to do with Karen's death—every single bit erased like the night before the perfect brilliance flowing from an empty tomb where a stone was left behind like a child's toy.

And he stood there in the desert and cried for the second time, not because he never really understood it all before, but rather because he knew God now, inside and out, for the first time, something so much larger than himself. And he knew he didn't have to stay in the darkness, in the barrenness of the desert. He heard it from the voice of the desert, and he knew that only in God's strength could he fly, mount up with wings like the eagles that lay out effortlessly in the rifts of river breezes. He knew he could walk—with Helene—that both of them could walk into what life still stood before them, slowly, hand in hand, into the quiet assurance of what years still remained before them, and that in that walk, the two of them need not be weary. In Christ's own love he was forgiven for what he'd done to Karen. He was.

He felt the sting of thinner against his cheek when he brought his sleeve up to his face again to dry his tears; but he turned around, put the desert behind him, and faced the mansion with the music in his soul.

The Facts of Life

Countless times I've watched Verona Worth dole out extra chicken strips to Mandy, her granddaughter, the only third grader in Greenwood School she wouldn't dare to touch. I've worked with her ever since she started in the lunch room, and a hundred times, I bet, I've seen her dawdle over a cup of applesauce just to keep Mandy at the window for an extra second. Sometimes she'll scrape beans off trays for twenty minutes on the chance the girl will give her only the slightest glance when she files by the tubs of dirty silverware.

Every noon she stands a countertop away from that child and sees her own son's eyes—strong and bright and quick, blue as heaven. And when she does, what she feels is written so deeply on the lines of her face that it doesn't take a gypsy to read it, only another grandma. She loves that child, even though Mandy doesn't know her from Martha Eshuis or Sylvia Brantsen—or any of the girls who work the lunch lines with us.

Mandy is my granddaughter, too, my seventh, out of twelve in all. She's the daughter of my Kelly—and Verona's son Jeff, who wouldn't marry Kelly, even though my daughter surely would have had him. But at school the whole affair has never come up between us, even though Verona and I work side by side, baking chicken, spooning chocolate pudding into the Charlie Brown pies, and scrubbing out pots once the sixth grade is through the line come 12:30.

It happened at college, like so much does, and the night Jeff and Kelly came to tell me and Ted, Verona came with, alone, like she's been since her husband died trucking a dozen years ago or more, killed on an interstate in Utah, I think, or maybe Nevada. My daughter was pregnant, we found out, but Ted and I jumped the gun ourselves way back in the olden days, so I've been through some of that hurt myself, even though it's a whole lot worse when it's your daughter, let me tell you, and when she doesn't have a husband.

I love Kelly, and I always have, but she's been a chore to bring up, headstrong as she was from the moment she wouldn't take a nook. But that night it wasn't Kelly that scared me, it was Verona, who sat with her legs crossed in a rocker beneath the clock and couldn't stop crying. She didn't bawl really, just whimpered constantly, kept dabbing at her eyes, so that whatever she said, or tried to say, came out off-key.

She'd taken Jeff over to apologize to us because he'd already made it clear that he wasn't about to marry my daughter. Lord knows Verona tried to do everything right, tried with a passion, but she was so broken that night, all she could do was mumble.

We never talk about Mandy on the job, even though what happened is eight years behind us. It never comes up because Verona is embarrassed about what her son did to Kelly. But that isn't all of it. She's embarrassed about that night, too, about how she couldn't do much at all but slobber when she tried to be the mother—and the father Jeff never had.

I feel the same way around the nurse that stood by me when my Tom was born. When that boy didn't want to come, I know I made a horrible rucus. If I see that nurse on the street—even today—I look away. She saw me in a state I'm not proud of, the way I saw Verona pinched in the rocking chair, in perfectly helpless pain over her only child.

Jeff's gone on to be someone, but he's never married; and if you ask me he doesn't pay much attention to his mother. He lives in Virginia and works in Washington D. C., does something with numbers, financial, works for the government, Verona says.

My Kelly took the next best thing once Jeff said no. When Mandy was a year old, Kelly married Reggie Ellenson, who stands first in line to inherit his father's masonry company. Reg never went to college. He's a fine man, but Kelly runs him, and she knew darn well she would. There's already two little boys—two little masons—behind Mandy, the princess she had with Jeff. I'm not proud of saying this, but I pray more for my Kelly today than I did eight years ago, the night she told us she was going to have a baby. She's not finished growing up, even if she doesn't know it herself.

She came over Tuesday, mad as ever, because Verona had sent Mandy a new dress for her birthday. Verona's sent things anonymously for years—at Christmas she writes "Santa Claus" on the tag. First, it was rattles, then stuffed animals. The last few years it's been clothes, school clothes.

"You've got to do something about it, Mom," Kelly told me. She stood at the door and didn't even unbutton her jacket, left the car running on the driveway, the boys inside. "It's driving me nuts, I swear it. Mandy's getting old enough to where I'm going to have to explain it, you know. Here's this big package comes in the mail." She draws the lines with her arms. "The boys don't get anything extra. Mandy's going to wonder—you know she will."

"What can I do?" I said.

"You know her. You talk to her everyday at school. Tell her it's got to stop—it's for Mandy's own good, Mom."

Like I say, I've seen Verona's long face whenever Mandy goes by with an empty tray. Ever since the girl's been in kindegarten I've seen that look.

"I've talked to Reg's lawyers—the business, you know—and they claim I can get a court order—"

"My goodness, Kelly," I said.

"Listen to me! They said I can get a court order that would keep her from contacting Mandy in any way. It's the law."

"You going to arrest her for sending a pair of socks?"

"If I have to," she said.

Somewhere it's written, I think, that once they leave the nest a mother's supposed to stop worrying. You think that's the way it's going to be, but it isn't.

"You want me to tell her?" I said.

"I'm right about this, Mom. Maybe someday when Mandy's old enough, you know, when she can take the truth. But she's only eight years old." She ran her fingers through her hair like she always does, front to back, her father's thick dark hair. She's beautiful, my prettiest daughter. I've never quite figured out where she came from—such a beautiful girl at the end of the line.

"Mom," she says, "please? I just can't think of Christmas in another two weeks. Besides, she's getting so extravagant. This outfit must have cost forty bucks."

"What was it?" I said.

She rolled her eyes. "What difference does it make?"

"Really?" I said. "Tell me about it."

She let out this long, grieved breath. "A black, cotton jumper with suspenders and a bright yellow tube belt—"

"Sounds cute," I said.

"She even sent a pair of panty hose and a turtleneck."

I waited for her critique. "Well?" I said.

"I just won't have it anymore," she said. "I don't care if it's cashmere. You've got to tell her."

"Why me?" I said.

"It's either you or the lawyer," she told me.

Her father used to say that if Kelly got up a head of steam, she could carry the Chicago Bears on her back and still get where she wants to go. In her entire life, the only thing she wanted but never got was Jeff Worth.

* * * * *

On Mondays we spread more peanut butter sandwiches than we normally do because sometimes kids don't get enough to eat over the weekend. Of everything we do in the kitchen, spreading sandwiches takes the most time. We go through more than a gallon of peanut butter every day.

Verona and I sat there together for almost an hour while the others were out setting tables and getting the lines ready. It was almost 11:00, time for the second grade. The vegetables were already up in the roasters, ready to serve. It's almost Christmas now, but we were talking about the March menus. Planning school meals isn't any different from doing the job at home—it's hard to come up with something new. And it's got to be likeable, of course. The waste here is a sin you never quite get used to.

"We could use tons of apples," Verona said.

Sometimes government fruits come thick during the winter, if there's a surplus.

"You never know if we'll get them for sure," I told her.

"You never know anything for sure," she said.

"You got me there, I guess," I said.

It was already the fourteenth. I knew that if I was ever going to say
a thing, I had to now. So I didn't wait for something easy. I kept telling
myself it was me or the lawyers. Kelly doesn't just shoot off her mouth
about things like that. So I charged in right there in the middle of menus,
and maybe I shouldn't have. Like I said, we've never said a word about
it before.

"Verona," I told her, "Kelly says that jumper you sent for Mandy's
birthday was just darling."

You could feel cold seep into the room as if someone had just opened
a window to winter.

"I've been waiting to see it on her," I told her. "She looks so cute
in dark colors."

Government peanut butter isn't the texture of Peter Pan. Sometimes
towards the bottom of the can it spreads in chunks and rips the bread.

"Verona," I said, "I wish there was some other way we could do
this. I know what that child means to you. I mean, I can see it when
she comes through the line."

She wasn't looking at me at all. She reached in the bag and pulled
out a half-dozen slices, then jammed the spatula down into the tub for
more peanut butter.

"I know we never talk about it," I said, "but if it helps at all for
me to say it, I think I know how you feel."

She turned to me, her eyes full of glass shards. "How dare you say
that?" she said.

It was pointless for me to argue, so I let it go and the both of us kept
on spreading.

Martha finished up on the tables and came up to the window wondering if she ought to start slicing up cheese for tomorrow's lasagne. When
I told her to check the napkin holders, she knew something was sticky
between us.

"It hurts me to have to say this," I told Verona, "but Kelly's always
been her own person and I long ago gave up trying to fight her. Maybe
she's got a point here too. She says it's got to stop—your presents."
I didn't know whether or not the woman was even tuned in to what I
was saying. "You listening to me?" I said.

She never moved.

"Well, you're going to hear me because I'm the one who's got to say it.'' I was shaking myself, I'll have you know, maybe even a little angry because Verona just couldn't be civil. "Kelly says you've got to stop sending presents because Mandy's going to wonder where they're coming from. That's what I'm supposed to say. And you know it's true. You've watched her grow.''

Verona's eyes stayed down on the bread. She turned hard as the counter top.

"She's right, Verona. Mandy's no baby, but she doesn't have to know the whole story, not yet. You know that too. She's too young.''

Miss Brigston from the second grade came through the door all smiles. "It's five minutes early I know," she said. "But I figured you might not mind if I brought the kids down a little early. They're so excited. Did you see the beautiful snow?''

I hadn't even looked outside since seven.

*   *   *   *   *

That was Monday, a week ago, and Verona didn't say a word to me in all those days together. Everybody in this kitchen knows we aren't speaking—and they know why, too, even though I never told a soul, and neither did she. We're all grandmas here.

It's not easy living in silence. You go about the day-to-days and even laugh and joke with the others, but the whole Mandy business—and she's such a sweetheart herself—sits in your craw. It hovers over everything, every minute on the job, every last minute. But I wasn't about to break the silence because it wasn't my problem. Maybe that's pig-headed of me, too, I don't know.

On Saturday, Kelly was back at my house with a big box in her hand, mad. "I took the jumper," she said, "but I'm not taking this—Christmas or no Christmas." She flung the box over to the couch, where it slipped off the pillows and fell to the floor. "It's got to stop. I told you to tell her, Mom. I told you.''

When Kelly gets angry, her face sets, almost like Verona's. She tries to mask her anger as if its only determination.

"What is it?'' I said.

"She must have paid a fortune for it. Look.''

I put down my coffee, walked over to the couch, and picked the box off the floor. "Whyn't you stay awhile?" I said.

But she turned around and walked right out, leaving the door wide open. What was in the box was magenta ski jacket with corduroy trim and a snap-off hood, nylon, light as a feather—plus a matching hat and mitten set tucked into the hood. The price tags were all neatly cut.

Now they were both mad, I thought.

Kelly showed up at the door again with another box she set down on the step. "Take the whole mess," she said. "I've had it. You talked to her, didn't you?"

"I mentioned it—"

"Then nothing's worked. She's pushed me too far now. I didn't want to do it this way. I tried to avoid it, Mom, you know I did. But she's driven us to it now—she has. It's her fault what happens."

"What's in there?" I said, pointing at the other box.

She gave the box a little kick. "Matching boots and a bib pants. She doesn't even need it. We just got her the whole outfit ourselves in November."

I hadn't seen her so angry since she was thirteen when I told her eleven o'clock was late enough, county fair or no county fair. She spit then too. She's spit quite a bit in her years.

"Let me try once more," I said. "You just hold your horses awhile longer. You don't want to be Scrooge. Let me try again." Sometimes I think if Kelly would just cry, I'd feel less scared about her myself.

"All right," she said, "but once Christmas is passed, it's got to stop." Mad as a wet hen.

"Don't you forget who she is," I told her. "Don't ever forget."

"You're her grandma, Mom," she said. "I won't hear it."

"Then you won't hear the facts of life," I told her.

All she came for was to yell about the presents, that's all. "See you tomorrow at church," she says, and then she leaves again, just like that.

I'd do anything for that girl, I swear, but she can grieve me no end—always could.

There I sat on the floor with my coffee up on the table, that cute little jacket all in a bundle, half out of the box. I picked it up and held it by the shoulders, then flipped the hood back. It was pretty, so little-girlish. I couldn't help thinking that Verona must have held it up before her eyes the same way. She must have pulled it out of the box it was shipped in just to hold it in her hands, to feel it, let the whole sweet outfit inflate with Mandy's imagined body.

I got to my feet, kept ahold of the jacket, and kicked the other box over to the coffee table beside the one Kelly had thrown. Then I sat on the edge of the couch and opened it up. I shoved my hand up into one of the boots, probably the same thing Verona did, imagining Mandy's feet, warm inside against January cold.

The hat was cable knit, thick stripes, with a thick tassel. I put my hands into the mittens and that's when I found the little brown bag. I opened it up and a smaller bag fell out, a tiny plastic bag holding the thinnest gold necklace.

Verona just couldn't stop herself, I thought. Even if she tried—even if her conscience told her that what I'd said was gospel truth, she just kept on going because she couldn't stop. Giving those presents was all she could do for eight years. I could just see her paging through J. C. Penney's—"this, and this, and this, and, oh yes, this too." She probably already had the whole outfit when I'd spoken to her a week ago. She probably took it all out that afternoon and laid it on the dining room table, the whole outfit—jacket over pants, hat tucked into the hood, mittens snuggled up into the cuffs on either hand, boots down at the bottom. And then she probably laid that gold necklace beneath the collar. She probably had it all in her closet since October already, two weeks after the winter catalogue first showed up in her mailbox. I know Verona.

* * * * *

It was my turn to host the girls for our Christmas party this year. It's one of those things you enjoy only when it's going on, not when it's ahead of you. Years ago, it would have kept me awake nights. I would have wondered what to serve and how to be sure everybody has a good time. But I don't care so much anymore; and now that I don't, I wish I hadn't got myself thick with nerves for so many years.

I made some chocolate pretzels and some blitzes and spread frosting over a host of Christmas cookies. I made a batch of sea foam and even a couple dozen gum drops, and the whole time, I tell you, I ate way too much, way too much. I'll bet I spent twenty dollars on Chex mix, since my own kids eat it by the pound whenever they come over during

Christmas because I'm the only one who makes it with real mixed nuts. I took out the pine cone wreath from the closet and an old Christmas tablecloth that Ted claimed he didn't even remember. The only thing new for the party was a pair of Christmas CD's Ted picked out himself, only because he couldn't resist buying himself a new toy this year, that new CD player, when the tape deck he bought not that long ago still played very well, as far as I'm concerned. Boys will be boys.

It was Martha's idea to sing. Usually the girls each bring a five-dollar present, and we throw them in a pile in the middle of the room, pick a number, and everyone gets to choose—or trade. After that it's cards. But Martha says that this year we ought to sing a little for a change, since everybody likes to sing anyway.

"Whyn't you get Mandy over to play for us?" she says. "Didn't you say she was already playing carols?"

Martha plays ragtime like Al Jolson, by ear too yet. If she wanted to sing so badly, she could have played every last carol herself. There was something up her sleeve.

But I played the game. I asked Mandy to come over around 7:30 or so—it was a school night, after all—and play those carols she'd been practicing so all the cooks could sing along.

By then, I figured, I'd have my sandwiches served, and we'd have gone through the whole presents thing. It sometimes amazes me what we can do to each other. We all had a good time that night, even though Verona never said a word to me. I didn't try to pry her loose, because I think she's got a right to what she feels. We all joked with each other, we all had a good time, but the two of us never said a word.

And bless Kelly's soul. I can get so angry at that girl sometimes, but then she just comes through and does something just like an angel. When Mandy came in that night, she was wearing Verona's black jumper, the whole outfit, even the yellow belt. She took off her jacket and every one of the girls was just stunned. But she is a beautiful girl. I know I'm not to be trusted, being her grandmother, but I've got twelve and that makes me somewhat objective.

My Kelly's hair is dark and straight and cut short like that famous ice skater's. What hair Reg has left is thin and red. But Jeff has his mother's hair, blonde as beach sand and very thick—and so does Mandy. She wore it up that night, in a single braid.

And we sang. We could have done a whole lot better with Martha at the piano, but grandmas don't really care that much about their kids' fumbling. Mandy brought along her own book, a starter, so the melodies of the old favorites—"Silent Night," "Little Town of Bethlehem," "Come, All Ye Faithful," the only six she knew—came out slowly in one-finger jabs.

And all of us, even Mandy, sat around the table afterwards, eating candy like none of us should. Twenty minutes, maybe, we sat there, when Martha said she had to leave.

"We haven't even played cards yet," I told her, but she got up from the table and went to the closet herself for her coat.

"I got big things to do," she said, "and tomorrow's Christmas dinner." It's the biggest meal of the year at school.

"But you just stay on here and have a good time, okay? Don't mind me."

See, they had it all arranged, the girls did. One by one they left—Anne had a brother over from Texas, Millie was worried about getting her call from her son in the service. They had it all arranged so that the three of us were left, Verona and Mandy and me. That was the plan. I finally figured it out.

"I suppose I ought to be going myself," Verona said, once Millie was up and at the door.

"You stay awhile," I told her. "It's still early."

Those were the first words I spoke to her in a whole week.

"Mandy," I said, "I bet Verona would like to hear those carols again. Whyn't you go over and play them—you two together. I got to do a little cleaning up here or Grandpa will have a fit."

I winked at my friend Verona, and she didn't have to say a word because what was in her was written over her face like it always is. She looked liked a child again, with a face full of Christmas wonder. It was all Martha's idea. I just played along.

I took my time cleaning up because what I saw on the piano bench, the way Verona touched her for the very first time in her life, then hugged her when she'd make a little mistake somewhere, was just about the best gift I could ever have imagined. I love Mandy, maybe more than some of the other kids, the older ones sometimes, but I got this great big joy in me from giving her to Verona that night. It was Christmas joy, giving being the blessing it is. And that's something a human being never stops learning either, I'll tell you.

I let them go for a long time, picked up all the food, did some of the dishes, even dumped the garbage, then I got out the present. I'd wrapped it up, complete with a bow, and I told Mandy I was giving it to her for playing for us, for all the cooks—for being our accompanist.

But it wasn't her eyes that I watched when her fingers fumbled with the paper. When Verona saw the necklace she'd bought herself, I put my hand on her shoulder to shush her up—and because I wanted her to look at me right then, at that very moment, to see my own eyes, so that once she saw my tears she'd know she didn't have to cry.

"It's beautiful, Grandma," Mandy said. "I love it. It's gorgeous." She lifted it out of the little box with her fingers and let it dangle. "I want to wear it," she said, and she turned to Verona without even thinking. "Help me put it on."

That moment was Verona's whole Christmas, let me tell you. Nothing else, no present, could possibly come close. I can't tell you what I felt.

I shooed Mandy out the door at 8:30, which was already a half-hour too late, but her mother never once minded time in her whole life so she's not one to complain.

That left Verona and me.

She didn't say a thing. Her lips were shaking, and her eyes were glazed. She hunched her shoulders as if there really were nothing at all to say, and then she walked to the vestibule and pulled out her coat.

"Thanks for coming," I said.

Then she reached over and kissed me, hugged me too. I wonder how long it had been since she'd done that to anyone.

She had her hand on the knob when I remembered the jacket and the boots and the whole winter outfit. I could have let it go too, in the charm of that party and the blaze of joy in her eyes. But I know there's more to life than Christmas candy, and I figured if my Kelly could dress Mandy up for her ghost grandma that night, then Verona could learn to bend a bit herself.

"I got some stuff here that belongs to you," I said. "I think you better take it along." I had it in a couple of shopping bags on the floor of the vestibule.

She had no idea what it was. I know she didn't. She was still in a dream. She looked at me strangely, then reached down to slip open a box.

I don't think I can really describe exactly what happened right then to my friend's face. Maybe the best way to say it would be that it moved from heaven back to earth—but not to hell. She took this deep breath, as if the whole time on that piano bench she hadn't even taken a minute for air. And then she bit her bottom lip, and smiled. I know very well it wasn't easy for her to say anything.

"It's something how easy it is to take things back nowadays," she said. "It's so simple, don't you think?"

"Wasn't always that way," I told her.

"Sure wasn't," she said. She looked up at me almost as if she didn't want to leave, but she did. It's Christmas dinner at school tomorrow, after all.

Once she was out the door, I pulled out what was left of the chocolate-coated pretzels and ate all of them, every last one. Not once did I feel guilty either. I ate the whole works. It's no holiday at all, if you've got to watch yourself every last minute. What's a holiday for, I figure. Joy— that's what it is.

Paternity

Somewhere today a woman named Cassandra Something-or-other is telling a little different story, I'm sure, because she was rich and likely still is.

What do I remember of her? Her hair—the way she turned her face up into the brisk, beach sun and swept the long bronzed bangs across her cheeks. The way she laughed, always hard and full, embarrassingly sometimes—for me, not her—and the way she never giggled, even though she was only sixteen. The sharp fortitude of her eyes confronting yours and never once backing down. I remember her body very well—and her tan, both where it was and where it wasn't. Her face, really—the exact shape of her nose and the thickness of her eyebrows, even her lips—has gone from my memory, but a part of her will never go, the ever-urging boldness that knew no fear.

The fall of her sophomore year she and her mother moved, all year round, into her parents' cottage on the lake. She was what we called "lake people." I was a townie. Her father owned a Chicago company that turned out fifty fiberglass boats per day. My father milked thirty-five cows. Twice she'd been to Europe. I'd been to Indiana three times to Bible Camp. She was going to college in Vermont, she said, because she hated Chicago, where she'd lived for her first fifteen years.

We were both sixteen. I was an athlete, tall and muscular from years of farm work, and blond, like a beach bum, from the burning sun and long hours in the alfalfa fields that still lie like storybook meadows between Easton and the woods that belt the lakeshore. I wanted her all right, but she just wanted. That was the difference between Cassie and normal Easton girls. They never really wanted. Cassie did—sincerely and truly.

Once I told her how—when I was a boy—we'd seen a train flatten a penny we'd laid on the track. A half hour later she stood, holding a handful of unruly hair to keep it out of her face, while only ten feet away a huge freight exploded by. The miniature football I'd hung on a chain from my rearview mirror swayed in the lurches of the coal cars across those ties, and I was in the car fifty feet away; but she never raised her eyes from the spot on the steel where she'd planted a nickel herself.

I wasn't really Gary Dirks to her. I was merely the boy she wanted. Eight times we made love. I could probably still list them, by place and degree of success, in order. And we really didn't quit each other, at least not until the next summer, when she became pregnant and went back to Chicago to have our baby.

She had no desire to marry me, the son of an Easton Hollander, a small dairyman. So she finished high school in Chicago, I suppose, and I never heard from her again, just as she had promised. When I say she left Easton, I don't mean that her parents forced her to return to Chicago. She simply determined herself that she would leave, then told her mother of her plans. Back then I thought of Cassie's having free will in the theological sense my father talked about "free will"—as the opposite of being predestined for salvation, almost as sin.

Yesterday, I sat on a crowded curb in my hometown as a Dutch Festival parade marched up from the memory of my sixteenth summer in Easton, one float after another, the Lions Club's old black and gold, papier-maché feline still mounted on the same crepe-papered hayrack, First Presbyterian's same black Bible open to the same John 3:16. Only the faces of the queen and her court had changed; even their Dutch costumes seemed handsewn replicas of what I remembered. My children were off on the Tilt-a-Whirl and the Ferris Wheel because a silly, small-town parade doesn't entertain ten-year-olds who have been brought up on cartoon excesses. So I sat there alone and watched another parade too: a score of Easton high school kids dressed down for the sun, performing for each other. And I remembered who I was back then, sixteen years ago.

I remembered Cassie and our child and my own father, who yesterday was out baling hay somewhere, just as he was during the Dutch Festival in town that summer I became a father myself. We'd had a New Holland baler for four years already and developed a list of farmer-customers long enough to call ourselves the Dirks' family custom balers—my two older brothers, Andy and Darrell, and myself. The three of us usually set things up and took turns working in the mow or in the field; then there was the boss, my father, of course, who always finished the milking at home before getting out to join us; and my little brother Jesse, eleven-years-old maybe, who usually drove the wagons back and forth and loaded bales on the elevator. Three cuts we made some years; some years only two.

Nothing remarkable happened the afternoon Cassie and I told my parents about her being pregnant. Cassie's mother was there too, the collar of her lavender blouse lying open, tastefully, over her tanned chest. When I remember now how strange that woman looked in our farm house—with all our fans churning up the air—I can see in the collar of that silk blouse what it was that determined, finally, my father's nodding silence: he didn't know how to talk to a woman who looked like she'd just stepped from a television screen. My mother, in her kitchen smock, smiled the way good women can when they have to; but my father sat and listened, his hands folded in his lap as if he were in church.

Cassie controlled the conversation. It was her style to talk, to reason out what must be done, and she did, with such coolness that she disarmed my mother's usually hair-triggered emotions. She explained how she knew it was Easton tradition to marry a couple of kids at a time like this, but how that would be foolish, neither of us even seventeen and neither of us really seriously in love. She told my mother how she was going to move back to Chicago and have the baby there, and how she didn't blame me for the baby because it wasn't my fault alone any more than it was hers. It was, simply, what had happened, she said.

At that point my mother reached for her handkerchief.

"Of course, we expect to be able to cover the entire financial picture," her mother threw in, as if it were the line that Cassie had allowed her to say.

At five, my father, taking his cue from the tolling of the clock in the family room, went out to the barn, sensing, I'm sure, that nothing more could be said anyway.

If I'd scour my high school annual I could come up with two or three other Easton girls who got pregnant that summer, but the story that unfolded in those cases would have been completely different. Once the news was out, Cassie packed her bags quickly for Chicago; as a result, the elders from my church never did visit with us together, as was the custom with the other shotgunned couples who'd violated the seventh commandment. Since she was already gone, they visited me alone, three of them, all men; and once they had nudged the word sin into and out of the conversation, we spent the rest of the night talking about football, my senior year upcoming.

I never saw Cassie again, nor the child—wherever he or she may be— if, in fact, that child exists. Cassie had money like I'd never seen. That was 1970, before Roe vs. Wade, but the Mikklesons had the kind of money that could pay for illegality.

Some summer nights a few years later, when I was home from college, I drove slowly down the lake road past their home late at night, maybe once a week or so. I'm not sure what drew me back so frequently to that path through the birch just a couple hundred feet off the lakefront—lust maybe, but I don't think that's the whole reason. Maybe I wanted to know that what had happened was all real.

But what I remember best about that summer is what happened after Cassie and her mother made their afternoon visit to our dairy—what I saw that night in the barn, and what my father said the next day, when he finally opened up.

He caught me once, maybe a year before, beating a cow with a hoe. I don't remember the provocation anymore, but a milk cow, like a wife or a sister or a brother, can make you feel that bloody kind of hate you can feel only for those you live with, day-in, day-out. He came up from behind and grabbed me, lifted me off the cement and kept me up there until he'd stopped my thrashing.

"You ever do that again, Gary," he said, "and so help me I'll use that hoe on you."

That's all he said about it, ever.

When Cassie and her mother left late that afternoon, I went out to the barn, maybe a half hour after my father picked up and left in silence. I pulled on my boots just outside the parlor and unlatched the door. I was young then, cocky. I figured I'd take my licks and have it over. But I found him beating a cow that night, whacking away, the milking machine lying awkwardly in the gutter like some overturned turtle. He had a dowel he'd picked up somewhere, thick as his finger, and he was thrashing that cow like I'd never seen him do before.

When he saw me standing there where the rest of the cows were already stanchioned, he stopped, frozen in the act, a vacant, stunned look on his face. We both knew that nothing needed to be said, so we milked beside each other all night long and never spoke a word. I felt almost excused, as if what I'd done with Cassie was lost in some big harvest of sin.

The next morning we were out baling hay at the Trillian place, an old farm with hundreds of acres of land and a sprawling, ramshackle barn with 1904 painted just below the point of the eaves.

Today, the baler my father bought is obsolete because people say a crew of five or six makes baling hay too labor-intensive. Today, with the right kind of equipment, one man can do all the haying and never leave the air-conditioned comfort of his cab. Back then, haying employed our entire family, locked us up in dusty mows, forced us to gulp ice-cold lemonade from a common-cup canning jar, to work long, hot hours in stagnant air, thick with dust, and to talk to each other, even when we may not have wanted to.

When my father came on the job that morning, we'd already started up. I was stacking bales on the wagon when I saw his pickup roll into the yard. My brother Andy was driving the baler, while old man Trillian himself shuttled the first load back to the barn where he and little Jesse unloaded. In a matter of minutes, half hour maybe, Darrell rode out on the empty wagon and told me Dad wanted me to work with him in the barn.

My brothers hadn't said much to me that morning. They knew what had happened the night before, but on the ride out to Trillian's I'd found a corner in the back of the wagon and they let me be. Maybe they were disappointed in me, I don't know. Maybe they were jealous. Whatever they felt, they didn't say much. Maybe they felt as I did—it was all water over the dam. The way I saw it, Cassie was leaving. Now it was her problem.

My father is a tall, gaunt man with very dry hair and proud features, a wide nose that, come summer, reddens almost daily. His arms are long, and his hands carry muskmelons as if they were softballs. He resembles the picture we have of his grandfather, the North Sea sailor who, eighty years ago, decided to leave the Netherlands and cut a life for himself and his family from uncut Dakota grasslands.

My father has mellowed in the years that have passed since that summer. He laughs now as he watches his own grandchildren play on the rope swing he hung, not four years ago, from the maple I remember as a sapling. Back then, with three teenage boys and six children in all, with thirty-five milk cows, with all of that life riding the back of the cold and dreary lakeshore seasons, he seemed to me to be driven. I remember unforeseen spurts of temper during harvest, nervousness in unexplained silences during early spring planting. Whole nights passed in October when he didn't speak a word to my mother or to us.

Although he was a man to be feared then, it would be wrong to say that I was ever afraid of my father. He was to be feared the way he himself talked about fearing God. Each of us, I think, lived in a kind of awe of him. Darrell, the oldest, still wrestles him: if Dad says Darrell shouldn't use herbicides, Darrell claims he'll go bankrupt if he doesn't. Andy simply follows Dad. He's learned to live with him the way a good Marine feels comfort in a well-defined chain of command. I don't claim to know about myself.

"You know," he said to me that day when I'd climbed up in the mow beside him, "I always thought it would be Darrell and Gloria, the way they neck. I didn't think it would be you."

Little Jesse was loading the bales on the elevator that poked its nose into a square door maybe twenty feet off the ground. Trillian was helping him. We were putting hay up in the corners of the east loft, and the air was hot, full of chaff and dust, even though it wasn't past ten or eleven in the morning.

"We're all capable of it," he said. "I'm not throwing the first stone either."

He pointed me over to the place where he'd been packing. "Watch out for those kittens there," he said. His stacking had uprooted four of them, gray ones—farm cats—certainly no more than a month old, from their nest, so he'd put them up beside a rafter that he likely didn't mean to cover. The end of the yellow elevator, anchored with twine down to the wall, protruded from the open door behind him, sunlight cutting through the maze of dust in perfect geometric shafts.

"You know you shouldn't have done it," he said, not meaning it as a question.

I nodded.

When he didn't hear me reply, he looked straight up at me.
"Yes," I told him.
"Our bodies are the temple of the Lord," he said.
I really didn't feel any less healthy having made love eight times. It didn't seem somehow like a desecration.

When a bale came up the elevator, it fell, end first, down to the floor where it grazed off the edge of another set deliberately below, then flipped over completely, landing flat, strings up, four, maybe five feet closer to the spot where we were trying to fill in the last of the holes in that corner of the mow. He'd grab them from the spot where they'd finally come to rest and heave them at me. Jesse was sending them up plenty fast.

"I've been thinking for hours," he said, "and I just don't know what to say to you that you don't already know."

I didn't talk back. I was sorry for letting them down the way I did, but Cassie wasn't really a girl I'd marry anyway, I thought. I'd miss her. I knew I would. But I didn't love her, not love like you're supposed to, I thought. Besides, she really wasn't one of us. She was "lake people." And she was leaving.

"Slow down, Jesse," he yelled down the open hole. "We're finishing up up here."

He motioned with his arm for me to climb up and take the bales from him when he picked them off the floor. His was the heavy work; mine was simply tedious: fitting them into what spaces remained.

"The church calls it a sin," he said.

"I know it," I told him.

"I don't know if it's a bigger sin if it happened a hundred times, or a little one if it happened just once," he said, "but you and this girl, how often did you do it?"

I don't know why I said what I did, but I told him it had happened four times. "But she let me do it, Dad," I told him. "Every time. She told me that it was okay, that nothing would happen."

"You and Adam," he said. He picked up a bale and heaved it up to me off his knee. I was standing on a ledge of bales maybe four feet above him.

"Well, you saw her," I told him.

"Sure I did."

"She let me."

"Slow down, Jesse," he yelled again. Bales were piling up after flipping over the end as if they were riding a waterfall.

He pulled his handkerchief out and wiped his face. "So you just go and do whatever that thing you got in your pants says?—is that it?" He stopped and stared at me, bales still falling heavily to the floor.

I threw one in a hole without looking up at all. But I didn't talk.

"Does it say somewhere in the Bible that it's all just fine and dandy if the girl says yes? Is that a verse you read somewhere?"

I was up high, I remember. I reached up and scraped away cobwebs so thick with dust that they could have passed for yarn. But he stayed there at my feet, staring. I wouldn't look at him.

He turned around and grabbed for another bale. That's when I said, "Any guy would have done it, and you know it."

"Does that make it right?" he said, shoving another one up at me.

I twisted around, keeping my feet straight beneath me as I picked up the bale and swung it into a hole at the corner of the roof line.

"What's the big deal?" I said. "By football season it'll be all over anyway."

I'm not sure where that came from.

"Football season," my father said, in a tone without emotion, as if he were repeating it in order to get me to verify that what I'd said actually came from my lips.

"That's what I said," I told him.

His face turned suddenly into some fierce mask. "It'll all be over, will it?" he said, laughing in a biting, mature way that I'd never heard him laugh before, as if I wasn't his own boy.

Behind him the bales kept falling all over the spaces where he could walk. He twisted around quickly, as if he had forgotten what he was about. He scrambled down two levels of bales to get to the window, then dug his knees into the hay to look outside. "Slow down, Jesse— didn't you hear me?" he yelled, and he grabbed the end of the elevator and shook it. He stayed there for a minute, ripped four bales from the track and stacked them, one atop the next, to keep them out of the way.

Seated over there, he had to yell for me to hear. "You think it'll all be over, do you?" he said. "Just like that—like the mumps. You think it'll all go away, just like that. Like a sore knee, is that it?"

"What?" I said. "She'll be gone. She's rich. You saw her old lady.

She'll take care of the whole business."

The floor at the end of the elevator was cluttered with bales. He pulled himself up from his knees, grabbed the end of the elevator, and twisted himself around it; but his foot slipped in a crack, and he twisted his back when he couldn't keep his balance, finally falling to all fours. Just like that, like a slap in the face with an open hand, another bale came off the end and slammed to the floor over his twisted foot.

He came up swearing under his breath, something he rarely did, and he grabbed that elevator and twisted it, wrestled it loose from the knot Andy must have tied to anchor it, the chain jangling like loose bells, then turned it completely upside down, dumping every last bale off the track and to the ground between the barn and the wagon. "Now slow down!" he yelled again at Jesse.

"You don't have to lose your temper," I said.

"You shut up," he said, pointing back at me. "You talk like a child— it'll all be over—" he said. "It's no big deal at all because once you make a touchdown nobody will remember."

Anger and hurt twisted his mouth and narrowed his eyes, pouring out in something close to tears. "We're talking about life here. Don't you understand that—or is all you care about getting laid."

I never heard my father use that kind of language.

"Life," he said, and he put both hands down on a row of bales and climbed up several levels, lifting himself to the nest of kittens he'd laid at the beam. He grabbed a kitten from the pile that he'd found up there, took it in his huge hand and held it towards me like some circus magician, the kitten's round head protruding between his thumb and forefinger, the rest of its body in his fist, small and gray with long fur. He raised it higher and higher towards me, then jerked down suddenly, as if he were snapping his fingers, as if he were a kid snapping a lead pencil in half. When he opened his hand, the kitten was perfectly dead.

I couldn't believe what he'd done.

He didn't say anything just then. He looked at me and tossed the kitten across the mow somewhere. If his eyes could have spoken, they would have explained everything, but his eyes were vacant. He just stood there and stared, almost as if I could be next.

"Dad—" I said.

"You two made a child," he said, "not a kitten."

And just then Jesse came up the ladder, almost crying himself. "I tried to get that old guy to slow down, but he just kept on going," he said. "I tried."

"That's what you made," my father said, pointing at Jesse. "And who's going to be nice to him—who's going to dry up his tears, Gary? You going to be there?"

Two years ago, I was divorced. I could give you a hundred reasons why, but none of them would be any good really. Anyway, I see my two kids on weekends, and I take them places but you get tired of amusement parks and malls. So I took them to the Dutch Festival in Easton yesterday, a half day's ride north of Chicago, where we live.

Today I'm a teacher, special ed, in the schools there. My students are kids who don't understand why it's important to show up for work in the morning if you want to keep a job. And every year I get new ones, a new crop of sixteen-year-olds. This year I will too. And I wonder sometimes if I'd recognize that one of Cassie and me, the one I never saw. Maybe it was a girl.

Somewhere, I imagine, Cassandra Whoever-she's-married-to is telling her story too, and it's probably not at all the same.

But I couldn't help thinking when I was sitting there yesterday on the curb, when I saw all those Dutch kids around town, all those preening girls and the boys with the developing shoulders, that somewhere someplace there's this tall, gaunt, half-Dutch, sixteen-year-old, who could just as well be up in a stuffy haymow somewhere with my father, wearing out overalls by hoisting bales on his knee, his face sticky with sweat and chaff, and sometimes talking, sometimes talking.

Harmony

We've got these friends in Illinois. I grew up with the guy, went to school with him. We were the best of friends. We went to college together, but I lasted only a year or so before I realized education wasn't in the cards for me and went off to Vietnam. My friend Harry finished up, got a teaching job in Illinois, and never once donned a uniform. For a while I held that against him, but time's long ago taken the edge off all that—twenty years' worth of time.

The thing is, Joyce and I don't take many vacations. I'm the auctioneer in town, and you just don't leave so easily on weekends, not in these days when people are moving out of the Midwest as if there's nothing at all out here but a world of trailers in a feisty wind. So, when we get a day or two, we can't roam all that far. Joyce and I are happy for a weekend at the Holiday Inn in Sioux Falls, if you know what I mean.

So at least once a year we go to Illinois, usually in the early fall when the trees around the Mississippi dress up in their finest. We drive up along the river bluffs, singing the same old hymns, like we used to when our kids were younger. We make music—maybe somebody with class wouldn't say so, but it's what we do, the two of us. I used to hold a pretty even bass in the high school choir, and Joyce always did have music in her. She still sings for things in town, mostly funerals. There's something strange about harmonizing that I just can't put my finger on. You feel as if you're holding yourselves together with melody. But that's a whole different story.

Every year we go out to my friend Harry's place for a day or two and try to snag a catfish off the bottom of the Black Hawk River. We're friends, real friends.

So I call Harry this year on Sunday afternoon, and I tell him we're coming. And he's just as lighthearted as he always is. "Sure, sure

Woody,'' he says, "you just come on up.''

"Probably Wednesday we'll be there,'' I tell him.

"Wednesday—you bet,'' he says.

"You sure it's okay?'' I say.

"Wednesday—sure it is,'' he says. "I'll tell Lois.''

I've been over that conversation a hundred times since, and I swear I never felt a thing could be wrong.

For all those years that Harry and Lois have been married, they've been living in a trailer house, not just a little one but one of those double-wides set in a little country grove of scrub oaks on the side of a hill. I don't know why they stayed in that place, but they did. I suppose you just get your roots down, and it's hard to pick up so easily.

So Joyce and I drive up to his place late Wednesday afternoon, about the time I'm sure that Harry must be home from school, and the place looks deserted, leaves in bunches up against the garage door and a wad of advertising papers jammed in under the front door handle.

"They moved,'' Joyce said. She's half-looking up in the mirror on her visor, trying to get herself ready.

We sat there for a minute in the driveway. The sun was already down far enough to let a chill back into the air, but there wasn't a whisper of smoke from the chimney.

"Why don't you go up and knock on the door?'' Joyce said.

I had this feeling something was wrong, that maybe we should just head back to the state line and find some Motel 6 near Dubuque. "I don't like it,'' I said.

"Maybe they didn't see us yet,'' she said.

"There isn't anybody home,'' I told her.

"Maybe they left a note.''

Joyce was right. They'd already put the glass down on the combination front door, but right behind was a typed note taped to the storm. I still have that note. Here's what it said.

> Dear Woody and Joyce,
> We're sorry that this had to happen this way, right at this time, but it did. Our marriage is over. We're separated now, but we're getting divorced. It's a painful time, and yet it isn't. We still think of you as our friends, and we want you to stay

here overnight if you have no place to stay. I'm in Freeport,
and Lois is gone home to her parents. Please, call me. I want
to talk to you to explain.

                                    Harry

He wrote a telephone number in beneath his name. I took the note
off the door and brought it back to Joyce. I didn't say a word to her,
just handed her the note, and she read it.

"He left her," Joyce said.

"How do you know?"

"Because he wrote the note—and because that's the way it always
goes," she said. "When you're a woman—"

"That's hooey," I said. "It always takes two. Why blame him?"

"I didn't blame Harry. I just said that he left her. That's all I said.
Look here: 'It's a painful time, and yet it isn't.' He left her, Woody,"
she said to me. "I know it."

She was right.

I've never liked trailers. I don't know why. Maybe it's because they're
perilous, sitting there on top of the earth without a dime's worth of
footings. You can get some that look like a million bucks inside—fancy
curtains and furniture, all modern appliances, just about everything you
can get in a real house; but it doesn't make any difference. There's
something mobile about house trailers, and I've seen enough of them
go at auctions to know that people rarely get their money out of them.

"Well," Joyce said, "are we going in?"

"The place is haunted," I told her. "Forget it."

"I want to look around," she said.

Now Joyce isn't subject to morbid curiosity. More than once people
have called us in to assess what's in an estate after some death, and it's
Joyce who gets chills walking up long, narrow staircases, looking at oak
commodes or old brass beds, poking around in bedroom secrets where
nobody should want us.

"What's the deal?" I said.

"You can't just turn around and go home—and you know it," she
said. "The guy's your friend and he's asking for us to understand at
least." She folded up the letter and stuck it in the glove compartment.
"It's not why we came out here, but we can't turn around now."

"What happens if you're right and he just up and left her for some dish from Freeport? You still want me to talk to him?"

She looks up at me and twists her lips. "It's not a communicable disease."

"Hah!" I say, "there's lots of it going around."

"We're just going to have to chance it then," she said, "because he's almost like your brother."

It's like her to spin the Cain-and-Abel story on me because she knows that'll do it.

So, in we went. Up on the wall near the phone a couple dozen greeting cards were tacked—including one from us—each congratulating the two of them on their twenty-fourth anniversary. You might think I'm making this up, but I swear they were there. We read them, every one of them, including the one Joyce had written.

"Here's yours," I said when I found it beside one with a glossy picture of a bouquet of flowers.

She'd written how happy she was for them, how living twenty-four years together in this world of broken marriages seemed like it was a real miracle, how she and I were thankful for their friendship, and how they should be thankful themselves for the blessings of a life without terrible storms.

"You did a good job here, honey," I told her.

She was reading someone else's. "I did it in about two minutes," she said. "I almost forgot about it, so I ran downtown and picked it up from the drug store. On my way home I stood in the post office and scribbled something down and sent it. I don't even remember what I said."

"You want me to read it over?" I said.

"Please don't," she said, picking up one of those odd-looking cards, a couple of cartoon mice on the outside, sitting against a fancy pillow and opening a box of chocolates. "Look at this—'Looks like love really agrees with you.'" She read it out loud. "I can't imagine having to look at these things now," she said. "We'd do them both a favor by burning the whole lot."

"It's lucky nobody takes these things very seriously," I told her.

"Some people do," she said, meaning herself.

That's how it went.

"You know," she said later, "you ought to call him. He left a number." She was paging through a magazine she didn't give two hoots for. But I knew she was trying to listen in to the old voices that both of us thought we might hear in the trailer.

The phone sits on a corner table right beside an imitation Lazy-boy. Harry and Lois were the type to have lots of little tables. None of them would bring an eighth of what they'd paid for them. Corner tables. K-Marts. Particle board.

So I'm thinking about what I can say to my old friend, when Joyce goes to the organ and opens the bench. "There's nothing in here but "Moon River" and stuff like that," she says, "nothing but Andy Williams. No hymns or anything."

"People got their tastes," I said.

She starts playing loud enough that I can't call Harry right away, something from her memory, and then her hands wander up along the stops.

"Listen to this," she says, and she punches a button and suddenly we're in Mexico. She bounces through "Autumn Leaves" in a calypso beat.

"You're murdering the song," I told her.

"The organ's doing it," she said.

So I tell her that if she's just going to fool around anyway, she can just as soon soft-pedal it a little so that I can call my friend Harry.

Here's the way the conversation goes, nearest I can remember:

Me: Hi, Harry. This is Woody. How's it going?

Harry: Oh, Woody, it's you.

Me: We made it all right.

Harry: You found the note?

Me: We're at your place right now.

Harry: Good, good. (Long pause.) How you doing?

Me: We're on vacation, like always.

Harry: Got no work, huh? (It's right here that I hear this voice of a woman in the background asking who it is. And I can't help it, but that woman's voice irritates me.)

Me: I got plenty of work—that's why we're on vacation.

Harry: (laughs out loud) Good, good.

Me: (So I came right out and blasted him.) What the hell you go and leave Lois for, Harry? (Joyce is listening to me say all this, of course.)

Harry: (breathes big) It's a long story—
Me: I'm sure it is.
Harry: I can see how you can be angry.
Me: I'm not angry. We don't understand.
Harry: You're right. (Waits—and so do I.) I'll tell you the whole story, but not over the phone. Tonight yet, I want to talk to you. I'll meet you at this place on 18, just outside of town. Nine-ish. Called "Soupy's." Just after nine.
Me: Soupy's? (I say it, as if it's a dumb name.)
Harry: That's right. Joyce there too?
Me: She's playing the organ.
Harry: Woody, you got to come alone. I don't want to tell you all this with Joyce around—you know?
Me: No.
Harry: Just come alone. Trust me.
Me: (We're in bad shape, I figure, if my old friend has to tell me to trust him.) It's a deal, I tell him.
As Harry puts the phone down, in the background I catch the sound of supper frying in a skillet.
"You're right about the woman," I told Joyce. "I heard her talking. They sound like they're married."
"What do you mean?" she says.
"Well, they're cooking supper."
"That doesn't mean they're married. He's not even divorced. Harry's gone and moved in with some other woman. I told you."
"He wants me to meet him tonight. Some place called 'Soupy's,'" I told her. "Just me."
"Sure," she said, "leave me in this haunted house alone."

* * * * *

"You don't know what it's like to get up in the morning and be excited about what you're going to wear—you don't know what that's like, Woody," Harry says to me that night. "You forgot it long ago. But you get it back and you can't believe how great that is."
It's all there in that one comment, I figure. Harry thinks he's in heaven. Maybe he is.

He shows me these two pictures. In one of them he's with this new girl—he calls her "Ang." She's maybe ten years younger than he is, that's all. It's not that he's robbing the cradle or lecherous or anything. The woman's got lines around her eyes and she's no petite little dish or anything. But he's got these two pictures, and he brings them along just to show me.

"Look at this one," he says, and he hands me this picture of himself and Lois one Christmas, not more than five years back, the two of them sitting on that same couch that's still in their trailer, Harry's arms bent like an ape over his knees and Lois sitting there right beside him with her legs slanted away from her. It's no great shakes, I'm thinking.

"This is our Christmas picture," he says. "Look at me."

So what?—I figure. What does it prove? Somebody snapped a picture and it ends up looking like the bumper sticker you see around nowadays—"Are we having a good time yet?"

"Now look at this," he says, and he shoves this little polaroid shot at me.

I know exactly what he wants me to say because it's all very clear. In this one his face is full of energy. The flashbulb caught like a little explosion in his glasses, but you can see in his face that this man is no cadaver.

"Two pictures," I tell him. "Big deal."

"You can see what she's done to my life," he says.

We're sitting in this place called "Soupy's," the place where he and Lois probably used to go for dinner, and right there above our table a huge coyote pelt is spread out over the wall, outlined in a rim of heavy scarlet pad.

"Listen, it's just a picture," I told him. "And soon enough the honeymoon's going to be over."

"Oh, no," he says—this guidance counselor, this man who tells young kids how to deal with their problems. "You're wrong as ever on that one. You don't understand," he says. "It's everything I've ever wanted. I married Lois in college. I didn't know what I was doing—"

"Don't bother going on," I said. "You aren't telling me anything that I couldn't have guessed you'd say."

"Okay, okay," he says, "but you know how I always loved photography? You remember that? Now I'm doing it. I'm taking these pictures. Me and Ang, we've been riding all over just taking pictures. I know I'll sell them. We've been to Galena when the leaves were perfect around those mansions. And I took hundreds of pictures,'' he says, ''hundreds of them. Just shot and shot and shot. You realize that *National Geographic* photographers shoot thousands of shots just for one single slide? That's right,'' he says. ''And Lois never liked that camera because it cost so frightfully much. You know what I mean?''

''So what'd you do, rob a bank too?'' I said.

''You don't understand at all,'' he says. ''You don't know what it's like to live, to do the things you want—''

''You're right about that—me and Joyce are just now on the way to the graveyard.''

He turned away and wiped his fingers through his eyes. It didn't take a genius to see that this Harry wasn't the one we'd visited last year. His hair was cut shorter than it had been and restyled. He wore this thin gold necklace beneath his open collar, and his eyes were burning up with energy and fever—I don't know which. We sat in that booth and talked for more than a half hour, I think, and he never once looked away or over my shoulder to see who might be around. He didn't seem paranoid one bit, but he drank too much. He didn't slosh it down, but we went through more than a couple of drinks.

''My life has changed completely, Woody. You got to believe me. I'm close to God now, I swear it.''

Harry and I were born and reared in the same church, a church in which divorce was the next thing to murder. ''Sure,'' I said. ''I'm thinking of killing Joyce just so that I can get some peace in my soul.''

''I'm serious,'' he says. ''I've prayed in ways that I haven't prayed for more than twenty years.''

''You should,'' I said.

''Every day, Harry.''

''I hope that you're asking forgiveness in there sometime too.''

''I'm forgiven. I know that. The Lord's given me a new lease on life now. That sin is behind me, I'm sure of it.''

''What about your kids?—they behind you, too?''

If I'd hit him flat in the face with my fist I don't think I'd have stopped him as cold as I did with that line. He's sitting there with both hands around his glass, and he raises them both up together, almost like he's

throwing in the towel. "There's some broken pieces around, Woody,"
he says. "I'm no dreamer. This isn't anything that's going to be easy.
For heaven's sake, I never thought it would be easy."

"What about Daniel?" I said.

Harry turns his glass so the ice tinkles.

"What'd he tell you?" I ask him again.

He leans back and looks up to God or something. Then he shakes his
head. I can see I'm breaking him, but it wasn't just me either. It was
what his own boy had told him, something he didn't want to hear but
something that wouldn't go out of his mind so quickly. He started maybe
three times or so before he finally got it all out. "Lois said he told her
he was going to burn down the cottage," he said. "We got this place
on a lake in Minnesota. Had it for years. That's what she told me."

"He's telling you just exactly what you've been telling me," I says
to my friend Harry. "He's saying that your whole life has been a frick-
ing lie. That's just what you told me."

"I pray, Woody," he said. "I pray and pray and pray that it's the
right thing."

"You're a fool," I said. "You're a damned fool." That's what I told
him. And then I left.

He was still sitting there with his own half-filled drink when I just
walked out on him. I don't know now if it's what I should have done,
but I did. I figured I'd got him to a place where there wasn't an image
in sight for those roaming eyes of his, only the vision of his own damned
worthlessness. And it wasn't even me that had to tell him. It was the
voice of his own son, who claimed he wanted to destroy every last plaster
slat in a place where he had found so much boyhood joy.

When I got back, Harry's trailer was all lit up. It's unlike Joyce to
waste power, but the whole place is glowing. I don't know why, but
I stand outside for a while and try to figure out how we'd run the auc-
tion, where I'd put the flatbed for the little things, and where Joyce would
sit handing out tickets and taking the checks, how we'd line up the furniture over the front lawn so that the people could wander back and forth:
the dining room set out by the three evergreens along the driveway, the
sofa, the Lazy-boy, the TV console, then the lawn mower and the snow
blower, right down to shovels and rakes and what's still in the bag of
last year's grass seed. I'd sell it with a vengeance, I figure. Sometimes

you try to milk a crowd, try to get every last cent out of them because you know the owner needs something to live. But this sale I'd hum through. Harry's not thinking of money. He's taking pictures now and really living, he says. What does he care anyway? Just get rid of the stuff. It's all bad memories.

When I get back inside, Joyce is sitting there on that cheap sofa, watching the news with an afghan wrapped around her feet. I'm not sure I want to tell her what he said because it's the same old story. "You were right," I tell her. "He's got this other woman, and the whole world is singing."

She looks down at her nails.

So you see her there, see? And you think to yourself that this is the woman you've lived with for umpteen years, through three kids and four dogs and eleventy-seven rabbits; through banged heads and skinned knees and late nights when you're sitting up because the kids should have been home an hour before; through that ugly time when all the kids do is mope and complain—if you're lucky enough to get that out of them; through long, long years of no more than an hour a week at most you've got to talk about yourselves.

And first you wonder how anybody could leave that kind of investment. But then you tell yourself that you know you're kidding, because you know that it's always possible to leave her lying back there like some unclaimed freight, because you can't help wonder yourself what it would be like to get up in the morning and look in your closet and pick out something a new woman will think you're handsome in. I'm not that old that I don't know. That's what scares me, I guess. Like I say, you can never tell about people—not even yourself.

"They're going through with it, then?" she says.

"It's already over," I tell her.

Neither of us give two hoots about what's on TV.

"We could leave, you know," I said to Joyce.

She glances down at her watch.

"We could get back to Dubuque in less than an hour."

"We ought to talk to her yet," Joyce says. "I mean, we talked to him now, but we really ought to talk to her. She probably needs us. She probably needs somebody."

The afghan's probably hand-knit, I figure. Maybe it's not for sale.

Maybe Lois did it herself. Ten bucks anyway, twenty, I suppose, at most.
"How you going to get ahold of her?" I said.
"Her parents' number is in the back of the book. I looked," she said.
"You try to call already?"
She said she figured she'd wait until I came back from Soupy's with
the news.

So there we sit listening to some weatherman go on about how perfect
an Indian summer we're going to have, the trees in the river valley and
through the hills outfitted in all their blazing splendor. That's why we
came. I've got to remind myself.
"What's here for us?" I said. "What's to prevent us from just kick-
ing the dust off our feet and going home?"
"They're your friends," she says. "Maybe we can do some good."
I'm not in the mood to be scolded. I don't know why. "A guy gets
tired of making other people feel good," I said.
She doesn't say anything. It's like her not to. It means that I'm so
dumb that I can't see my hand in front of my face.
"I didn't take a vacation to play marriage counselor," I tell her.
"There's people that need us here," she says.
You can't imagine how that boiled me. I'll tell you what I was think-
ing: I'm thinking that I'd been blessed with a sufficiently good conscience
from the Lord himself, and I don't need Joyce to tell me how to keep
myself pure.
"Sometimes you get tired of other people's need," I say.
"You sound just like your buddy Harry," she says.
She had no right to say something like that because she didn't know
how I made him fry. She was thinking how I'd sympathized with Harry,
how I'd got myself sucked into the usual male song-and-dance. She didn't
know that the reason I didn't tell her, word for word, what went on is
that all the whole mess would do is make her mad. The sordid specifics
she didn't need.
There's something I didn't say about our meeting at Soupy's. I didn't
think I needed to mention it, but maybe it's important. Harry says to
me that this new girlfriend of his really knows how to love. What he
means is that she's an acrobat in bed. You know what he means when
he says something like that. He didn't say it that way, but you know
what they're hinting at when their eyes flash. Sex is always part of it,

always.

Anyway, when Joyce said that about "you and your friend," I figured I'd already been through one storm that night, and one was all I needed. "I'm going to bed," I said. "You want to call Lois in the morning, you go ahead. It's a good idea. But I'm going up," I said. Of course, there is no "up" in a trailer.

I took my clothes off, snapped off the lights, and got in bed. Joyce knows what I'm saying when I tell her I'm going to bed. She knows that I'm miffed.

Fifteen minutes later she got up off the couch and started hitting switches. When I looked up at the clock, it was closer to twelve than I'd guessed. Quite a vacation, I'm thinking.

Joyce crawls in the left side and lies there on her back, the two of us like a couple of tombstones, side by side. "I shouldn't have said that about you and Harry," she says. "I'm sorry."

"It hurts me too," I tell her. "The guy's somebody I grew up with."

"Is he in love?" she says.

How do I answer that one? I pull my hands up over my head. "He thinks he is," I tell her. "He doesn't know what love is anyway."

"You sure?" she says.

I figure I've got to be careful now. All I've got to do is underline what I'd already told her. "Of course," I say. "He's living in the beyond somewhere. Sometime he's going to have to come down. You know that. They all do."

Then she waits long enough to make me take this breath just to fill in the silence. "Why?" she says. That's all. And she turns to me. She turns on her side and her hand comes over my chest. "You really think he will—or do just you want him to?"

I don't know why of course. Sometimes maybe it seems as if you get older and older and slower and slower, and things just get foggy—no sunshine and no rain, no storms and no heat at all, just a day-in, day-out haze. "Don't ask me questions I can't answer, honey," I tell her.

I don't always know what Joyce is going to say, and just then she comes out with another one: "I wonder what went on in this bed," she says.

I pull my right arm down and slip it under her head and around her side. "If you knew, you'd have the whole story straight—what happened and everything else."

She turned cold right away. "It's not all sex," she says. "You think that it's all sex, but it's not all sex."

I told her I knew that. "I mean, if Harry had one of those voice-activated recorders in this room somewhere—and if you listened to all those tapes, you'd know."

"There probably wouldn't be much on them," she said.

So I'm lying there thinking of sleeping in Harry and Lois' bed, and all of a sudden it dawns on me that that is the first time I'd ever been in a trailer overnight. "You know," I said, "I've never slept in one of these birds before."

Joyce didn't say anything.

I wondered if Harry had smoke detectors. There we were, both of us wide awake, in this halloween bed. At least they had an electric blanket.

"What's she like," she says, "this other woman?"

I told her that she couldn't be that stunning because I couldn't even remember her face clearly from that polaroid.

"She's young, I bet." Her fingers stopped moving.

"I don't think she was that young, but I suppose she's got something going for her."

And then Joyce starts into something that I think I only faintly understand. We stop talking all together, but her fingers keep moving, up and over my chest and down over my stomach, in a way that does more than suggest that it's not just nodding off that she's interested in. It's unlike her to feel that way because there's just way too much working against it. Here we are in this haunted bed, and the whole business of Harry's leaving is like a fresh wound. I can't believe that she's doing what she's doing.

So I put my hand over hers to weigh it down, to stop it from moving around. Then I twist over on my side and pull her hand along. We get into a cuddling position, like a pair of spoons.

It wasn't that I couldn't or anything. It wasn't that at all. But I didn't want her to have to stoop like that, to offer herself as bounty against whatever it was she may have been afraid of.

"Aren't you interested?" she said finally, when we're lying there, her arm around my side.

Nobody tells men how to say no well. But I didn't like her doing it for the reasons I thought were behind it right then. So I said to Joyce, "I'm always interested, but there's the whole state of Iowa between here and home."

She turned her hand into a fist and drummed it on my chest, as if she knew I was right. That's the way I read it anyway. I might be wrong. Maybe I shouldn't have turned Joyce down that night in Harry's bed. Maybe she needed me for herself. You never know about those things, I guess. We're all crazy.

* * * * *

It's after twelve when we get the call about Harry, and it was an awkward situation. Even the cop thought it was strange when a man answered the phone.

"Is this 46575 Bluebriar Road?" he said.

"I believe it is," I said. Joyce was sitting up right away.

"There's been an accident," he said, "and the man in the car has a registration which indicates that his place of residence is 46575 Bluebriar."

"Oh, no," I said to Joyce, "Harry's been in an accident."

"The man's name is Harry Lamberts, it says here, and his license says he lives there."

"Is he hurt?" I said.

"He's banged up some, but it's nothing life-threatening. Our procedure is to notify someone."

Right away I'm thinking how we're in the middle of something now. "My wife and I are staying at his place," I told the cop. "Harry's separated from his wife. Neither of them live here right now."

"Can you tell me how to get in contact with his wife?" he said.

I put my hand over the receiver. "You got that number of Lois's parents?" I said to Joyce. It's dark as pitch in the room and I can barely make out her outline.

"Tell him we'll do that," Joyce said. "And find out where he is— how to get there."

Joyce was already up and getting dressed when I hung up the phone.

"He flipped the car and took a bad bump on the head," I told her. "Drove his car right into a cemetery."

She was so busy changing clothes that I couldn't tell if she thought our being in the middle was as odd as I thought it was. "Let's go down there ourselves first," she said. "Then we'll call Lois."

I'd left my pants hang over the swinging doors of the bureau. "What about that other woman?" I said. "I don't know her name."

"We'll call her too," she said. She said we'd get it some way.

When we got to the hospital, a policewoman was out there to meet us, a blonde, fortyish. I remember thinking how those big pockets and the belt full of hardware didn't do much for her shape.

"You two family?" she said.

So we told her the whole thing—Joyce did. It's funny how I would have done all the talking if it would have been a man, but because it wasn't, Joyce told her how it was that we happened to show up.

The woman cop said that the doctors had cleaned him all up and set the leg already. The only thing was that the bump he took on the head was a li:tle worse than they'd thought at first and they wanted him to stay around in the hospital for a couple days, maybe to be sure that it wasn't something really bad. She walked us down to his room, and leaned in through the door. "Have you called his wife already?" she said.

Sure enough. There he was peaceful as ever with a dome of white over his forehead and his leg protruding from the blanket in a cast. He was asleep.

"I thought we'd call her from here. She's in Rockford—that's a couple hours away, isn't it?" Joyce said.

The woman cop nodded. Her name was Carol—Carol Brandes. It was pinned to one of those big pouch pockets.

"Say, Miss," Joyce says. "He's got a girlfriend too, but we don't know her name."

The cop put her clipboard under her arm, then she scratched her head. "You got a first name on that number?"

Joyce looks at me. All of a sudden I remember. "Ang," I said, "that's all I know."

"And she's married too, I bet," the woman said.

Both of us shrug our shoulders. "He's a teacher—or a guidance counselor or something," Joyce says.

"Sure," the cop says, "a guidance counselor. Where?"

"Some high school," I said. I looked at Joyce. Harry's my friend, of course. That's what Joyce's eyes say. "'Apple' something—Apple River, Apple Valley?"

"Listen, why don't you just call his wife? You can bet she knows this other woman."

"I got her number," Joyce says. "I brought it along." She takes the piece of paper out of her purse and sticks it in my fingers. "Here," she says, "you call—they're your friends."

I told her thanks a million. I figured Joyce could talk to Lois better than I could, being a woman.

The hospital is really new, so there are no booths, only those plastic bubble shells sticking out of the wall. Eight rings go by before an old woman's voice answers. It was almost one o'clock. I tell her I'm looking for Lois, and I thought she might be there. "This isn't Harry, is it?" the woman says.

When Lois gets on the phone, her voice is full of little squeals, as if she's been sleeping already, and the tubes haven't been cleared fully yet. This is how the conversation goes—I swear it.

Me: Lois, Harry's been in an accident.

Lois: He hurt bad?

Me: No, me and Joyce are down here at the hospital and everything seems to be okay.

Lois: What'd you call me for?

Me: (stunned) We figured you should know.

Lois: Call Ang—she's the one who cares.

Me: (I don't know what on earth to say, and I can't get up my courage yet to ask for Ang's number.) I'm sorry for disturbing your sleep—

Lois: Who sleeps nowadays?

Me: Joyce said you should know. (I figure if I bring my wife into this maybe Lois'll cool off.)

Lois: Well I'm not coming all the way over there unless he's dying or already dead.

Me: He's just got a nasty conk on the head. He'll be all right.

Lois: I'm sorry.

Me: (What's there left to say?) Well, we just thought you should know.

Now there's this long silence. Finally, she starts in again.

Lois: Listen, Woody, this has got nothing to do with you. I'm sorry that you had to get hauled into this mess, but he could have told you

over the phone that the whole blasted thing was going to break. He could
have told you that, but he was scared. And now, you know what he's
saying? He's telling everyobody that this is the first time he's really been
alive in twenty years. I tell you what that makes me feel like—pure shit.
Dead shit.
    Me: I'm sorry.
    Lois: I don't want him back either. I can't even lift up my head—
    Me: I can see—
    Lois: You just tell him that next time he gets in an accident, I hope
it's for keeps.
    Me: Lois, you can't mean that.
    Lois: I'll write him a card that says it. I swear.
    Me: (I don't w .nt to talk anymore.) I just won't tell him that we called
you.
    Lois: He won't ask either.
    Me: How do you know?
    Lois: I'm dead, remember?
    Me: Well, I'm sorry for waking you.
    Lois: Sure, sure. I understand. Like I said, Woody, this has got nothing
to do with you. I got wounds, you know. I could be in a hospital myself.
    Me: Well, tomorrow the sun will come up again.
    Lois: Sure it will. I know that.
    But I had to get the other woman's name.
    Me: Look, Lois, I don't like asking you this, but can you tell me who
this other woman is—what her name is?
    Lois: Sure, it's Angela Trumpy—sounds like a mistress, doesn't it—
Angela T-R-U-M-P-Y. You can find her number in the book.
    The whole time I was talking on the phone, Joyce was over on the
sofa with the policewoman. Who knows what they were talking about?
It wouldn't have been at all like Joyce to tell her the whole story. She
wouldn't have done that. Not Joyce. Me? Maybe, but not Joyce.
    "She's not coming," I told her. "She said a lot of other stuff too,
but none of it's worth repeating."
    "You got yourself right in the middle of a real soap opera," the woman
said.
    "She wasn't even concerned?" Joyce said.
    I told them that she'd said she wasn't about to come unless he was

dying or already dead. Just like that she'd said it, "dying or already dead."

"She's hurting," the woman said.

"It couldn't have even been a week ago that they broke up," Joyce said.

And all of a sudden this policewoman starts laughing. "Break up," she says, almost squealing. "What the hell is going on when we talk about a twenty-year-old marriage breaking up—as if they were nothing more than kids going steady?"

"You're right," I said.

"Would you come down here if this one had done that to you?" the woman asked Joyce.

And Joyce looks me flat in the eyes right then, and all of a sudden I know I'm the enemy again. She shrugs her shoulder as if to say that she can't give an honest answer in the presence of these witnesses.

"Well, my job is finished," the cop says. She gets up off the couch and tugs at her slacks with her fingers. "You've got to call that other one yet, I suppose."

I'd almost forgotten about that. I said to Joyce that she should do it since I'd been the one that called Lois. She knew I meant it.

"Happy trails," that lady cop said, and she picked up her clipboard from the coffee table and gave Joyce one of those little female hugs—you know the kind—before she left.

"She's a good soul," Joyce said to me. "She's seen a lot."

Joyce did the calling all right. I gave her the name and she went over to the same phone I was using, even though I was thinking that Lois's words still probably hung in the wires.

I sat there on a chair and paged through an *Outdoor Life* magazine, one eye up there on Joyce at the phone. I knew she'd be good at a job like that. It's hard for Joyce to be sour to anyone, no matter what, and I figured she'd be good as gold to this Angela.

"She's coming right over," Joyce said when she came back across the lobby. "She's upset, all right."

"Well, that makes four of us," I said.

I didn't know what to expect in Angela. By that time I could barely remember her face in that snapshot. I don't know why, but you always do get a picture of the other woman as being some kind of bombshell, somebody sexy and sinful enough not to care what she's destroying. And it's silly to think that way because you scratch anybody deep enough and there'll be nothing more down there than a human being.

"What'd she sound like over the phone?" I said to Joyce.

Joyce just sat there staring into her cup. "Perfect," she said. "To tell you the truth, she sounded like someone I'm going to like."

What's there to say, huh? There's nothing like life itself to screw you up royal.

She didn't look Spanish, not one bit. As a matter of fact, when she came in, the first person I thought of was my brother Henry's wife, Ann, who people say resembles Jane Pauley. She was definitely middle-aged, but her face had that same kind of little girl look. Her hair, even though it was graying, was cut straight and kind of mid-length, to a curl at her collar. She came in in jeans and a turtleneck sweater, and she was no Jane Mansfield. She wore a cape-like thing over her shoulders for a jacket. You could see she was single. That much you could see.

"Joyce?" she said, as if she was afraid of asking.

Joyce nodded and the two of them shook hands, not just formally either. Joyce took her hand in both of hers, and the two of them went to the nurse's station to get someone to take them to Harry's room, and right away Joyce had her arm.

The first thing Angela did was put her purse in the chair next to Harry's bed. Then she leaned over him, put one of her hands on his chest and the other on his shoulder. There she stood kind of straddling him with her arms, not saying anything.

The nurse told her everything—how he was going to be all right but that the doctor had simply said that he should stay around a day or two just to be sure that the bump on his head didn't amount to anything more than a good strong headache, how the break in his leg had been clean and the bone was set well already, and how he'd have to take it easy for a couple of weeks maybe before he'd get strong enough for a walking cast. Angela stood over him, not crying, just staring down into his face.

Joyce took Angela's arm once the nurse started moving toward the door. It was no big traumatic scene or anything. We're talking about a grown woman here, not some giddy teenager.

"Are you his wife?" the nurse said back in the hallway.

"Not yet," Angela said. You could tell that she was embarrassed. I mean, you could see it in her face that it wasn't something she was proud of.

Then the nurse asked her some other questions, questions about insurance, questions that Angie didn't seem to know much about.

Joyce and I went back to the lounge area to wait.

"She's nice, isn't she?" I said.

"Yes, she is," Joyce said stubbornly. "She's very nice."

As far as I was concerned, it was all too clear how Harry could fall for her. On top of everything else, she knew how to love, he had said. Lois's steam was still in my ear, and here was this other woman, not young either really, but caring at least. She never cried at all, not once the whole time we were there together. Strong woman. No bimbo.

"What gets me is what happened," she said later when she and Joyce sat together on the couch. "I mean, driving into a cemetery like that— what on earth got into him?" She had her hands up on her cheeks when she talked. "You were with him—what happened anyway?"

And all of a sudden in my head this whole business is my fault, if you know what I mean. "He was sloshing it down pretty fast when we were at that restaurant," I told her.

"What did you talk about anyway?" she said.

Actually, the question was just slightly aggravating. What did she figure we talked about anyway?—pea soup? "He told me the whole story," I said. "He said he wanted me to know."

"There must have been more that he wanted to say to you or he wouldn't have been going down that road," she said, "back towards the trailer."

The thing is, it wasn't easy for me to get angry with her. There was no sting in her questions. It wasn't that she was trying to accuse me of anything, of being overly righteous or something. "He's a very fine man," she said. "Harry's about the finest human being I know. I love him."

When I think about it now, I know that Angie wasn't as starry-eyed as he was. Everything about her smelled authentic.

"This whole business has been very hard on him," she said. "You can't imagine how hard it's been. Maybe you don't have any sympathy—I can understand that too. I mean, you knew Lois and him together, didn't you? I mean, it's hard for you to think of them not being together—just as hard as it is for you to think of yourselves not being together.''

Joyce is sitting there without saying a thing.

"I'm happy you were here anyway. Otherwise, I wouldn't have known where he went. No one would have got in contact with me. How could they? I'd have been up all night wondering—and the thing is, Harry's just so sensitive.'' Then she said something that made her eyes go down. "He's so full of guilt.''

There were so many things I could have said right then, some sharp things that could have cut out that woman's heart right there in the hospital. And you wonder sometimes whether you should have. But I didn't. And now you wonder if maybe not saying something made her feel as if what the two of them had done was somehow right in the eyes of God and Lois and the kids and even Joyce and me. But the woman was sweet, and in my ears I still heard Lois's anger. It's a broken world all right. There ain't nobody whole.

"Everything is so mixed up,'' she said. "You can't believe how mixed up it can get.''

When we left, Joyce stood there and hugged that woman, stood there and held her as if they'd been through the war and held each other up for the whole tour. I wouldn't have ever believed it if I hadn't seen it myself. And it wasn't just the woman either, it was the pain that did it. You get to feel the pain and it doesn't matter who it is that's suffering, you get to feel like it's something that's got to be stanched—like a fire. You got to do your best to get it out, and, failing that, keep it from spreading. There my wife stood holding that other woman, neither of them crying either, just holding each other as if there weren't any other arms in the world by which a person could be held up. My Joyce and that other woman. "She knows how to love,'' Harry had said, and I'd read it all as if she was some bedroom contortionist, which she dang well might have been. But that wasn't all he meant either.

* * * * *

Joyce and I started back west somewhere around three in the morning, and we crossed the river at Dubuque seeing nothing but lights from the city. I don't think we said much for a long time. Joyce had her pillow along and she leaned up against the window on the passenger's side as if she were sleeping. I knew she wasn't. She was just like me, trying to settle some kind of uproar down deep in the soul.

We had breakfast in some small-town restaurant. I had pancakes and she had an omelet with orange juice. But the fact that we'd had no sleep didn't really catch up to us until mid-morning or so, when we were about halfway across the state of Iowa—Mason City, in fact. By then we were talking a little, Joyce going on and on about Angie, and how she couldn't help but like her for some reason, even though she wanted to hate her.

"It's a stupid thing," I said, "this love business."

"It's not always what you think," she said.

"Ain't that a fact."

"Do you love me, Woody?" she says.

Maybe we're like most people. Maybe we don't say it often enough. Maybe when we do it's for some reason other than really meaning it, too.

"Sure," I says, "I love you more than anything."

She's not even looking at me when I'm saying it. She's lying against the window of the car and looking straight out over the road in front of us. It's as if she doesn't want her eyes to throw too much weight on my answer. "Why?" she says.

I think for a minute, thumb through some answers. "Because you're good for me and—"

"I don't want to hear any selfish answers," she says, patiently kind of, not as if she's mad. "Really, why do you love me?"

That's not so easy to answer because there's things you can't just put into words so easily, like why. It's because you're you, I would have liked to say, but I figured she'd guess that sounded too much like some cheap lyrics. So I said what I could. "It's a different thing, you know—I mean it's different than like love when we were married. It's just a lot different," I said.

"You get old," she said.

"You get old and things change and it's just not the same."

And then she says it again. "But you still love me?"

It feels like it's just not enough this time for me to say yes. She's fishing for something more now. So I try my best to come up with something. "You're nothing but an old woman, and I'm nothing but an old man. And someday the both of us will drive into some cemetery somewhere

and be parked together in the ground. But that's not all bad, Joyce—the
way I see it, that's not all bad.''

She lets that sit for a while, as if she were typing the line out in her
head. Finally, she says, "We'll park, huh?" And she laughs a little.

"What do you mean?"

"Like we were kids?"

"That kind of park?"

"Yeah, that kind," she says.

Mason City's about the only city of any size along the northern route
through Iowa. Right about where you run across the Interstate there's
a ton of fast-food joints and restaurants and motels. But it's Joyce who
says it—not me. "Why don't we see what's up in Mason City?" she
says, and she's yawning as she says it. "Let's just get ourselves a room."

"It's the middle of the day," I said.

"I'm not blind," she says.

I like what she's suggesting. I'm dog tired, but I got an idea of what
she's after here, so I play her a little. "What's some clerk going to say
about an old couple coming in in the middle of the afternoon?" I ask her.

"Let her think what she wants," Joyce says, and her arms are up
behind her when she stretches.

So I take a right into a Motor Lodge and drive up through the circle
at the front door, check the prices, and go back out to the car. I can't
believe it's as much as that woman says. "It's sixty bucks," I tell Joyce.

"How many honeymoons you get in life?" she says.

So we take it.

Now this is embarrassing. It's not even noon, and here we are in bed
together. Tired? You can't believe how tired the both of us are. Old
folks. But I've always thought that being really tired isn't so bad when
it comes to love. I don't have to go into all of the juicy details either,
but we did all right, believe me. For a couple of almost-fiftys who hadn't
slept more than a wink the night before, who'd been through all the crap
that we'd been through in the last twenty-four, we did just fine. I'm not
sure why Joyce wanted it done that way, whether it was some kind of
gift or pledge or some way of making her feel as if we weren't already
parked there in the cemetery. Maybe it was all of those.

We napped for awhile, and then, in the afternoon we spent an hour
or two at a little prairie museum, we did some shopping, and we found

this great Chinese restaurant for dinner. And then we went back to that motel and started over. Honeymoon.

We really didn't get to singing until the next morning, once we started to home across western Iowa.

And that's the story of our autumn vacation.

But the thing is, I just got this call from Harry. It's almost Christmas now, and it came in out of the blue, out of nowhere at all. He says that he and Lois are going to get back together. He says he went to their preacher and the preacher said the only way it might work was if they both went out to some neutral turf somewhere and tried to talk it out.

So Harry says that he wants us to host this peace-talk. He says he's bringing this preacher along, and Lois is coming out too—he all by himself and Lois with the preacher. He says that our place is good neutral turf. He says he figures he could count on us because we've always been the kind of friends that tell the truth, the kind he can trust, even if he doesn't see that much of us.

Joyce is sitting at the piano in the den. I'm going to tell her now, but I think I know what she'll say. She'll be sad about Angie somehow, just like I am. She'll say she wonders how it was that that thing could ever have broken up. She'll be shocked, really, just like I was, and not shocked either. It's hard to get shocked about things anymore. Mostly, she'll hate Harry for what he's done to two women.

But then she'll say to tell Harry that we'd be glad to serve as hosts for whatever it is he's got planned this time. "What are friends for?" she'll say. Either that or something about "brother's keepers." I know Joyce. She'll swallow something back, but she'll know darn well that we can't turn the guy down, even after what's happened. He's in a cast on top of it.

And then we'll sing something together, just the two of us. Probably some hymn that we've sung together for the last decade or so. We got our favorites. Joyce'll sit there and play, and I'll stand behind her with my hands on her shoulders, and we'll sing like kids. Like we always do. Singing is something you can do until you die.

November's Thursday

When he awoke, Gary heard the silly wind chimes the neighbors had hung from their back porch in July—queer tinkling in an early winter wind. The shock of feeling her gone again had awakened him, his leg stretched uphill to the cold sheets on her side of the bed, just like October's Thursday, and September's before that. He pulled his hands back behind his head, running through a conversation he didn't want to have, his eyes following cracks in the ceiling that were barely visible in what light squeezed through the shades from the street outside.

The cracks had been there for years already. Nora had spotted them the first night they slept together in their new house. "Look at that," she had said, pointing. Back then, Nora had loved to whisper in those quiet moments when it was over. "Why didn't you see those when the realtor showed us through?"

He had pulled the sheet up so it half-covered his chest. "Right then I wasn't thinking about the ceiling," he had said.

"The realtor says 'master bedroom,' and you see visions—you turn into an animal," she had told him. Her old laugh was something like a naughty growl.

"I guess I'm the one who would see it," she had said. "I'm usually the one awake when it's all finished."

Nora would never say anything like that anymore. That was the first night in the new house and the new bed, amid the sprawl of boxes and half-emptied wardrobes, no rugs on the floor and nothing but shades over the windows, one of those nights that seemed so long ago now, before the cancer and the treatments.

The ceiling cracks had opened only slightly in the years they had lived in the house; they still didn't amount to much more than a dollar can of spackling and new coat of paint. But everything was on hold now.

Maybe they should take on a repair job together some Saturday, he thought, like the old days. That would be a great idea, something he might tell her tonight yet.

He lay there motionless, in the sound of the storm and the noisy smiling chimes. Nothing seemed so vacant as the empty bed she'd leave behind when she'd sneak away and sit downstairs, miles of stairway, like an open field of silence between them.

He couldn't sleep with her down there, and he couldn't lie awake and pretend he was—not even for her sake. But he couldn't move either. If she'd hear one sound from the bedroom, her guilt for being gone would wither whatever strength she had. Down there over the Bible, she'd cry to hear that her weakness had awakened him.

But he had to go down. Nora was his wife, after all, and he was her husband. He had to. Some things had to be said.

He swung himself out and pulled on his robe, then walked past the kids' room, until he stopped at the windows overlooking the neighbors' back porch and the chimes. By now she knew he was coming down, so he waited, watching the northeast wind's cargo of wet snow fall heavy as manna on the driveway next door, melting on the cracks and piling up between in perfect rectangles.

He put his arms up on the window. Tomorrow the neighbors would know she was up, even though now the house next door was dark. "So, you had somebody up again last night, Gary," Ben would say when they'd be outside with shovels. "Got somebody sick?" The old couple knew it was Nora's day for treatments; they knew the whole story of Thursday nights.

The light from the kitchen glowed in the stairwell beneath him. Nora was bracing herself now, he thought. Maybe praying.

He drew his finger through the steam at the corner of the window. The storms needed caulking yet. There was still a lot of Saturday work before the real winter.

To go back now would only make her cry again. Once she'd heard his footsteps through the hall, she'd blame herself for everything, even his not coming down. They had to talk now.

"I wish I could take on what your Nora's got," Ben had told him one spring Saturday in late spring when the both of them were out spraying dandelions. "Nora's so very young yet. Me and Trudy really had our time already.'' That was no more than a month after diagnosis, and Ben meant it.

Cancer was something he wouldn't wish on anyone, of course. But he had thought a lot about surrogates since then, about horrible people in the news who maybe deserved what Nora had.

When Gregg was born, he and Nora had gone to pre-natal classes, where some stocky feminist nurse told them about some strange jungle rite in which the husband would writhe in pain while his wife was in labor. That night it seemed funny. But sharing seemed impossible when he stood beside her and watched and listened as Gregg was born. On treatment days that strange picture would return, him lying there in pain on her bed, while she could sit and watch. If only it could be done, he thought.

In an even cadence he marched down the steps and through the dining room and found her in the kitchen, the hanging lamp pulled low over the open Bible. She pretended not to hear him, her elbows spread over the edge of the table, her fingers pushing through her thinning hair, a habit of hers.

He used to joke about the hair thing. As long as she had to wear a wig, he said, she might as well start her life over as a platinum Hollywood starlet. Once her own hair would grow back in, she'd never have such glorious options. But Nora didn't want to think of the whole business being over. That was a big part of the problem.

He walked up behind her to the refrigerator and opened the door, and just like that she closed the Bible. ''I put the cat out,'' she said quickly. ''You know how she gets when she wants to go out. I woke up—I guess I've got this sixth sense about her.''

The light from the refrigerator swept out over the linoleum that arched around the appliances, just the way she wanted it laid when they re-modeled the kitchen. Baloney sat there on the shelf next to turkey in Saran Wrap. ''Dagwood makes these huge sandwiches in the middle of the night, a foot thick at least,'' he said. ''You've seen them—mammoth things.''

''Gary, please—'' she said.

The cold slid down over his feet. He hadn't intended to talk about food. The Dagwood stuff was just something to say. ''I'm sorry, Nora,'' he said, turning to her. ''I wasn't thinking.'' The lamplight drew a perfect circle over the grain of the table. He put his hand up against the freezer compartment to make sure the refrigerator closed quietly.

"I think there's ice cream in the freezer," she said. "Mint—your favorite."

He knew it was hard for her even to mention food, and he wanted to hug her for her courage. It was a good sign. "I think I'll have some," he told her. "Maybe we'll both have just a scoop—"

Her head dropped slightly from the square lines of her shoulders. She picked some tiny crumb off the table, flicked it off on the floor, and shook her head slowly, her face down. It was still too much to ask of her, he knew—even that small bit of food. The lamplight bathed her crown where the bald patches flashed just like they did in the dreams he never told her about.

"I'm not so hungry myself," he said.

She turned to see him standing there, but she kept her fingers up around her eyes, as if she were looking into some brightness she couldn't bring herself to face. "I'm sorry, honey, but I can't even take the word *hunger*. Don't even say the word, okay?" She tried to laugh at herself.

He couldn't take silences because they fit him wrong somehow, so he came up behind her and took her shoulders in both hands, squeezing them hard, as if he were holding her down. "Think of yourself in a desert, honey. Nothing but sand and a thousand silly Arabs on camels. Some fat director's out there with a cigarette in one of those fancy holders—" He let go her of shoulders and sat down beside her. "Like this—" He took a toothpick from the glass picnic basket on the table, and he stuck it between his teeth. "You know what I mean?—like those old pictures of FDR with a cigar—"

"Gary—" she said, like a scolding given to a child.

"But here comes this Buster Crabbe-type in a perfectly white uniform—"

"Ah, yes—the star!—"

"That Arab with the black goatee wants my wife for his harem, see—"

"I think I know the handsome hero—"

"You've seen the show?" he said.

"A thousand times, at least."

"You recongnized those rippling muscles I bet—"

She took his arm. "He's going to get them, isn't he?—every last one of those Arabs—''

''It's a piece of cake. But, the whole time he's got his eye on the babe, see?''

''Oh my, whatever happened to the great, old movies?'' she said, leaning toward him.

''The hero pounds the bearded guy, scoops up the sweetheart, and the two of them drive off into the sunset in the shiek's silver-plated Mercedes—''

''Nice touch. A silver-plated Mercedes—''

''—and they stop off at the Riviera where they make love all night long for about a hundred years—''

She turned her head away and raised both hands. ''Too much sex,'' she said. ''Take me home this instant—it's horrible and disgusting and absolutely sinful—''

''Nonsense. Sparkling clean stuff. Lights out the whole time—''

For a moment she tried to hide her laughter with her hands, but finally it cam up free. She slid her hand beneath the table and dropped it to his thigh. ''I can't imagine going through this without you, honey,'' she said. ''It's actually made us stronger, you know.''

She looked so healthy now.

''You and I, honey—we could sit here in the middle of this storm and have one little scoop of the most delicious mint ice cream ever made on earth. You know that?'' He pretended to tip his hat like a circus barker. ''Yessiree, this here ice cream's guaranteed to be the world's finest— now what do you say, ma'am? You going to turn down this once-in-a-lifetime offer?''

Nora inhaled, the smile still there. Her eyes left his and scrambled over the table top as if to find something to steal her attention.

''Now as for me and my house, I could horse down a half gallon,'' he said. ''It's so blame hot out there in the desert.''

He knew she wanted to. He could see desire push lines across her chin.

Finally, she shook her head hard, one hand over her eyes. ''I can't,'' she said. ''I'm sorry. I just can't—''

He loved the softness of her arms. He moved both hands up and down from her wrist to her elbow, as if he had never taken the time to touch her before.

''I don't need it,'' he said. ''Man gets to be forty and he's got to cut down on calories—''

''You're only thirty-eight, Gary,'' she said.

''I've been lying to you for all these years.''

She pulled her hand back to the Bible and rubbed her fingernails against the leather grain. ''You're not really hungry either, are you? That isn't why you got up—''

''So what? You didn't get up to put out the cat.''

''So we're both guilty, aren't we?''

Only the wind chimes sang through the silence. He wondered how the sound could seep in through the storm windows. It seemed like such a dumb idea for Ben to put them up at the back door, not more than thirty feet from the neighbor's kitchen. ''I'd like to rip those chimes down,'' he said. ''You hear them? They drive me nuts.''

She was working her fingers through the thin hair at her temples again, looking away, as if she didn't deserve his attention.

He wanted so badly to have her back the way she was. He dragged the chair over the floor to be able to look into her eyes. ''How about this?'' he said. ''The jungle's wild and there's a woman swimming naked across this African lake. A herd of hippos spot her—''

''Hippos are vegetarians—''

''—and there's this handsome guy in leopard skin—''

''Please, Gary—'' She held the edge of the table with both hands. ''You don't have to—''

When he looked up at the clock, he thought it hadn't moved since he came down. He put his elbows up and felt the sting of his unshaven face in his hands. It embarrassed him to think of what he must look like.

''Just go back to bed, honey. I'll be there in a minute—''

''Hey, I already caught you once in a lie,'' he said. ''Great white woman speaks with forked tongue—''

She pushed back her chair and stood, the Bible clutched to her chest. ''We've been through this before, Gary. There's five down, seven to go. Seven horrid Thursdays and seven awful Fridays, and seven awful Saturdays. Seven more. That's all.''

He rubbed his sweaty hands against his pajamas.

''I've got to face it, Gary. Monday it'll all be over. I've got to think of it that way.'' She stood there leafing through the wall calendar. ''Go on—say it. Go on—''

A thin sheet of cold lay over his skin, as if his thighs were sugared with light snow. He had to say it. Even she knew he had to. "It's only because I'm trying to help, Nora. It's not to hurt you." He wished she would let him see her eyes more clearly. "Your being up like this only makes it worse. Try not to think about it. If you could just put it out of your mind—"

She looked up into the darkness as if there were someone standing in front of her. "I can feel the elevator lifting me up to that room," she said, "and right now I can even smell the room." She turned around to face him, holding the Bible with a balled fist. "The doctor says it's not unusual—"

"I know that—"

"If it was just a matter of my mind, Gary, don't you think I'd talk myself out of it?" She crossed both arms over her chest, her hands clutching her elbows. "I can't help it. I lie there next to you and I hate myself for being awake." She stared at the floor. "I try to settle my nerves, to make myself quiet and calm. I let my shoulders drop, let my head float—" She tried to hold back the thrusts in her breath.

He wished now there had been some way by which he could stay in bed and pretend to be asleep. Maybe he shouldn't have come down at all, he thought.

"You're angry at me, aren't you?" she said.

"How can I be angry?—"

"Because for the life of me, I can't control it!"

"Nora, I'm not angry with you." He stood quickly. "It's the cancer I hate—that blasted cancer." He wanted to hold her now, but he didn't know if he should. He didn't know if instead she should stand there on her own.

What angered him was that in fact it was Friday already; the IV's were already in her, her face blanched and distorted, and all around them the too-sweet smell of the flowers he'd brought threatened to choke him with his own lie—something pretty and bright and full of joy like the stupid windchimes—dumb flowers she never even saw. There they both were already, the two of them: he in the chair, Nora cramped up in bed. Sometimes he wished he could writhe like the savage.

"It's like a nightmare you can't bang your way out of," he said. Every one of those damned cells—every single blasted one, Nora. I hate every last one of them—''

''Please don't say it that way—''

''You want to know real sin, Nora? Cancer is sin—the word itself is obscene.''

''I won't let you say it that way,'' she said. Her arms dropped to her side when she came back to the table and sat down. ''I saw Alvin Fischer again today, Gary.'' Her hands begged him to sit again. ''I've prayed for that man—you know how long—and God is hearing me now. For the first time in that man's life he sees a need for something he doesn't have. He's got faith, honey. Don't you see that?—''

He picked up the basket of toothpicks and turned it in his hand. Like soft rain, the snow pelted the storms outside.

''It was my cancer that brought me into his life. Without my cancer I would never have the courage to talk to him. He may have died without knowing God.''

They'd been through all this before, he thought. All of it. ''I know the whole story,'' he said. He had seen the feeble old man lying in a hospital bed, an old man ready to die. ''I'm happy for you—and for him too, but that's not the point.''

''I thank God for my cancer,'' she said. ''I see things so much differently now. If I hadn't had cancer, I would never have met Alvin, and he would never have heard—''

''I know all that—''

''Then don't damn my cancer, Gary—''

''I'm sorry,'' he said. He stood again and went to the sink where the kid's ice cream dishes were stacked awkwardly, spoons still sitting in the bowls. The snow melted as clear as rain against the window outside.

''I'm scared that you're going to overinvest,'' he said. ''You're sticking too much into this, and you're going to lose yourself, Nora. You're going to lose your own sense of reason.''

''Losing yourself is what faith is all about, isn't it? You're as much a believer as I am, Gary. Look at me.''

The pain was there in streaks coming right through the steel resolve she tried to hold.

''I'm sorry,'' he said. He wiped his cheek with his shoulder. ''It's just that sometimes I can't take hearing you talk the way you do—I can't—'' He put his hands behind him and leaned up against the counter.

"Yesterday you said it again. 'Cancer has been such a blessing to me. It's changed my life.' Right in front of the kids, you said it—"

"It's true—"

"I don't care if it's true. How can I give thanks for some wretched disease eating away inside my wife's body?"

"It's brought me closer to Christ, Gary," she said. She crossed her legs and pulled her housecoat over her knees, smoothing it over her legs.

"Just don't ask me to paint halos on those damned cells," he said. He went back to her, took her shoulders, stiff as dried clay, in his hands. "I'm sorry. I'm sorry, I'm sorry—" He leaned over and kissed her cheek, but she held herself rigid.

He tried to think of working long days and nights in piles of piles of lifeless papers, claims and policies lying there in the chatter of typewriters around his desk.

She wouldn't speak now, because she'd already said everything there was to say. But for her sake, he had to explain himself.

"You see all of this in such spiritual terms," he said. "I want to feel you here on earth next to me. I want you to feel close to God—of course I do. But I want you to feel close to me and the kids too."

"We've got to rely on God—don't you see that, Gary? There's some things we can't do on our own. You know that—"

"—And there are some things God gives us strength to fight," he said.

She rose immediately. "You think I'm weak, don't you? You think this talk about God is just a crutch—"

"Nora, please—"

"You don't feel what I feel." She rubbed her arms with both hands, then walked toward the dining room. "Last week—it was just like you to say what you did—you remember? Insurance on that car accident with the burned man? You remember that?"

"Of course—"

"You described it all—how they had to bathe him, what?—twice a day, three times, I don't know—because the skin was gone over most of his body. 'Man loses that much skin in a fire, and he can't live,' you said. So proud you were, so knowledgeable, everything down to a science. 'Skin does all these things for us,' you said. 'Skin holds out infection. Man doesn't have skin and the other organs work overtime to do the job. Ecology of the body,' you said."

Emotions—anger, fear, guilt—twisted her lips. "It was all so clinical: pancreas and kidneys and lungs and heart. Such perfect sense it all made: this one goes and that one; then the whole body—like a house of cards. 'That man can't live without skin—can't live two weeks,' you said." She pointed at him. "You think you know everything, Gary. You don't even believe that God could still save that man—"

"My God can do anything," he said.

"Then can God save that man or not?"

"Of course he can—"

"Then how can you say it like that: 'That man can't live for two weeks'? What gives you the right to build walls in front of God's own hands?"

He could lie or tell her the truth. The burned man couldn't live, but he shouldn't have told Nora that way.

"Answer the question, Gary. Can God still save him?"

The only place he could hide was behind the truth. "The man died, Nora," he told her, "Tuesday morning". He could feel right away the ripping through her soul. "I'm sorry," he said. "Lord help me, I'm sorry." He could feel it in his own ribs, slashing through like shards of a broken window pane. "All I'm trying to say, Nora, is don't make this stuff we're fighting holy."

When her face lifted, her breath came audibly in anger and frustration. "You're right, of course," she said. She turned away from him completely, toward the darkness in the dining room. "You're always so very right."

She stood there alone with the Bible still held under her arm. Holes like yawns were worn into the elbows of the housecoat he bought her years ago at Christmas, a heavy cotton flowered pattern, high at the neckline, when she had expected some sexy nightgown. He had thought she would like it, admitting as it did the way their love had matured.

He heard the wind outside, and he wondered how thick the heavy snow was on the evergreens, whether or not he should go out and sweep the branches.

At the cupboard, he took out an orange tumbler, filled it with water and drank, then poured what was left quietly down the side of the sink. He knew he needed her back now. Even if she would go up, she wouldn't sleep a moment after this. He had to do something. "Nora, tell me," he said, "tell me about Fischer?"

She tested him with her eyes. "Don't condescend," she said. "Do you really want to know?"

"Please," he said.

Once again she came back to the table, because he knew, like she did, that this was simply no place for it all to end.

"He's very weak, and he doesn't talk well anymore." She laid the Bible back on the table, and her hands dropped to her lap like a schoolgirl's. "They've taken most of what he had inside him, I think. He's done fighting now—I suppose that's why I say he's so close to accepting Christ."

"What you've done for him is saintly, honey. I mean it."

Fischer's memory eased the tension from her face. "It's so fulfilling— I've never talked to anyone about faith so easily before. He needs me too—"

"I know it," Gary said. "We need you too—me and the kids."

She sat there nodding. "There's not much else to say," she said, rubbing her fingers through her eyes. "It's such a blessing to me." She laid out both her arms across the table. "I think I want to go to bed. Big day tomorrow—right?" Her lips tightened and she looked up at the top edge of the curtains over the window.

He stared at her as closely as a sweetheart, as he used to, at the familiarity of her eyes and the lines across her forehead, at the way she held her lips. It had taken five years of married life for him to learn how to love her, five years for things to get strong enough so their marriage didn't need guy wires. It took him five years to know how she wanted to be loved. Then it got so much better, he thought.

She reached for his arm. "Sometimes I think it would be much better if it was all over—for all of—"

"Nora! Don't you dare say that." Right then he could have hit her. "You've got to fight it. You aren't Alvin Fischer."

She tried to bring both hands up to her face, but he wouldn't let her. He held her wrists, both his arms straining to keep her from hiding behind her hands, and they sat there wrestling, Nora's face gone into storm again, him holding her, her wrists quivering, then slowly relenting, going limp and soft, her forehead flattened above the tears that squeezed from the corners of her eyes.

Maybe he could take her away. "Nora, listen," he said. "Just listen
to me. This is something. This guy with a long mustache grabs a beautiful
woman in a blonde wig, see?—and he takes her off to this mountain pass
where there's a railroad—" He let her use the backs of her hands to
get her tears.

"It's been done—" she said.

"He's got nothing but horrible thoughts about this babe—"

She jerked free from his arms and stood, staring angrily.
"In all of these cute little escapes of yours, I'm always half-naked,
because it's always only physical with you—isn't it, Gary? Admit it.
It's always physical. What you fear is the loss of my body—"

"That's not true—"

"I'm no sex goddess, Gary." Her hands were clenched as if tied over
her stomach. "I know that—"

"Nora, listen—when this is all over, you and I are going somewhere
for a month at least—"

"Stop it," she said.

"I'm just trying to—"

She came at him angrily and wrapped her fingers tightly around his
arms. "When are you going to understand that right now I can't see
any farther than tomorrow afternoon?—"

He stood and faced her, holding her just as she held him. And he felt
the truth of what she had said welling up like a giant fist and pounding
away inside him. It was his own rotten needs that pushed him sometimes,
his own pain. He pulled her tightly into him, her head against his chest,
her fine hairs against his cheek, and they stood there together in one
another's arms.

Finally it was Nora who backed away, wiping her fingers through her
eyes as she took him back once more to the table. "Sit here—" she said.

Steam rose from the open door when she took out the ice cream. With
her back to him, she took a bowl from the cupboard and reached in the
drawer for the scoop.

"I bought it because it's your favorite," she said. "Mint."

She took everything to the table and set it before him—the carton, the
bowl, the scoop—and she scooped out a dish full, the temper of her
breathing rising.

"Nora, please—I know how you feel—"

"Go on," she said. "Go on and eat it, Gary. I have to learn to take it. I can't let it get me."

Nothing stood before him but a wilderness of snow. He sliced a wedge from the side of the mound, put it quickly into his mouth and let it melt there, not moving his jaw, not giving her any sense of it being in him. She watched him, holding herself stiff against her own weakness.

Each sharp mouthful seemed sour, rancid. It thickened in his chest as if it wanted to come up again in a ball, his stomach tense and shifting, so that it wouldn't go down. He felt a rush of heat in his face, and a sudden chill over his skin. His heart quickened, and his hands felt light and shaky, as if every muscle in his body were tired from fighting.

When he looked down into the bowl, the ice cream seemed vile, repulsive. Simply to have it there seemed more than he could take, so he got up quickly and slammed what remained in the sink, then ran water to wash it away, closing his eyes and turning his head away as if to avoid even the smell.

And he stood there alone at the window, both arms braced beneath him on the counter, trying to regain his strength.

She came to him and held him so long that she turned soft in his arms, the tightness finally gone. He felt his arms sink slowly as his strength flowed into her, as hers had come into him, and together they stood in the silence.

Through the darkness they walked back to the stairs, then up into their bedroom, in the music of the windchimes and the rush of wet snow hitting and melting against the storms outside.

The Gift

Smiling radiantly, the woman pointed at a table full of craft treasures—tiny Santas aboard tiny black matchbox sleighs on runners of candy cane, pine cones painted like snowmen, and twenty or so assorted Christmas tree decorations, each of them pretty and precious.

"The great thing is that none of them cost more than a dollar or two to make," she said. Even her frilly apron was cross-stitched. "God bless you this holiday season," it said across her chest, the kind of print, deftly sewn, one might see beneath the print of a horse-drawn sleigh in a winter wonderland. "A lot of these things are nothing more than trash, really." She picked up the Santa. "This guy is an old sock I would have used to wash my windows." She laughed at her own joke. "My husband's old sock."

Julia sat on a folding chair with twenty other wives of school administrators, while their husbands, in freshly washed socks, she assumed, were busy in another room, talking about budgets. She'd never given two hoots about crafts, hadn't the time or the inclination to sit for hours with needle and thread. She was a captive to her husband's job tonight. Most of the administrators were men. Tom had wanted her to come along to the banquet, so she did, knowing full well that coming along probably meant sitting through something like this, some perfect housewife in frills explaining what could be done with Baggies, old socks, worn panty-hose, and empty Kleenex boxes—how to make treasures out of trash, for Christmas this time, the holiday meeting.

She introduced herself as Melody or Melanie or something like that. "They make such wonderful gifts because you're giving something of yourself," the lady said.

Julia knew she was right about that. There likely was something special about giving some little thing you'd spent hours working on. But she never had that kind of time, not with her own teaching, her twenty-four second graders, kids whose noses ran daily during December, whose snow boots wouldn't snug up over their sneakers, whose zippers got stuck in their underwear. And not with her own children, even though there was only one around now that Amy was off to college, only Missy anymore. Pregnant Missy.

She'd bought Missy her first pair of maternity jeans on Tuesday, but that pair of pants had lain upstairs on the chest of drawers in Julia's own room because she couldn't bring herself to give them to Missy—Missy not even sixteen years old. So that pair of pregnant-lady jeans lay there beside her and Tom's wedding picture for four days, the crumpled edge of the shopping bag still bunched where she'd carried it in her fist for an hour in the mall; it lay there until tonight, not two hours before, when Julia knew she had to give it to her daughter.

"I could have had an abortion, you know," Missy said. "I could have just gone through with it and you would have never known."

That was probably true. She may well have lined something up on her own and taken care of the whole business like so many young girls did, even those as young as Missy.

"I'm glad you didn't," she had told her daughter. "It would have been wrong. You know that."

Missy sat on the bed with the nylon panel in her fingers, not crying— oh no, not crying, because their second daughter was always too tough to cry—just angry, angry like she always was, angry at the world.

Missy had never told them she was pregnant. Somehow Julia just knew. It seemed strange to her that she could know as surely she did, be gripped by the conviction that her little girl was going to have a baby. It was strange because Julia had never had a child herself. But there was this pudginess in Missy—not just physical pudginess either—but her hands were looking strange, her voice had lowered almost, as if she were a boy at puberty. And she was nervous, brittle in the way she could be spoken to. Not like Missy at all. Tough little Missy.

Julia had caught her at the door, just after breakfast, her school bag already up over her shoulder. Tom was in the dining room with his coffee. "Missy," she'd said, "I think you're pregnant. Am I right?"

Missy hadn't said anything. Just left for school. Walked out the door and never once turned around. Didn't deny it. So all that day—through second grade spelling bees and recess bruises—she'd thought about her little daughter, a sophomore, going to have a baby, a baby she herself had wanted like nothing else in the world for all twenty-five years of marriage.

For years she and Tom had avoided department store toys at Christmas, kept themselves from the pain of seeing tractors and dolls and tinker-toys, a pain so great that she couldn't speak of it. Tom had always insisted that there were thousands of couples who couldn't have kids, that it wasn't the end of the world; but she had given long stretches of her life, hours and hours, to unanswered questions about why it was this woman's body of hers couldn't bring forth life.

The questions had never stopped. Even when they adopted Amy, then Missy, even when they brought those two little bundles home to a real children's bedroom and laid them so carefully into cribs, even then the desire never left her because she'd heard so many stories about adoptive parents who suddenly, out of nowhere, had conceived once the nervousness had passed, once someone else's child slept soundly beside them, just a wall away.

Now Missy, her own daughter, was fifteen and pregnant with a baby that she'd never once thought of conceiving.

"Everyone loves wreaths," the frilly woman said. "If you walk in the woods at the lake you can still find pinecones lying all over. And they're so easy to make. All it takes is time."

Time was running out. Missy's middle was growing daily. That's why she needed the maternity levis. But no one knew yet. No one but she and Tom. Tomorrow Amy would be home for Christmas. They hadn't told her yet because Julia told Tom that it just wasn't something that she could sit down and write—something like the fact that it had been a terribly cold winter back home and that the basketball team had won five games in a row.

"Why don't you call her then?" Tom said.

The thought of that kind of news out on some slender copper wire stretched from Wisconsin to New York seemed too public.

"She'll be home in couple of weeks," she'd told him. "I'll wait. Missy won't be showing yet anyway. She doesn't have to know."

"How can you not tell her?" Tom had said.

She and Tom were different that way. Tom was the one who had to talk, as if talking would make the whole thing go away. Years ago, when she couldn't get pregnant, he had told her to get some counseling—not told her, asked her in a loving way. But the thought was the same: if you talk about it, maybe you'll feel better. But talking never made her feel any better about anything. Tom was like a truck full of cargo—once he'd got all of it off his chest, he could sleep. Just like making love. He was always the first to sleep.

"Just let me wait," she said. "I'll tell Amy when I pick her up from the airport."

"I don't know how you can sit on it that long," he said, as if it were some kind of explosive charge.

Maybe he was right. Maybe Tom was right about so much. She never knew. You get to feel as if your mind is like a child's board game, a square-by-square path that angles and twists and winds around like a labyrinth because you're always second guessing yourself, she thought. Maybe it hurt so bad because she could never have a baby herself. Maybe it was simply selfish of her. Maybe if she had had children herself, she wouldn't be so constantly reining her tears. Maybe it was her fault somehow. And in all of it she was forgetting Missy and her problems.

That's when she'd pray. Sometimes there weren't even any words, just grief and guilt and anguish that came out in a single question—why? What did I do? Was it because she loved Amy more than Missy? She had always tried so hard not to. Sometimes she'd be angry with herself for favoring Missy—overcompensating for what she knew but hated horribly to admit: there was something about Amy that was easy to love, something about Missy that was so very hard.

Why?—was it her own frantic need for a child of her own when the Lord himself had given her two very healthy children? Maybe she'd spent too much time frozen in desire. Maybe she hadn't loved them, not really. Maybe she'd adopted two kids only because she thought they might be just what she needed to have her own. Maybe down deep she'd hated them, really hated both of them, because they hadn't delivered what she thought they promised. Why?—she said. Just a one-word prayer.

And now it was Missy pregnant, her own child having a baby.

Sometimes she'd wait for an answer from God. In the middle of the lunch hour, all alone in her room, her kids outside in the snow, she'd sit, eyes open and staring, waiting as if somewhere on the blackboard

God himself would write an answer. When the bell would ring, all twenty-four kids would bounce back in, their hands parched and red, stung by the cold. "Reading time," they'd say as they'd take their seats. After lunch it was reading time, and for twenty minutes, surrounded by all those loving kids, she could lose herself in boxcar children and velveteen rabbits.

Maybe she wanted to teach in order to try to find that child she never had. She'd thought of that too. She'd thought of every angle.

"There's lots of places where you can get things laminated," the frilly lady said. "Look at these." She held up three placemats adorned with stick figures throwing snowballs and sledding. "I had my kids draw these. Then I took them down to the frame shop and had them laminated. I think they make wonderful Christmas placemats—even for Christmas dinner. And think of what Grandma will say—"

Just three hours ago, Missy had been sitting there on the bed holding the jeans. "I want to keep the baby," she said.

She and Tom had talked about it before, but not for more than a half hour because Tom had said it was not a good idea at all. She knew he was right. At fifteen, even with their help, keeping the child wasn't a good idea. Missy would lose so much of life that way. She'd graduate from high school with a kid in the terrible two's. She and Tom could raise the child, of course, but it wasn't right.

"I don't think that's a good idea," she told Missy.

Missy laid the levis on the bag and stretched her hands behind her. "It's my baby," she said.

"I know that."

"I mean, I don't have to listen to you because it's not really yours, is it?"

She pushed the levis aside and sat next to her on the bed. "You're mine," she said.

"But I'm the one who's going to have the baby."

She took Missy's hand. "Honey, listen. Your father and I have talked it over and we agree that keeping the baby just isn't the right thing." She squeezed her fingers hard, bounced her hand on her thigh. "You've got to trust us."

"It's my baby."

"It's not a toy, Missy."

"But it's mine."

"It's God's.

"Well, that's easy to say. What's God going to do when it's dirty?" She pulled her hand away, lay back on the bed, then rolled over on her stomach.

Julia reached over and felt the soft denim. "God's got ways of changing diapers—"

"Don't be weird, Mom," Missy said.

"I'm serious."

She could feel the thump in the bed when Missy hit the mattress with her fist. "I want to keep it," she said.

"You're fifteen."

"What else is new?"

"You can't be a mother and be fifteen years old."

"There's lots of girls who do. You read the papers."

Julia felt herself about to cry, and it was always that way with Missy. Ever since she'd been old enough to think for herself they'd had disagreements, and every time they'd try to talk them out, it would be Julia who would be the first to break. "You've got to trust me," she said. "You've got to trust your father and me."

"You're not even my real parents," she said.

At that moment it had taken Julia every last ounce of her strength to twist her body around and lie down next to Missy, to try to hang on to her daughter even when Missy was working harder than she knew herself to fling her own mother away. "I'm the only one in this room right now who loves you," she said. "You've got to trust me."

"I can't just give this baby away," she said.

"I know that."

They were lying there together, their two bodies across the bed.

"You don't know what it's like to have a baby," she said.

She had tried to be as tough and strong as her own little girl. She pulled herself up again and sat beside her daughter. "I know what it's like to have a child," she said.

"But you don't know. You're just getting back at me. You don't want it because you couldn't have one."

There they were at the bottom line, she and her dark-haired baby girl. She felt as if there were something tearing her out of that room then,

something that wanted to protect her own daughter against what her
mother might say. But she knew what was right. She held herself.
"Missy," she said. "I don't care what you say. I love you."

Missy sat there with her face in her hands, her arms propped up beneath
her. She wouldn't cry. She couldn't. If Missy would ever cry, it would
be alone.

"That's all I can tell you," Julia told her.

Missy stared at the eighth grade graduation picture tacked to the wall
beside the bed. The silence felt like thick clay between them, thick, cold
clay. But she had said everything she could say. She knew that. Now
it was up to Missy. So Julia let the silence sit there like some half-formed
wall between them, just sat and waited. She would have waited for hours.

Missy's hands dropped, stretched outward toward the wall, and she
turned her face away toward the lamp at the head of the bed. Her bare
feet swayed up behind her so her skirt fell in a puddle of plaid over the
quilt. She was barely old enough to shave her legs, and somewhere inside her this baby was growing.

"Mom," she said, finally. She swallowed something back. "Mom,
sometimes I just want to die."

"I know, Missy," she'd said. "I know very, very well."

The woman in the frilly apron stood directly in front of the table full
of Christmas treasures, one arm tucked beneath the elbow of the one
that was gesturing. "As I've said before," she said, "these holiday
decorations can be put together for hardly a cent. I'd guess the whole
table cost me no more than twenty dollars. And they make such great
gifts."

Julia had no time to make things.

When they drove home that night, Tom asked how it had gone.

"A girl showed us how to make decorations for Christmas," she said.

"Wow!" he said, guessing she'd be bleeding frustration. "Did you
pick up any goodies?"

When she told him she simply hadn't heard much of what the lady
had to say, he lost his gaming sense.

Julia said she wanted to pick up Amy alone, so Tom stayed home with
Missy. He was refinishing an old oak commode in the basement,
something he figured he'd give to Amy for Christmas. He wasn't so
much in love with antiques himself, but on Saturday afternoons he en-

joyed stripping down old pieces and making the old grain redefine itself, all the time watching some ball game on the little black-and-white he bought for thirty dollars and stuck downstairs in his shop. He called it his therapy, but Tom was, in fact, far more "crafty" than she was.

Julia didn't teach in Tom's district, not only because it would have been against the rules but because she knew well and good it wouldn't be a good situation. She taught in a town named Garland, about fifteen miles of old snaking highway away from Bartlesville, where they lived. In the five years she'd been back at teaching, she must have driven those miles a thousand times, so often that she knew ᵗʰe people she'd meet every morning at half past seven, even though she hadn't the slightest idea who they were or where they were going.

What's more, she knew every mile's worth of farms, from the abandoned place just outside of town, to the ramshackle place a mile from school where an old man tethered a goat to a front yard pole. There were old acreages and new A-frames on the steep, wooded hills that couldn't be farmed. Halfway between home and school, a tiny little place named Ranslik, a town of no more than two hundred, was slowly dying on the very spot where it had been settled a hundred years before—nothing much more than a foundry there, just off the highway, its metal walls cast in a glow of orange from the rust that crept farther up every year, like red ivy, toward the cupola.

The old foundry stood on the banks of the Pecatonica River, a lazy old muddy thing that emptied into the Mississippi just less than a hundred miles west. By Christmas, the river was covered over with a foot of ice, and from where she daily crossed the bridge she could see the belted paths of snowmobiles that cruised its winding path through naked lowland farm acres.

In a patch of woods on the hill above the river, an old leafless cottonwood jutted up above the trees around it, its silver branches reaching, like talons, into the sky. Every day Julia saw that tree, and sometimes she wondered why it hadn't fallen. Lightning had cleaned it of its bark, so it stood there like some skeleton, some symbol.

It had always looked to her like aspiration itself, like a picture of desire. The trees beneath it were content to be no more than what they were created to be, but this cottonwood had wanted something more. It had reached higher. But when it did, it was subject to the wind and rain and ravaging lightning. She saw herself in that tree—a woman rendered lifeless by her own excessive passion for a child, by her inability to accept the fate which the Lord had given her.

On her way to the airport, she passed the tree and wondered once again if it wasn't her own sinful jealousy eating away down inside of her, somewhere deeper than her hurt at what Missy'd done, deeper than anger, deeper even than the fear of losing her. And again, right there on the road, she prayed for herself, for Missy, for Amy, for Tom, for all of them—her eyes wide open, her mind so tangled in emotions that she couldn't put anything into sentences; she prayed, knowing full well that God would hear the words in her sighing. And then she looked along the road, hoping for some kind of finger-painted message in the wide swath of snow clinging to the naked hills.

The airport was full of holiday traffic, carols ringing through the terminal like so much holiday clatter. She'd arrived just on time, but the flight had been delayed in Detroit, so she had an hour to sit.

She knew people who hated airports, but she hadn't flown often enough to dislike them the way others did, the people who carried or wheeled baggage around as if the place was just as familiar as a backyard alley. She walked through the gift shop, looked at the last minute trinkets people bought—sweatshirts, calendars, souvenir pens, fancy chocolate bars, a hundred different horribly overpriced toys to satisfy any parent guilt-ridden for not thinking of his or her kids: stuffed animals, or a fancy car—fifteen dollars—that ran into walls, then backed off as if some smart little driver inside knew enough to turn around. She picked up a Danish chocolate bar—two dollars for less than ten ounces—then took two and decided that she and Amy would eat them together on the long ride home.

The Lord had given them one perfectly lovable daughter. Amy was everything any parent would want—bright, mature, blessed with a loving disposition, talented, respectful. The two of them were three years apart, but Missy had stayed behind a year in grade school. Amy had always tried to be a mother to Missy, another mother, and now that Amy was coming home, Julia was afraid of how she would react to what had happened. Amy was likely to walk into Missy's room and tell her where she went wrong, not in a righteous fashion either, just honestly and lovingly. But it would be something that Missy didn't need from her always-perfect older sister.

She looked up at the monitors once again, at the flashing time behind Amy's flight number, then checked her watch and walked over to the gate where the plane would arrive. It was always a shock for her to be in the airport. There were so many people, all of them nameless, all of them moving back and forth constantly, people always leaving and always arriving, hundreds and hundreds of people, so many of them absorbed in magazines or some airport novel, or just walking, walking, walking. She sat across from a man wearing a bolo tie and a cowboy hat. He wore one of those half-pairs of glasses, and he was reading *Business Week*.

People began to gather around the gate adjacent to Amy's, groups of people in families, ready to welcome some member back home. You could read anticipation in their faces. She wondered how she looked to the others, whether it was clear on her face that all of this reception wasn't only Christmas joy.

A whole battery of young couples, maybe thirty years old, were standing and sitting around the east edge, some of the men staring out of the window and holding their kids, as if to try to be the first to spot the plane. They were friends. You can tell the way friends talk with each other because it's not forced, she thought, it's not just so much small-talk, so much being polite. These were people who loved each other. In Tom's job there wasn't always such good opportunities for friends. His job was lonely. She had friends herself, of course, at school, but she didn't live in the district so "they" didn't have friends, not friends like the couples who were there at the gate together, awaiting someone.

Four couples. All of them well-to-do. You could see it. The men looked clean and well-dressed, the women proud of themselves without being pompous. Two of the women were holding hands with the one in the middle. Two old couples were there too, like grandpas and grandmas, all of them waiting together, it seemed.

She thought there was something nice about airports, something nice about the hugs and kisses at the gates. She'd hug Amy too when Amy would come in. It was always so easy to hug Amy. Even when she was a child, she loved to snuggle up next to them—either of them—with a little book; she loved to be held on a lap.

There was a whole group of people all right, and they were all waiting for someone. Some of them had children. Some of the kids were tugging away at their fathers' pantlegs, pointing at the gift shop or the water fountain or some other attraction. But they were all together, like a whole, large family. Maybe there was a European tour or something just getting over, Julia thought. Maybe they were all from the same church.

She leaned back in her chair and thought about eating her chocolate bar. She reached in her purse, then decided to wait for Amy. The man in the half-glasses had fallen asleep across from her, the magazine folded against his chest.

From out of nowhere she heard the announcement for an incoming flight. It registered in her mind because she heard the voice say—it was a woman's voice—"Gate 22," the one right next to Amy's.

The couples rose simultaneously. The women still held hands. It was odd, Julia thought, the way they held hands like that, as if it were grief they were holding back. The woman in the middle looked back at her chair to be sure that the package she had taken was still there. It was precious.

Julia decided to get up and walk over there. It wasn't more than fifty feet. She would watch the package for her. The woman in the middle wanted someone to watch the package for her. It was something you could see in her eyes.

A uniformed man opened the door to the gate. The first people off the plane were rich. You could tell it by the way they folded their London Fog coats over their arms, by the way they toted their bags, and by the fact that no one was there to greet them. Then came the others— college guys in levis and sport coats over madras shirts, college girls with fancy earrings, holding the kinds of books you can't buy in airports. Julia looked down at the package beneath the seat to make sure it was there.

The woman stood over at the door, waiting. They all stood around together. One of the grandmas hugged her again. Her husband came over and took her hand. When she looked back at the package, Julia waved her fingers just to let her know that she was watching her things. The woman smiled, nervously, almost as if she were crying, but happily.

Almost every passenger had deplaned when what they were waiting for came in a perfectly white bundle of receiving blankets, a baby, a brown-faced Korean baby, all wrapped up as if it had just come from a bath. It was a child they were waiting for. All of that love, all of that anticipation, the nervousness, even the thin tears around the woman's eyes, all of it for this child. The woman carrying the baby handed it to its new mother, as if the bundle of blankets were the most precious gift in the world. She slid her arms out carefully, once the mother held the child firmly in her arms. Then she kissed the mother, and the grandpa kissed the mother, and the husband kissed his wife, and everybody kissed and hugged, and Julia stood there keeping watch over the package at her feet.

Tears flowed more easily now. The husband dabbed at his wife's eyes with his handkerchief because she couldn't reach them herself, and she didn't seem to care anyway because there was no reason not to cry. She simply stood and held that child, stared into its round, brown face as if by noting every single wrinkle and line she would bring it into her soul. And Julia knew exactly what was in that woman's mind, because she saw herself there once again, holding both of her children, both Amy and Missy, for the very first time, in pure disbelief that this child —that these children—could really be her own, their own, Tom's and hers.

The woman suddenly looked up as if she had forgotten something very important. She stared at Julia, at her feet. And Julia picked up the bag and brought it to her.

The woman held her bottom lip in her teeth and smiled, her tears washing down her cheeks. "Thank you," she said, when Julia brought her the package. "Thank you. This is my baby."

"I know," Julia said. "I know."

"Will you get it out for me?" she said.

So Julia reached in the bag and took out a tiny stuffed bunny. "He'll love it," she said.

"It's a girl," the woman said. "She's a girl."

Julia didn't want to be crying. "She'll love it then," she said, remembering how she'd waited in the school room and she'd waited on the road, watching blackboards and stretching fields of snow for someone's clear handwriting. But now she knew that God had given her the message here in the airport; and it had come in the tears she felt brimming in her eyes, the tears of a mother who never was and yet was, even today; the tears of a grandmother who would give her own child's baby away into arms no less loving than these that hugged all around. To see it, to remember, to know again, was God's own gift to her at

Christmas.

An hour later Amy came bounding off her flight, third person off, even before the businessmen, a huge student bag flopping around her shoulders, her hair cut short—short and kind of sassy, a little too short maybe—her own face bright with anticipation.

"Mom," she said and the two of them hugged the way it means something to hug.

"Oh, Amy," she said. "It's so good to have you back."

Amy pulled herself away quickly, poked her lower lip out with all the resolution in the world, and held her mother at arm's length. "It's so good to be home. I know it's going to be a good Christmas, Mom," she said. "I just know it."

"So do I, honey, so do I," she said, because she could feel grace in her arms and her fingers, and in her heart; grace that strengthened her, built her up once again the way only the Lord can do, grace in a brown-faced gift of love.

The Land of Goshen

Sometimes I wonder what it must have been like for old man Emil to stand out here on the prairie and see nothing at all but grass and sky, because when the Branderhorsts came here there were no trees. Ten miles west, scrub oak have always grown like weeds over the hills that shoulder the river valley, but here there was nothing. They're here now, elm and cottonwoods and ash like shadows around the houses and the church, the elevator and the store. There are few poplars around, because in Goshen nobody's ever been short-sighted. If you plant at all, you plant long term—maples and elm—and shore up the saplings until they get twelve feet or so.

But if it weren't for the trees, there'd be little to distinguish Goshen from what it might have looked like seventy-five years ago, a little settlement of frame houses surrounding a country store, a church, and a school on the town's only paved street. Of course, the school is shut down now. Years ago already Goshen's kids were vacuumed up by the Meridith district when the state put on pressure to consolidate the smallest districts. So the kids are gone. The trees are grown up and the kids are gone. Otherwise, Goshen's just about the same.

Once your tires crack the gravel at the end of the town's blacktop, if you stay with the road, if you follow its sweeping curve through the fields and over the culverts, you'll find that same big house that's been there for years—Emil's own American dream. It's always been painted white, and it stands out front of the barn and sheds, facing east so that it catches the face of the dawn, a glossy mirage against the long tawny grain fields stretching west to the river. The home place is the only house in the county with four two-story pillars out front, the kind of pillars that bring to mind a Southern plantation set down here on the bleak northern plains by some freakish, drunken whirlwind.

Emil Branderhorst had money when he came from the old country at the turn of the century, money and kids; and he built the home place first thing to stand up on the knoll like a castle just west of town. In those days, of course, there was promise in the land. Goshen had a couple hundred people, and the sweep of prairie, west and east, sprouted farms where hundreds of immigrant families cut through prairie turf as if, with proper cultivation, they could grow their own fortunes. Last week Emil's great-grandson sold three hundred cattle at a hundred-dollar-a-head loss, and in ten minutes of sluggish bidding lost himself thirty thousand dollars. Emil's castle cost half that much to build.

In the thirties already the land shook off excess settlers as if God himself, like a farm wife, picked up the topsoil like a dirty carpet and shook it in the wind. Some of the immigrants left the land of Goshen—those who took up farming in America because they thought it was the only new country occupation; those who were simply not predestined to take the rigors of milking; those whose vision of the promised land hadn't included the burning heat of a prairie summer or searing winter winds spun from a continent of snow to the north; and those whose ambition climbed beyond a barbed-wire fence strung around eighty acres of black soil, no matter how rich and sweet it smelled come May's annual re-awakening. The land itself evicted its unsuited squatters, and those who were left dug in like survivors, planting elm and ash and maple south of the house for balm from the sun, north and west as a shield from the wind.

By the forties Goshen never saw new faces, save a new schoolteacher or a preacher, transients for the most part, in a community of not more than a half-dozen extended families who met on Sunday, as was Emil's custom, in the frame church in town to drink their own brand of old-country Calvinism. Good sermons, folks thought, were something like cod liver oil, a potion one needed to stay healthy, not necessarily good-tasting but morally, spiritually healthful. For years Goshen thought a good sermon was one that laid a scar across your back, one that kept you smarting through a week of fieldwork.

What Reverend Heerema did the day of Earl Branderhorst's funeral was nothing out of the ordinary for the place. There's never been a fire in the Goshen church, but its walls are thoroughly scorched. What Heerema said that day is well within the traditions of great-grandpa Emil's own Calvinism, but it laid proud welts across his descendants' backs, opened up some thick skin that had long ago lost sensitivity to the scourge of a stringent sermon. What I'm saying is that in some ways little has changed in Goshen, and yet there is a difference. Emil Branderhorst's great-grandchildren still take some pleasure in an old-fashioned whipping from the pulpit, but only for the searing sound of the whip in the air—not for the open flesh across the back. It's the sound alone that rings true to a deep sense of tradition—"give me that old-time religion." They like the pitch of a blistering sermon, but the fierce gospel itself doesn't tune their lives anymore. That's what I mean. Heerema gave them what they wanted, but the amplification smashed right through their precious stained glass.

The Lord only knows why folks called Earl, Emil's wealthiest grandson, "the Beagle," but they did for as long as anyone could remember. In Goshen men have a way of nicknaming each other as boys already, assigning each other tags and poking them in a kid's ear the same way they tag cattle. Earl was one of a couple dozen of Emil's grandchildren, but he wore the Branderhorst features as if he were cut out of the exact pattern—wide shoulders above a long and stocky trunk, with squat legs and no rear end whatsoever, so the back pockets of his jeans hung down from his waist like a pair of empty bags. Like most Branderhorsts, Earl's face had the puffy red glow of an alcoholic's, a thick nose and a broad forehead, his cheeks shot full of tiny red veins, his full head of hair still dark and wavy when he was nearing seventy, refusing to gray with a Branderhorst's perfectly stubborn determination.

Earl lived on the home place for one reason: unlike many of his cousins, he never went to war. If he had had his choice, he likely might have; but his father kept him back, even though, like all the rest, Earl had this fervor to go to Europe or the Pacific and do what he could—at least that's the story as he tells it. Reluctantly, he got an agricultural deferment when so many other boys were already gone, and the war, for the most part, treated him well. By the time his cousins returned to Goshen from Guadalcanal and Anzio, the Beagle had, as they say, a leg up on the field, his operation expanding throughout the war years whenever land came available in the area. He learned how to deal on the black market, picking up implements when the government claimed they were unavailable, buying tires when the Co-op said there were none to be found. He had no trouble rationalizing his wheeling and dealing, because his operation turned out more milk and beef and grain, with more efficiency and in greater supply than anything seen in the county. He was doing his part at home, he thought—and said. That's what his father told him, and that's how he dealt with his guilt over not carrying a gun into Germany. But he made enemies, lots of them. Somehow there's room for enemies in Goshen, even though the town itself is no more than six blocks long.

I know all of this because I'm an outsider, one of the last teachers to come into Goshen before the school shut down. What's more, I married the Beagle's daughter, Julia, who was, and still is, a startlingly beautiful woman with her father's thick head of hair and her mother's charm and grace and slight build. Goshen was my first teaching job, just out of teacher's college. I was single then, and I went at teaching with all the zeal of a true believer setting a course to change the world and starting right here on the plains. Back then I loved Goshen because I loved its children. And Goshen loved me; in fact, it offered me one of its own favored women to marry. When I think back on it now, I sometimes see it was one of those prearranged feudal marriages. When the Beagle decided I was good enough stock to stay in Goshen, he offered me his daughter as a surety, even though I wasn't about to farm. It wasn't done that blatantly as I remember, but I understand now that nothing got done in town without Earl's approval back then in the early sixties.

So we were married. Then the school closed up, and I took a job at Meridith. Even though we lived in Goshen, Goshen forgot about me, and once more, I became an outsider. "The land of Goshen," my friends in Meridith call it. It's a dead town on the prairie now. Last month Herm Beernink died, and his place was sold—a decent house, two barns, one good shed on a five acre plot at the edge of town—for four thousand dollars. They were lucky to find a buyer.

I'm a Midwesterner at heart, but I grew up far north of here, where dozens of inland lakes mirror the woods and patches of farmland that sit on their shores. I grew up in a church, but somehow we didn't take faith so seriously as the Goshen people do. Maybe I say that because I lived back there only as a child, but I don't think so. I married into this place, for better or for worse, as they say; and their faith has eaten into me too now, although it's not easy for me to admit it.

But I've never regretted marrying Julia. She's a Branderhorst in ways that I'm not always proud of, but she's got roots like an elm or an ash—like her whole family. The old Calvinism buried itself in her soul, and she sees her calling clearly. She invests her devotion in our family the same way her brothers invest their sweat in the land. I like that. Maybe I'm old-fashioned. Maybe Goshen's got into me. I loved her when I married her, and nothing's happened since to make me stop. You've got to believe that. I really do love her. History tells us that those feudal marriages didn't always work, but this one has. I swear it.

It's early March now, the time of year when everyone thinks it's supposed to be spring. One day the temperature can creep up to forty degrees and make the farmers restless. "You can start to hear the seed rustling around in the bag," some farmers say, but what they hear is the echo of their own anticipation. It's still too cold for a farming operation to come out of its long winter's nap, but there's this feeling all around. Everyone's out in the machine shed with grease guns.

Beagle died on New Year's Day, in the afternoon, with his boys just outside his bedroom watching bowl games and his wife and daughters drinking coffee, their laps full of kids, around the cleared kitchen table in the slowly dying heat of the stove that had just cooked up a holiday ham. He couldn't have designed a better way of dying if he'd sat down one day and decided how he wanted to go.

The Beagle was reared in a day without television football, and he never really understood the game at all, so it was no surprise when he picked up and left the den, explaining that he felt like lying down for awhile after dinner. Julia herself found him when her mother claimed it was unlike him to take such a long nap and maybe someone should check to see if he was feeling okay. He was lying there on his back, stone dead, one leg up over the other, as if he'd just decided to die like some gentleman he never was.

"Dad's not breathing," Julia told us, almost whispering, when she came into the den. Her eyes were glassy, but something in her, instinct maybe, warned her not to tell her mother right away. So she came to the den. "I took his arm and everything—" she said.

I don't know how to explain what happened next. We all left for the bedroom, of course, and Julia kept her mother outside while the men hovered over his body. Randall grabbed for his wrist to feel for his pulse. Then he jumped up on the bed and held open the old man's mouth and breathed his own breath into him—in even, almost machine-like breaths. He jerked open Earl's collar and popped the buttons down the front of his shirt. The old man's left arm fell like dead weight off the side of the bed, the back of his hand landing limply on the rug, its fingers uncurled just enough to reveal a pallid, bloodless palm.

"Call an ambulance," Randall said right away, so I did, right there from the phone on the nightstand. You feel so helpless when something like that happens, and you remember the thousands of times when you tell yourself it would be useful to take some classes or something, learn how to deal with that kind of crisis. Right then and there, I swore to myself that I'd take the time to learn how to deal with emergencies. It's something I've forgotten now, two months later.

Methodically, Randall kept forcing breath down into his father's lungs, one hand pinched over the old man's face. But it was clear that there was no response, so he straddled the body and fiercely ripped open the shirt as if somehow the fabric itself were locking up his lungs. "Come on, come on," he said, one hand down on the old man's chest, pushing and pumping, as if what was inside was nothing more than an engine too tired to ignite.

By then mother had made it into the bedroom. She stood there with her hands up to her face, Julia and Mary Nell holding her arms as if she might bolt.

Your mind spins so far out of control in a time like that. Images roll like leaves tossed in a whirlwind. I remembered the time a cow had calved on a Sunday afternoon, and Randall had stood over her and hammered her to her feet once she had delivered, Julia sitting there explaining it all to our Kevin. That's almost the way it was that New Year's Day, Randall banging away on his father's chest.

Randall spent a year in Vietnam growing callous to death, the way he explains it. Maybe it was that year that made him swear the way he did. "Come on, come on you son of a bitch!" he said, not loud but emphatically, as if his words could shock that heart into pumping. "Come on, come on," he kept repeating, his hair falling down from around his temples over his ears.

But you didn't need any experience with death to see that Earl was already gone. His mouth gaped and his head fell slightly toward the arm that had fallen from the side of the bed. Randall kept working anyway, kept pushing and pounding at his chest, his anger growing so high in frustration and grief that his own sweat fell over his outstretched fingers and wet his father's chest. But Earl was gone.

There were no dying words from him, no final injunctions, no assurance of faith. I'm sure he would have planned it without any dramatics himself, if he could have. It would be like me to try to tack some moral on the span of my life; it's the teacher in me, I suppose. But Earl Branderhorst would have thought a last word or two redundant, I think, nothing more than useless talk. For all his sins—his pent-up anger, the roll call of grudges he carried and those that were carried against him, for the years of petty deceit, the livestock miscounted, cutthroat deals spun out at another's expense—for all of that there was no Calvinist's last rites and no forgiveness-begging. Earl Branderhorst slipped out of life with what I expect was a conscience pumped full of rationalization and his own brash self-assurance that sometimes crossed over the thread-thin line that separates well-muscled will from plain, sinful pride.

I'm sure that when he stood up before his Maker that day, he expected nothing less than an extended right arm showing him the way to glory. A lifelong Calvinist, Earl, comfortable in his election, knew little of confession. If someone had told him that he'd spent his entire lifetime selfishly building his own kingdom, he would have thought the notion nonsense. What he was building, he thought, was a family. But he wouldn't have said that either. It wouldn't have been right for a man.

In January, darkness spreads over the plains long before supper, so it had been dark for hours before the family left the home place that night, the moon already up in silver over the glowing ribbons of snow between the empty fields' stubbled rows. Kevin and Shelley sat in the back seat in silence, old enough to know that the world had grown both smaller with the death of their grandfather, and larger, more complicated, more dangerous than it had seemed just that morning when the holiday began.

"Grandpa's with Jesus, isn't he?" Buddy kept saying. He sat up between Julia and me with his hands stuck between his mother's arms. "Grandpa died and went to be in heaven."

His mother unloosened his arms and took her son up on her lap, even though she held Rudy, the youngest, already sound asleep, in her right arm.

"Everybody sings in heaven," Buddy said. "It's just like Sunday School."

The clock on the dash said it was just before ten.

"Grandpa went to heaven in a chariot," Buddy said. For the first time that day I thought about what Buddy had imagined when the EMT's wheeled the body out of the house. I remembered the whirring red lights dancing off the sides of the machine shed out back.

I poured us both some brandy before we went to bed, so we sat at our kitchen table with most of the lights out in the house, listening to the constant whirr of the furnace fighting the press of cold against the outside walls.

"I wish I had known somehow that I was going to be the one to find him dead," Julia said. "I mean, I never thought of anything like that happening to me. I just wish I had known somehow."

The smears around her eyes that were there in the afternoon were long gone by that time. If anything, she looked somehow younger than she had, her eyes sharp and jumpy, as if she were walking slowly through a field of alfalfa, looking for something small but important she had lost.

I stood with Julia at the births of all our four children. She wanted it that way. But after the first, I had little desire to be there again, because I hated the uselessness of my own presence. Who knows what some analyst would say, but I stood there and hated myself because it seemed to me that what she was fighting was so much of an individual battle, her body writhing to release this new child, while all of her sense fought the searing pain that simply had to be. All I could do was stand there and hold her hand.

What I hated then was exactly what I felt that night, the horror of having an immense, solid oak door locked up tight between yourself and someone you love, and the frustration of having no means—no possible way—of opening it. Julia's grief, like her pain, was ultimately a private matter, and every word I could offer seemed nothing better than what any do-gooder had ever said in scenes like this—bland and chilled. My greatest gift, perhaps, was the brandy.

"If I'd have only known this was going to happen," she said again.

Every one of a dozen responses sounded frivolous when I rehearsed them in my mind.

"What do you do with a dead father anyway?" she said. "I mean, what's there to do now?"

"Probably you just remember," I told her.

"It doesn't seem like it's enough," she said. She turned the glass in her hand so the brandy rode the sides of the glass and left a tinge of bronze. Some tight Branderhorst emotion stretched itself thin at her lips and cheeks.

"You never really loved him, did you?" she said.

There was a lawyer's dispassionate ring to the question, as if she were only searching for a fact, not a criminal indictment.

"He gave me his daughter," I said. I thought it was as good as I could do.

"But you never really loved him, Howard. Admit it. You never really understood him at all."

It was no accusation, merely a statement of fact.

II

Jeff Heerema, is a youthful thirty-five; he's a late-sixties type who spent half his life being altruistic—first the Peace Corps, then several years in a hospital for kids with emotional problems—before taking on the ministry. He grew up in a manse himself, but he claims he fought the call to the ministry with a raised fist for a nearly a decade. He says he finally left the hospital and went to the seminary because he grew so tired of trying to work on symptoms that eventually he became confident that God was telling him to retool and go for the disease itself. I've been around the Calvinists long enough to know the language—disease means sin. What he meant is that the best way of handling the emotional problems wrought by broken homes is by wrestling pride itself to the canvas.

Goshen was his first charge, even though there are no broken homes around. It's a record people are proud of. I've been a member of the church council long enough to know that there have been more than a few indiscretions, but divorce is unheard of, for the most part, because the price one pays is simply too high. Where such heavy pressure to stay together exists, the real problems, quite literally, go away—that is, families in significant crises simply pick up stakes and move to Sioux Falls or Denver or Phoenix, where the divorce occurs, out of sight, at least, if not out of mind. Thus, Goshen stays clean.

Heerema began his ministry in Goshen with the objective of ministering straight for the sinful heart; what my wife's family felt at the funeral was an outsider with an education going instead for the jugular. Heerema grew up in Michigan, in a time when a preacher was still looked upon like Moses the law-giver, just descended from the mountain with an armful of God-ordained truths; and he came to the Plains, full of righteous passion, and found Aaron and the Israelites dancing around a golden calf—which is the perfect image for Goshen's kind of idolatry. But understanding Heerema is easier than that; simply, Heerema still has a rookie's zeal. I remember teaching with the same kind of emotion.

What he never understood was that in a little church like Goshen, the power battles have been fought long ago, even if they've not been forgotten. Today Goshen doesn't want a Jeremiah; all they want is someone to perform their religious rites, a witch doctor maybe, a voodoo man—someone to baptize their children and dole out the bread and the wine, someone who can deliver sermons that harmonize with their own sense of truth.

Heerema operated under the mistaken notion that he could change things in Goshen, when the natives needed him only to perform their tribal rituals. I don't want to misstate all of this. Maybe I'm getting too sarcastic. I've been in but not of the land of Goshen for so long that sometimes its strengths and weaknesses become indistinguishable. My own wife is so thoroughly "Goshen," that she hasn't a clue what I mean when I tell her she is.

And perhaps I'm overstating the case. What I'm trying to explain is why Heerema said what he did at Julia's father's funeral. If you understand the man himself, what he said was consistent with his own approach to the problems of life itself. And if you can see that, you'll accept his own explanation. His sermon was in no sense at all vindictive.

The church was packed, of course, full of family, friends, and enemies. Even if some folks hated the very ground Beagle worked, they would show up to see him off. It was a matter of common courtesy.

At the family meditation downstairs before the service, Heerema was soft and loving, empathetic and gracious, meek in a New Testament way. Herm, Julia's oldest brother, sat next to his mother, who had balled-up handkerchiefs in either hand but wasn't crying. She spent most of her life in silence. It took me ten years to understand that she wasn't a victim, some caricature farm wife with no power outside of the kitchen. Silence was her power and her witness, her means of illustrating to her children that her husband's way, all shoulders and elbows, demanded a counterpoint. At our fifth anniversary, she took both my hands when we were alone for a minute in the kitchen. "I'm so happy that Julia got you," she said. That's all. I've always thought that there are only x-number of words in her, which means that everything she says is carefully measured.

The rest of the boys—John, Adrian, and Randall—followed down the row with their wives and the little kids. Behind the kids sat the older grandchildren, and the aunts and uncles and cousins, anyone who counted themselves among the Branderhorst clan, even those who had fallen from grace. Uncle Pete was there from South Dakota. Thirty years ago he had left Goshen because he couldn't compete with his brother Earl. Beagle never hated his brother really, he just wrote him off for the lack of bite in his blood. They never talked again that I know of. Of course, Pete had a bad back. "You can't trust nobody with a bad back," Beagle used to say.

But downstairs in the church, Pastor Heerema didn't say anything the family didn't expect, so everything went smoothly. "We have confidence in the Lord's promises," he said. What he did was leave the door wide open for Beagle's salvation. He didn't try to judge that way, because he knows what he can't know. What the family doesn't remember was that Heerema never once said that Earl Branderhorst wasn't saved, not even when he got upstairs for the funeral sermon.

Downstairs his words had the traditional ring of a Calvinist eulogy, and the boys sat there approving, as if what he said were the patter of soft rain in mid-July, the time the corn gets thirsty enough to whisper in the wind. Upstairs, the public filed in solemnly, Earl's own favorite organist playing through familiar hymns that came through the floor as if the whole church was a wood-framed speaker.

But everything changed upstairs. My point is that he spoke the truth,

no matter what anybody says. The Beagle was my father-in-law, and
I think it's fair of me to say that no one knows his strengths and
weaknesses as well as I do, not even his own flesh-and-blood—perhaps
least of all his children. He was a loving father, a handsome provider,
a grandfather my own children will forever remember fondly. But he
was a bigot and a chiseler, a man who knew the law so well he could
turn it with a flourish to his own advantage. He despised weakness,
scorned the powerless, and never forgot—or forgave—those who
trespassed against him. He was a giant of compassion to those he loved;
a despot and a crook to those for whom he had no regard. Everything
Heerema said that day was true.

"Lord, you have been our dwelling place throughout all generations.
Before the mountains were born or you brought forth the earth and the
world, from everlasting to everlasting you are God."

He took his text from Psalm 90. Traditionally, funeral sermons stick
tenaciously to the text. Comfort is the antidote to grief, and to Goshen
people nothing brings comfort like the Word itself.

"You turn men back to dust, saying, 'Return to dust, O sons of men.
For a thousand years in your sight are like a day that has just gone by,
or like a watch in the night."

Today, prairie towns are full of old people. The Branderhorsts have
built a kingdom out here, but most families lose their kids; they're ex-
ported, often unwillingly, by the scarcity of jobs, and what's left are
so many old folks that any new preacher learns funeral homiletics inside of a year.

"You sweep men away in the sleep of death; they are like the new
grass of the morning—though in the morning it springs up new, by evening it is dry and withered."

Heerema was unpracticed at funeral preaching. Maybe that inex-
perience contributed to what happened. If you stick to the text, there's
often no need for application because the Word itself delivers its message
with a power that no preacher, not even the greatest of orators, needs
to compliment with relevancy.

"We are consumed by your anger and terrified by your indignation.
You have set our iniquities before you, our secret sins in the light of
your presence."

With that verse Heerema looked up and into the faces of the people.

He stopped momentarily, as if he needed to build up his own courage, and he leaned over the pulpit, his right hand coming up over the front and locking there. "We all know that Earl Branderhorst's life has been full of financial success," he said. "He's supported this congregation generously throughout his lifetime."

One could feel the beaming from the boys down the bench.

"We all know that he has a strong family who loved him dearly, a family that will miss his presence, generous as he was in love for them—"

I can't remember the words exactly, but the sermon itself began with that kind of homage, a testimony to the kind of powerful image that Earl had built and maintained in the community. But then things changed.

"But for Earl Branderhorst, life itself was war."

I remember that line because it struck me as perfect.

"The man found himself, throughout life, at odds with his fellow believers, angry, sometimes even belligerent with those with whom he prayed on Sunday, here in this church."

Right at that moment, my immediate impression was that what he said was inappropriate. I never once doubted its truth or his sincerity, but the truth made me uncomfortable, sitting there with the family.

"He never lacked means to pay for his joy, but as long as I knew the man, he seemed forever seeking true happiness, contentment, the kind of peace that comes with love and forgiveness."

Julia has this way of rocking the baby in church, back and forth, back and forth, her whole upper body swaying against the back of the bench. When I glanced at her just then, she was at it, her face tucked up close to the baby, as if she were whispering something in his ear.

"Earl Branderhorst's life should be a lesson for us—for you and for me, for all of us in this church. Let us understand the prison of our own guilt when we can't settle our old scores. Let us see for ourselves the way in which a lack of forgiveness rides each of us, keeps us from the kind of peace we all search for throughout our lives. My prayer is that each of us may feel the heat in our own lives when past sins—our own and those of others—are left to smolder in our souls."

By that time I knew that Heerema would be in trouble. He had never once said a word about Earl Branderhorst's salvation, but what he had done was proclaim the truth publicly. That was the deadliest of his sins. He took his cue from the Word and set my father-in-law's secret sins in the light of Goshen's presence.

"His death is an opportunity to all of us, because it serves to teach us something about ourselves, our motives, and our lives. Earl Branderhorst's life and death is a mirror in which we can see the strife on our own faces, a story in which we can feel our own unburied animosity; a portrait of rock-solid pride that is rooted too deep to admit weakness."

There's a story about the old Calvinist Jonathan Edwards. When he took the pulpit at his grandfather's church for the first time, he spoke in an almost effeminate way, clutching the sides of the pulpit, his voice strained to reach the corners of Northampton church. But the congregation waited breathlessly for every word. That's exactly the way it was with the folks in the Goshen church.

"God is Earl's judge, just as he is ours. God's mercy rises so far beyond our own that we can't but feel humbled at the measure of his grace. But let's use this man's life to change our own. Let us all learn in patience the lifelong task of forgiveness."

Forgiveness is what I remember, the linchpin between Earl's death and our lives. But I kept thinking then of how they were hearing it, the boys and my own wife. Even at the time, I was measuring the effect of his words in their lives. I thought even then that it was a perfect sermon for them. They're hearing what they need to hear, I thought.

"Listen to the words of Moses, the man of God," he said. "'Teach us to number our days aright, that we may gain a heart of wisdom.'"

With that he came back to the text again and ended with the last verses of the Psalm: "May the favor of the Lord our God rest upon us; establish the work of our hands for us—yea, establish the work of our hands." He left the text for no more than five minutes, but the sword he wielded for that short time cut to the quick.

Politically, I suppose, Heerema was wrong. But he wasn't thinking politics at that moment. He was speaking in ways he thought, I am sure, to be prophetic. There was nothing in what he said that wasn't true.

When it was over and the long line of cars headed out to the cemetery for the graveside service, Herm and John didn't even go. Someday they may regret not standing there at the open grave, but I'm sure they'll always blame Heerema for what they didn't do. Around here people say, "The apples don't fall far from the tree."

III

Three weeks later all the boys—Herm, John, and Randall—showed up at a meeting of the church board to demand Heerema's resignation. Julia would have been there with them if there were room for women in the kind of work they were up to that night. It's a mark of her Branderhorst nature that she didn't go, because it wasn't that she didn't want his scalp as badly as did her brothers. She did. Going to the church board was simply a man's job. It was something that needn't have been said.

I remember saying to her that night, "If you want his hide so bad, why don't you go too?" But she looked at me as if what I'd said were no more than a child's silly idea, as if I had no understanding at all of the way things were.

Things have been cold between us ever since that sermon. Silence builds itself into the kitchen and family room. You end up letting the kids do all the talking at meals. You each ask the kids questions about school and play independently, as if you are rival journalists at an interview, vying for the same story. There's no touching, no intimacy at all, and even sex is perfunctory, a totally physical act handled as if it were an obligation to each other's animal nature, part of a written contract that for whatever reason should not be broken.

But the three of them finally came to the church board a couple nights ago. I guess I expected that it wouldn't take two months, but it has. I knew they would come eventually. Even if I hadn't been privy to some of their anger, I would have guessed as much.

That neither Earl nor his boys have ever been on the church board is a fact that has always given me some reason to believe in God's abiding presence in his church. No one doubts the influence of the Branderhorsts in Goshen, but everyone understands that their kingdom has been built on something more than simply their own family's sweat, and for that reason the church seems to feel them unqualified for leadership. They're tainted by those very smears of corruption which have enabled them to reach what authority they have established in the community. Something wonderfully tragic exists in that paradox, but no one in Goshen would know what I mean.

It's possible, I suppose, that not being on the church board was one of Earl's last angry thoughts the day he died, because nothing upset him more than not being elected to leadership in the church. It's the custom here to install the new members on New Year's Day, so what he'd seen at church the morning before he died was another searing reminder of his own failure. Simply put, people in Goshen knew him too well to elect him to an office they respected.

The boys grew up with the ring of his constant resentment in their ears, but they never shared his frustration because they didn't seek the office. Somewhere in Earl's blood there must have been a vestige of the old faith, enough at least to make him aspire to the significant calling of holding church office, some remnant aspiration which he didn't pass on to his boys.

There's an old story about Emil that the boys are fond of repeating. I've heard it at least a dozen times, often when the Beagle's grandsons get old enough to understand it Herm's own way. It seems that Emil once employed a particularly irritating character named Jacob Smits, a cranky grain hauler everyone knew was a pain in the bottom. The story goes that one day while threshing Emil became so enraged at Smits that he almost buried him with one blow from his huge right hand. The boys laugh when they tell this one, of course; Herm gets up from the table and swings away as if he wishes he could connect himself.

But Emil apparently had something of a conscience in him. Smits went home once he picked himself up from the ground, and all day long Emil shivered away by himself out in the field, feeling guilty for decking the guy. Emil was a big man, the original Branderhorst.

So the story goes that at night he got to feeling so bad about what had happened, that his conscience gnawed a hole in his pride. He got out the horses and went over to Smits' place to apologize.

There he stands, at Smits' door, feeling sorry and guilty for what he'd done. Smits comes to the door, growls a bit, and they start to talk. The way Earl himself tells it, it took no more than five minutes and Smits was out cold again, right there on his front step.

It's a lovely story, Emil's great-grandchildren's favorite legend. But I think they read it all wrong. The reason they tell the story is to glory in its bravado, to relish a time and place when men handled problems with fists, and to exalt the masculinity of their own lineage. What they forget is that Emil had that conscience. What they forget is that if what happened to Emil in the field had ever happened to them, not one of them would finish the story the way Emil did. Beagle himself was never outfitted with his grandfather's conscience, even if he had the old man's sheer power. The boys miss the point of the story completely. I don't remember the exact words anymore, but once I remember reading something Cotton Mather wrote in describing the degeneration of New England piety: "Faith gave birth to prosperity, and the child devoured the mother." It went something like that. I'll have to look it up again sometime.

But I was talking about the church council. Beagle resented my being elected. I know he did, simply because he never brought it up. The boys used to joke about it. I remember John saying once at Sunday dinner how they couldn't talk so openly anymore now that Howard was an elder—how they'd have to ask me to leave if they wanted to talk business. Then the three of them—and Julia—laughed, chuckled really, superciliously, as I remember, in the same tone as if they were watching one of their kids trying to wrestle a sow. But Earl never laughed at all that time. That's how I know he felt humiliated at my having been elected.

But I've always felt that the church has retained some sanctity by not admitting them to office. It's remained the only institution in Goshen that didn't yield to the Branderhorst's bullying. Earl ran the elevator board for twenty years; John was an officer of the cattleman's association; and Randall came back from Vietnam and stepped right into authority in the American Legion. Only church office wouldn't admit them. Like I say, it's always made me feel good about the church.

It was the first week of February when I knew for sure how they would deal with their offence, that time when most of the sows have already farrowed and there's little work to be done on the farm. The only sound is the howl of heat rushing from gas burners over the farrowing pens and the crunching noise frozen snow makes beneath your boots. In February farm work goes dormant like everything else, so Beagle's funeral was all the boys had to think about.

One afternoon not more than a couple weeks ago Herm came to our place, and he was there when I came in from school. He was sitting at the table with Julia, his coveralls zipped down to his waist, his hair bunched up on his head from the way his stocking cap had been pulled over his ears.

"I'm here officially," he told me when I dropped my briefcase at the back door, "because we're coming next week. You tell them we're coming—"

I shook my head. Julia sat stone-faced while I took a cup of coffee from the airpot on the counter. The baby scrambled over her lap, unwilling to sit quietly or get off.

"I'm over here now because what we want to know is where you stand on this—after all, he was your father-in-law."

I stood behind the bar and leaned over towards them. Julia faced her brother across the table, looking outside through the windows over the deck. "You want him gone, don't you?" I said.

Herm uncrossed his legs and pushed himself up on the chair to straighten his back. He crossed his arms over his chest so his shoulders squared. "We think what he said up there at the funeral wasn't right at all for a preacher of the Word," he said. "We think it's unbecoming of the office, and we want him gone."

He used my own quiet tone of voice.

"What are you going to do if the board says no?—have you thought of that?" I said.

"Herm says that we're all going to resign our memberships," Julia said, turning toward me, her eyes hard as clenched fists.

"Daaaaeee," the baby said, looking up at me. "Daaeee, Daaeee." Her mother pressed her finger over his lips, trying to hold him straight. Sometimes you simply can't stop that child.

"That's your deal, Herm?" I said. "It's a case of you or him?"

"I can't sit there and listen to him anymore. It's useless for me to go to church when he's there. I might as well go somewhere else. That's all I'm saying."

I knew how they would say it, but it angered me to hear it anyway. Maybe it angered me more because I wanted them to be something other than what Beagle had reared them to be. Maybe I hoped Julia would help them, I don't know.

"Don't let me tell you how to feel, Herm, but if I were you I wouldn't come with any kind of ultimatum," I said; "you know what I mean? None of this 'it's either him or us' tough-guy stuff. It's intimidation, and it's not humility." What I was warning him not to do was exactly what his father would have done, and he looked at me as if he didn't understand a word I'd said.

"You know what I mean, Julia," I said. "Explain it."

Little Rudy kicked off her lap, then stood there beside her, taking cheerios out of her hand. "Daaeee home," he said. "Daaeee home. Daaeee—"

"All I'm saying is argue your case—tell them you think what he did at the funeral was inappropriate. Tell them you need an apology for Heerema's impoliteness or something, but don't try to strongarm anybody, for heaven's sake. We aren't steers—"

The baby tried to get back up again. He stretched his arms over Julia's waist and grabbed the belt of her jeans. His mother picked him up forcefully and set him down hard on her lap. But he wasn't happy there. He was in one of those moods when he doesn't know what he wants. Maybe even the child sensed what was in the air.

"Julia says she doesn't know where you stand," Herm said. "All of us want to know."

I pulled myself up from the counter and poured another half cup of coffee. What they wanted was a yes or a no. "It's not so black and white for me," I said. "And I hope you appreciate that I've got something other than this family's pride at stake. I got the responsibility of that church office too. You understand that, don't you?"

"Just as long as we know where you stand," Herm said. "It's all we want to know is where you stand on this." Unemotionally it was said, not as a threat but a simple statement of fact.

The sound of a cartoon war came into the kitchen from out in the den where the kids were watching television.

"I'm not saying I don't feel what you're feel—"

"You don't understand nothing. You don't have a notion for the way each of us kids feel inside about the way that—I can't say what I'd like to call him—for the way that guy shit on our old man. You don't understand at all—"

"Shi'," Rudy said. "Shi', shi'—" Julia tried to quiet him.

I needed both hands to lift my cup up to my lips. All the time I was thinking how things just had to come to this eventually, and how I was glad that at least now it was finally coming to a head.

I watched Julia wrestling with the baby. "Why don't you let him go in with the kids?" I said. "He don't know what he wants," she said.

I couldn't give them what they were asking for, and they knew it as
well as I did. "I'm not going to be pushed, Herm," I told him. "I'm
not going to let you push me around on this—I got the church to think
of too."

He swept cookie crumbs off the table with his stocking cap. "I guess
we know, don't we, Sis?" he said. "There's nothing left to say
anymore." He got up from the chair and zipped up his coverall. "All
these years and what the old man gave him and he ain't got a dime's
worth of loyalty."

"What is it you want, Herm?" I said. "You want my head—you want
my mind, is that it?."

"Daaeee, Daaeee," the baby said.

"You want me to get up and stamp my feet and walk out the door
with the rest of you?—is that what you're after?"

He stood at the back door and pulled his cap over his head. "It's all
we wanted was to know whether or not you was with us, that's all. I
think we know now." He pulled the door open. "We'll see you at the
meeting," he said, and then he left.

The kid was pulling and scratching and whining on her lap. Julia sat
there with no emotion on her face, nothing at all. He's teething again,"
she said. "I don't know what to do with him."

I love Julia. I always have. And when I think about it now, when I
remember how far we stood from each other just then, I can't help but
be amazed at what kind of immense distance can stretch between two
people that are one flesh; because right at that moment I didn't love her,
not at all. I hated her for her blindly stubborn allegiance, for her inability to stretch far enough to see her father's own weaknesses and her
brothers' bounding pride. I hated her, and I wanted to punish her for
taking their side and not seeing her husband's own position. I wanted
to punish her with every last New Testament passage about leaving your
father and mother and cleaving to your husband. I wanted to hurt her
with nothing less than guilt, to scar her for siding with them as if the
instinctive urgings of old hot blood were the strongest force on earth.
And that's exactly why I said what I did.

"There's a place I can stay in Meridith," I told her. It was my way
of punishing her. "Maybe it would be better that way for awhile." I
was determined that she take the blame for whatever happened to our

family.

She wouldn't look at me, because she knew I had forced the burden on her. The baby came down off her lap again and mounted her leg for a ride, but she picked him up angrily and set him back down.

"I know how you feel," I said. "Maybe it's better if—"

"You think you're so damn smart—you and your stinking education. You think you know everything, don't you?"

I let it go, thinking that she already knew what a dumb thing she had said.

"What makes you think you know how I feel? You never loved my father anyway. The whole time you were smiling at the funeral. The whole time. I didn't need to see you, because I know when you're laughing. You loved it, didn't you? It'd be one thing if you didn't smile, but I know you did. You always thought you were better than us. You always have."

"I always loved you, Julia," I told her.

"I'm not talking about me. I'm talking about them. You always did think they were nothing more than bullies, dumb old farmers who never went to college."

"It's no use talking right now," I told her. "I'll call you after the meeting." I pulled my jacket from the chair where I'd left it when I'd come in. "It's no use us talking anymore about it because the whole thing is poison right now." I stood at the back door, watching the baby still pawing at his mother's legs. I never left her before, not once in fifteen years. I have never even threatened like that, and neither did she.

"Go on then," she said. "Go on and get out."

I was thinking then that I know them better than they think I do. I was thinking that nothing would be so humiliating to Julia than her husband leaving. I was thinking that in her world there was no higher priority than to succeed at the calling of wife and mother, and that my leaving would make her sense her own silly hardheadedness, her stubborn Branderhorst pride. Julia's very identity was forged by her role. My leaving would force her to stare into her own dark and empty failure. That's what I was thinking. I can see now that what it was, was my own ultimatum.

IV

The meeting of the church board went off with less anger than I thought it would. My own three brothers-in-law came in and sat at the head of the table, laid out their case fully and not without emotion, then answered our questions for nearly an hour.

We have this custom in the board that when the meeting adjourns everyone shakes hands, as if the press of flesh will somehow fuse us back together as brothers in Christ. So once our discussion was over, Herm and John and Randall stood there at the end of the table while the rest of us filed past and shook their hands. I hadn't talked all night long, hadn't asked a question or tried to help them either. I was thinking that it might be inappropriate for me to enter into the discussion at that point, as if perhaps it would be some conflict of interest. So I was surprised that neither Herm nor John said a word when I shook their hands; only Randall spoke, and all he said was "Howard" out the opposite side of his mouth where he always keeps his toothpick.

Then the boys left. It took us a half an hour to decide that while it would be good for us to remind Heerema that some of his parishoners thought his funeral sermon was inappropriate, we wouldn't ask him to resign his position or seek a call to some other church. Officially, we decided not to accede to the request of the Branderhorsts—it sounds so clean that way, the way I wrote it into the minutes. There wasn't much discussion really, and for the most part I stayed out, except to vote. The decision was unanimous.

That's not to say it was easy. The fact that we acted quickly doesn't mean it was easy—not at all. We all sat there quietly for a while. Jake Vermeer maybe had the longest speech, and all he claimed was that nothing Heerema had said wasn't by the Book. He's an old man. He had his hands out in front of him, the way a child leans his arms out over a school desk to pray. He's rock-hard, unshakably conservative, doctrinaire enough to frustrate anyone who's on whatever side he opposes. But you always know where Vermeer is coming from. No matter what it is on the agenda, for the most part it's as if he doesn't even have to speak; in fact, he doesn't do all that much talking. It's just that what he says always counts. "The preacher's being right doesn't make this any easier," he said, his hands folded saint-like out in front of him.

I remember hearing a story about Queen Elizabeth sending Bloody Mary off to be hung. Temper your justice with mercy, people advised her, she's your own half sister. But the Virgin Queen knew that the decision had to be made. The law had to be followed; justice had to be meted out. But there was mercy too; it flowed from her eyes and down her cheeks. Justice was tempered by her own internal bleeding about what simply had to be done. Justice was the decision; mercy was there in the streaks down her face. So the story goes.

Vermeer sat there nodding his head as if to convince himself of what had to be done. "I don't like it much," he said. "Something in this whole business makes me feel for them boys." Then he leaned back and crossed his arms over his chest to signify that he had finished. "Lord Jesus, come quickly," he said. It's something he says everytime he's in that kind of place, as if he's throwing up his hands and asking for all of it to be over. That was the end of the discussion.

I told them it might be a good idea to tell the boys yet tonight of our decision, since I was sure they'd be waiting somewhere. Somebody asked, facetiously, if I wanted to bring the news. I told them how somewhere back in history the bearers of bad tidings were killed for merely bringing the news. Everyone laughed, and someone else got that assignment. I said I'd stop over at the preacher's to explain what we'd decided. Because he was so much involved in what was going on, he hadn't been at the meeting.

It was just past ten when I got there, and Heerema was sitting in front of the television in an old easy chair whose springs were so worn that not more than a foot was left between him and the floor, his legs outstretched over the braided rug, his boy tucked snugly under his. arm.

His wife let me in the door and led me through the living room to the den off the kitchen. The news was on just then, some news tape from South Africa.

"Look at this," he said.

A white guy stood in the middle of an immense crowd of blacks, trying to keep them off by swinging something at them wildly—what looked maybe like marbles in a nylon or something. But every time he'd turn his back, one of the blacks would push at him, try to knock him off his feet. On and on like some cowboy he whaled at them, spinning furiously, catching their blows and delivering his. It was a horrible thing to watch because he was so vastly outnumbered, as if the whole history of racism had been laid on his shoulders. Finally, he went down and the mob had at him, all the time the camera rolling, until some police finally came to his rescue and lifted him, bloodied, back to his feet. He was fortunate not having been killed. It was a horrible thing to watch, sickening in fact, no matter what you believe about South Africa. It was chilling and gruesome.

He got up from his chair and handed the boy to his mother. "We think we got it bad," he said, turning off the set. "Sit down, Howard. You need some coffee yet?"

I said I didn't need any, but I'd have some if there was still some hot. Nora had already left with the baby, so Jeff himself stepped out to the kitchen. "Well, let's have it," he said from the other room. "How did it go?"

I guess I felt uncomfortable yelling it through the open door, so I waited while he picked up the coffee. Up above the couch on the south wall was the only painting in the room, a Wyeth print of a old broken down wagon out back of some country home. It's late October or early November in the picture, and the sun is just retiring somewhere on the other side of the house, so the sky takes on this yellow hue. Half the picture is the long grass that grows out back of the house, like prairie grass, tall enough to come halfway up the spokes of the wagon wheels.

When I think about it now, I know that picture is itself an illustration of the affinity between myself and the Heeremas. It's not only that I liked the print, although I did. It's not only that its being alone on the walls, unencumbered by plastic angels or candleholders or vials stuffed with plastic flowers, was simply "right," unlike the usual Goshen wall-hangings, very tasteful—although it was. It's more than that. The print itself represents a commitment on the Heerema's part. When they bought that print and hung it, they were signifying their own commitment to live out here in the country, if to no one other than themselves.

It's not a sentimental picture either, no amber waves of grain, no patriarch husbandman with wisdom imprinted in the lines around his eyes, standing there as if he's wise enough to recite you half the *Farmer's Almanac*, and throw in some *Walden* at a discount. It's an unsullied portrait of real country life. But it's something that no one else in Goshen would put on their walls. Most places you'll find mountain streams or riverboats. But not at Heerema's.

They've made a commitment to a way of life. They think that commitment will enable them to live harmoniously with those whose roots go as deep as the broadest cottonwood. What the Heeremas don't understand is that in making the commitment, they have already externalized that way of life in a way that the Branderhorsts, and most other Goshen folk, have not. They've measured the possibilities of that way of life against other options—the opportunity of living in a city, even a small city, or the option of taking a charge in some sun-belt suburb. They've opted for this prairie life in a way that few Goshen souls do themselves. For many of them—even for Julia, really—there never were any options. It was simply understood that she would live somewhere around Goshen. In fact, it wasn't even understood. Choosing to live here was as much an instinct as choosing to breathe.

That's what separates us—the Heeremas, myself, and the handful of other outsiders—we've chosen this place. We know it in a different way than those whose whole histories are buried in this fertile soil. That knowledge is a blessing and a bane.

"They wanted your scalp all right," I told him when he came back in. "That's what they came for."

He raised his eyebrows and nodded.

"We took your side."

He took a sip of coffee and said thanks.

"There wasn't even much discussion."

What I told him was worth a grudging smile that didn't rise exactly from the center of his soul.

"So how are you taking this anyway?" I said.

He put down the cup and rubbed both hands over his face as if to wake himself. "I can live with myself," he said, looking down at his preacher's hands. "I think sometimes that maybe I was all wrong—not the substance of what I said—but saying it that way. I don't know—"

He's a young guy, even if he's only five years younger than I am. Goshen's his first charge.

"We're the ones who have to take the heat now," I told him. "You're not in the firing line anymore."

He nodded again. What I said was limp, and I knew it. Theoretically, I was right, of course.

"It's a terrible strain around here," he said. "Nora just never figured on anything like this. She never was too hot on being married to a preacher, and now she's got all this animosity on her back. She feels it, and it makes her defensive. She loves me and she hates the job—that's the whole thing—"

I wondered where she was just then. There had been some movement upstairs when she first left with the baby, but now it was perfectly silent through the house. Somewhere she was sitting up, her senses piqued, I was sure, trying to catch the emotional tenor of our conversation through the walls of the manse, trying to feel what we were saying downstairs. And I wished just then—you can't imagine how much I wished—that I could offer her Julia somehow.

"You've got the vast majority on your side," I told him.

"It's the fact that there are sides at all that gets her," he said. "I've stirred up the waters around here and everything's muddied now. It's not so much the nature of the bitterness as it is the whole blame quarrel itself." He sat there talking, staring at the TV as if he wished he could occupy his mind with something else, even if it was the terror of South Africa. "She's not like Julia at all that way. She's no fighter."

It made me wonder what might have happened to prompt him to say that.

"Nora just sits here and suffers, and I haven't got the slightest idea what to do about it. She can't feel whatever bit of assurance that I feel, and she just lacks the guts to fight. She wasn't built for it."

"Maybe this will help" I said, "I mean that we're on your side now, officially."

"The only thing that would help is full reconciliation. As long as there's sides, she's going to sit here and cry." The lines in his face broke just a bit and he looked away.

I wondered what Julia herself would think to sit there just then and watch him bite back his own tears. I wondered what the Branderhorsts would say to see him broken, if it would be enough for them to see him bleed from his wounds, as deep as their own maybe.

"It's a unanimous vote of confidence we've given you," I told him.

"I've always been taught that once you're in the pulpit you speak for the Lord God Almighty." He put his fist up to his head and hit himself lightly several times, as if he were trying to awaken himself from what he was feeling. "You want to tell the people something that will change them somehow, help them to see themselves in relation to the will of the Lord—"

"You did that," I told him. "Everybody knows it."

"But they never tell you how it feels when you come down from the mountain and take off your socks to smell your feet and know you're no God at all, when you smell that you're nothing more than clay and nothing more noble than those you want to change. What they don't say is that there's a part of every preacher that is supposed to be listening to the very words he's preaching." He smoothed back his beard with both hands. "You know what kind of burden that is?" He laughed as if he did. "There ought to be a law that every stinking preacher has to be a certified schizophrenic. Make it a prerequisite for seminary graduation: 'This man is a legitimate loon, fully capable of living two lives— one as a preacher, and another as a human being.' They ought to stamp it on every set of ministerial credentials. If you're not crazy, you shouldn't be part of it. Turn the rest into stunt car drivers or something."

I had nothing to tell him really, nothing at all. He swung his head around at all four walls, as if there would be a finger up there writing. Then he took this deep breath and grabbed his coffee.

"I'm sorry," he said.

"It's all right—"

"Here I am going on and on and I'm the one who's supposed to be the pastor."

There was something about him that was so precise and fine, so out of place, in a way, his perfect hair—so dark that it seemed almost black, except for the almost mahogany tones it would take in the lights at the front of the church; and his beard, trimmed low on his jaws, angled perfectly up the sides of his cheeks.

"So let's turn this around," he said. "Let me play the role here for awhile. You're the one with problems too, I'm sure. What's going on in Julia's mind?"

"Got an extra room?" I said.

He laughed. "That bad?"

"She's got so much of the old man in her," I said.

"Even if she wanted to see things in a different way, she couldn't fight her brothers' power," he said.

"She can't work up the strength to see things in a different way,"
I told him.

His face cleared and his eyes narrowed.

"I just don't think she can be objective," I said.

"Can you?"

I figured no one could be more objective than I could, knowing the
Beagle for close to fifteen years the way I did, being inside that family,
and yet outside too.

"Do you love her?" he said.

I told him I didn't think that was a question one asked of people who
were married for more than a dozen years, and he laughed.

"Are you two close?" he asked.

"What is this—a counseling session or something?"

"I'm doing a poll for *Redbook* on sex in the Goshen church."

I told him that I knew a lot of men who complained about their wives'
frequent headaches, but I wasn't one of them.

"You want my advice?" he said.

"That's not why I came here," I said.

"It's the preacher in me—I don't feel right about talking to people,
unless I can tell them what they're supposed to do."

I was happy to see him over his anguish. I figured his good mood
would do him well when he'd go up and talk all of this over with Nora.

"This isn't just one battle for you, it's more like three or four. Keep
them separate."

"What do you mean?"

"There's this big fight in the church—that's one. It involves you as
an elder. Then there's the private one with your brothers-in-law—that's
two. There's the silent one with Julia—that's three—"

I told him they were all the same.

"You're dumber than I thought you were if you think so," he said.

I wasn't sure what I'd said to deserve that. "Thanks much," I told him.

"I didn't mean it that way." He smiled, because what he'd said hadn't
been malicious. "What I'm saying is that each one of those fights is
a little different, and you can't lump them all together."

When I didn't have anything to say, he put up his hands the same way
Vermeer did at the end of our meeting, resigning himself to something.

"When I was a kid, we used to have these church bazaars—all kinds of games and food, a big money raiser," he said. "Thank goodness, no one's ever heard of them around here. Anyway, I was always terrific at throwing darts. I'd pick up one of these little old-fashioned wooden things—the ones with the real feathers—and loft it perfectly, put this sweet little arch on the toss, and bang! I could get balloons one after another. Usually walked home with whatever prizes I wanted. In fact, it got so easy that they kept me away. It wasn't fair, but it was church, you know?" He kept lofting imaginary darts into the air and watching them hit off the wall. "Lately I've come to think that's why I became a preacher. When a balloon gets nailed, it's just gone, you know. The dart never even slows down. It hits and sticks, and there's nothing left of the balloon but a knot of rubber pinned up there in shreds. That's the way I thought it was going to be with preaching. Softly thrown darts would just blow away the problems."

"Your problem was you read the Lord's signals all wrong," I told him. "He was calling you to be a quarterback."

He straightened out his back and pulled his arms up over his shoulders. "So where were you when I needed career guidance?"

"Marrying into the Branderhorsts," I said.

"You didn't marry a family," he said.

"Somebody turn out the lights in here?"

"I'm serious," he said. "I don't need a broken marriage on my conscience. I've got enough weight back there as it is."

"The problems are not related, remember?" I told him. "'You're dumber than I thought.'"

"Oooohhh," he said. "That one came home to roost."

I held up my hand and rolled an imaginary dart between my fingers, then lofted it up in the air in a perfect arch so it would land right on him.

"Pop," he said.

V

When I come home from late meetings, there's a light on in the kitchen. It's always been that way, even if Julia is already up to bed. But there wasn't that night. The house was perfectly dark, darker in fact on the inside than it was from the street. The sky, like the air, was crisp and clear and cold, lit almost hauntingly by the moon, a bright silver dish against the black field of stars, reflecting on the snow over the streets and yards.

Our house has no locks, but I knew what she meant by the darkness. I had said I could stay in town somewhere, and it was her signal that she understood what I had offered as no hollow threat. There was an entire dialogue in that darkened house, a full conversation that had taken place between us without a word ever having been said. Had I not brought up the possibility of my sleeping elsewhere, she would have kept the light on; but because I had offered it, she was only forcing me to live by my promise. She assumed I'd come home all right, but she was telling me by a darkened house that she had heard my threat. It had been her move, and she turned out all the lights. It's amazing how one knows every word of that argument, even though it's never taken place.

Had I not said what I did, I would have been angry to find everything dark; as it was, I had no right to snarl. So I stood there on Goshen's empty main street, jerking my collar up around my neck, while behind me, four houses west, the downstairs lights at the Heerema's had finally gone out. On the lot next door, the glare of the streetlight on the intersection lit up the twin entrances of the old white frame church.

I had only two options, of course; one was to go in the house, and the other was to stay out. Going in would be its own kind of statement. I was reneging on my offer to go elsewhere, and I knew I would be admitting to her that what I had said was nothing more than an empty threat. Even if I chose to sleep downstairs on the sofa, my going in would be my own loss. That's the way I saw it—win or lose. It was a matter of pride. I know that now. But it was past eleven already, and there would be nowhere to go anymore; not even the fast food places in Meridith stay open till twelve on weeknights.

I went to the garage anyway, because I knew that Julia wouldn't be sleeping and that she'd hear the whirr of the starter if I decided to leave. The sound of the engine was my reply to what she'd said by leaving the house darkened. I had told her I could sleep elsewhere; she had allowed me the validity of my threat. With the sound of the car leaving the yard, I knew I would push her one step farther, make her feel the deeper penetration of her own real fear.

By now she knew what had happened at church, of course. Her brothers would have called her and told her. I wondered what they would be planning now. It would be very difficult for them to leave the only church they had ever known. They had to be thinking that it was more their church than it was Heerema's anyway, and in a way, they were right. Without him, there would have been Branderhorsts in that church for a millenium. In a matter of years—four or five, maybe even less— Heerema would have gone on to some city church somewhere, probably out east, and the only remnant of his tenure would be a family picture hung in the basement in the gallery of the preachers who had served the Goshen church.

The decision we had made could serve only to increase their anger. Undoubtedly, that's what Julia felt when they called to tell her, and the anger made it even easier to turn out the light above the kitchen sink.

I'm not trying to excuse myself now, because I know what I did wasn't right—all I'm trying to do is to get you to understand what I felt. I'm not even looking for understanding; what I'm looking for is something else altogether.

I took the car out of the garage, backed out of the driveway and left town, going east toward Meridith, so if she looked out of the window at all, she would think I was leaving. The minute I started the car, the radio went on, as it always does, set as it is to a station that plays classical music. After eleven, there's nothing but jazz: the smooth, swishing rhythms, the muted complaints of the horns, and the almost endless tour of emotion only hinted at there in the temper of music. I'm not a jazz lover, but somehow it seemed perfect just then, an excursion into another world completely than the frigid, naked expanse of prairie beneath a perfectly cloudless night.

East of Goshen the land rises into one of those swells that a thousand prairie writers have seen as a wave in the flatland ocean. It's not a hill at all; a kid with a sled wouldn't do a thing from its summit. But it stands up high enough to let a person look down on the town of Goshen and count the three streetlights down main street between the bare bones of the maples and elms in the yards of its houses.

I pulled over on the gravel road, and stepped out into the cold, dousing the lights. It was one of those shiny cold nights when high school kids could brag about driving all the way back from Meridith without using headlights. In the dearth of wind, Midwestern cold isn't intolerable.

The dry air seeps like a wash of cold water into your lungs with each deep breath, and it's bright like a lamp's glow against your cheeks. Oddly enough, on a cold, moonlit night on the prairie, dark as it is, everything sparkles. Mercury lights at a thousand farms glitter like landborn stars; whole towns sit against the darkness like spilled jewels.

But it's impossible to catch the prairie's mighty beauty with a camera. I've seen many artists attempt to catch the depth of its grandeur on canvas, but I've not seen any that succeed. Probably half the homes in the nation have mountain portraits on their walls. Forests have depth and mystery; our own deepest human roots link us to the trees. But the beauty of the prairies lies in their almost massive naked power; it's a landscape without secrets, and it simply can't be caught in any kind of a portrait.

I was thinking of the prairie's immensity, thinking, oddly enough, of Red Chinese. When I was a boy the Cold War was being waged, and I remember being terrified of the communists because it was said there was no fighting with an army that would come in waves a million strong. March the Chinese a hundred abreast into the sea, it was said, and you would never deplete their population. Militarily they were ill-equipped, people said, because they had no sophisticated arsenal; but one feared their sheer numbers, the immensity of the force itself, thousands of corpses piling up on each other but still more bodies coming forward, while our best machine guns shot themselves into uselessness. It was part of the scare of the times, of course, but there is something in the immensity of that image that compares with the size and the force of the prairies, huge and relentless.

It was guilt in me, even then I suppose, that made me think the way I did.

I've never lived in a city, but I was thinking how it would be easy to hide from God in streets clogged with people. It's not so easy here. When that last trumpet sounds, no one will run to the prairies for cover.

There's a theory around here that says European immigrants to this area took the available land that most resembled the familiar landscapes of home. The Norwegians, for instance, took the land near the river, where the hills create sheltered pockets well-suited for farms. But the Dutch—men like Emil Branderhorst—put down roots where the land spread itself flat as a tablecloth, not unlike the land of the Dutch provinces from which they'd come. I've been part of Emil's Calvinist church long enough to feel that theory is only partially right. The old Calvinist forefathers took this land, I think, because they knew they couldn't hide from God, and, conversely, that God couldn't hide from them.

I stood there on that gravel road in the wind and cold and darkness, thinking that to be out there, alone, is like standing in judgement. Finally, faith is born out of our sad realization that we are not our own, that there is power beyond our means and ken, and that we stand like imps before that si.cngth, whatever our theology makes it out to be. What I'm saying is that it was, and is, humbling to stand out there and to sense the immense silliness of one's own pride.

I know all that. I know that very well, and I'm standing out there thinking that I would want Julia to come out here alone sometime, all alone, and feel what it was that I was feeling just then. If I were judge, I'd want Herm out here next, and then the other boys. What's more, it would have been good for the Beagle to stand out here alone too—forget about his cattle deals and his farrowing sheds and stand out here alone on a hill above all his blessed land and feel the kind of weakness I was feeling in my stomach and my knees. Finally, Heerema was right, of course. The family needed to hear what he said. They needed to know that it wasn't necessary to push one's life along with the kind of dogged ruthlessness that characterized everything Earl ever did. One must live with the humility necessary for forgiveness.

And I was thinking about a woman whose home I had visited a month or two before. The Calvinists have this custom of sending their officers around to visit members of the church once a year, and I'd visited a home where an older lady lived with her husband and her mentally impaired daughter, Evelyn, a woman close to forty years old but given a mental capacity that was no more than that of a three-year-old.

Evelyn is dying. The doctors have said that one of these days the disease she fights will clog her brain with blood and she'll have a massive stroke. She lies on a couch set for her in the family room. Mostly she watches television. Along the back of the couch are a dozen stuffed animals in assorted shapes and sizes, gifts from people in the community. She has no sense of her own condition, lives in the world of her stuffed animals; and when you sit there in the room, she smiles like a child without fear, lies there on the couch and smiles, just nods her head as if her life were nothing more than pure blessing.

She vomits nightly, her mother said, part of the curse of the disease she carries. But her mother usually knows what time it will come up, and she's there to catch it so that it won't soil the sheets. Her mother's done that for years already. And when she describes it, she's not conscious of saintly heroism in her own selflessness. She says it in the way other folks would describe thinning the carrots or sweeping the walk, simply part of the ritual of her own days and nights.

The goals of our visits is to ask about the family's level of spirituality. In a house like that one, such a question is silly, obviously. But the questioning has gone on for years, and the people themselves expect a certain kind of ritual. Not to ask the old questions is not to play the game according to its own established liturgy. So I asked her—you have devotions?

The woman says that her husband is usually helping their oldest son on his farm, so he's not around during the day. "It's just Evelyn and I," she says, "so I take her over to the table and I read to her from the children's story Bible, and I try to explain what I read."

Evelyn lies there on the couch, misshapen from so many bedridden years, tall and thick, her smile teased up by the sense of company somehow there in her mind.

And for a moment I can't say anything. Evelyn's mother is seventy. Florida is full of women her age who spend their lives at hairdressers, boutiques, golf courses, and posh sidewalk cafes, women—like their husbands—who make war against time itself. Here is Evelyn's mother spending the last years of her life reading Bible stories to her own grotesque child, as if time had stopped.

But she's expected the question, because what I'm doing at her house wouldn't be quite right if it weren't asked. So her answer isn't meant to illustrate her devotion to her child or to merit my praise. It's meant purely as an answer to the question; that is, it is an illustration of her own devotion to the God who has been with her in her miserable life for so many years. It's her way of saying, "It is well with my soul."

It's one of those incidents that stays with you. I've never told Julia about it, because we've not been open enough with each other since her father died for me to tell her. It's one of those stories which she would understand today as a reprimand. What's more, she'd be right.

But that story returned to me in the cold, almost like a standard of

186   *The Privacy of Storm*

humility and fortitude. So when I got back into the car, I felt armored with righteousness in a way, knowing that my job was to continue to work at settling what had become a crisis in our home. I was thinking just then how I could go home and tell Julia that story, give her a good shot of sincere righteousness.

When I think it all through now, I know it is important that you understand exactly what I was feeling—how I felt uplifted by the meditation I had done out there in the dark and cold, fortified by the odd sense of my own part in the task of rebuilding what sin itself had torn down. Julia wouldn't expect me home. My arrival would shock her now, and the shock itself would be sufficient reason to open up the whole business. I thought there was no reason that what had happened should ruin our family, and I knew that down deep Julia felt the same way. It was nothing more than her pride that was keeping us apart now, pure and simple Branderhorst pride, the exact specimen that Heerema himself had explained to them, offending it—and them—in the process.

I wondered whether she might still be awake when the wash of my headlights came over the wall outside our bedroom, but the upstairs bathroom light was on now. I thought perhaps one of the kids had been up to put it on. They'll do that if they wake up in the darkness and fear.

I shut the storm door quietly behind me and came up the back steps and through the back hall door to the dark kitchen, where I snapped on the light above the sink. As soon as I stopped moving, I heard the baby crying frantically upstairs, and I knew Julia was probably awake, up there herself.

I walked through the living room to the staircase. The light from the bathroom was squeezing out from the closed door at the top of the stairs. It was then that I heard two voices.

There may be no more wretched sound than a baby's slashing cry unabated. I was thinking how hard it was when Jeremy, our first, used to cry himself to sleep—how Julia and I would lie there in bed as if there were an ocean between us, waiting for it to stop, wondering how to stop it but knowing he had to stop by himself. Nothing could be said in those moments that sometimes stretched into hours of brutal, inhuman pain. I'll never forget feeling something bestial in me rise almost to the surface, unacknowledged but there, ugly as sin itself, in my fear and frustrated anger.

The baby's crying angered me. I waited for a moment at the bottom of the stairs because I knew that what I had planned was not going to work out smoothly if a crying spell were dropped somehow in the middle of the fray. I couldn't talk to her, not if her hands were filled with the kind of persistent crying that exasperated even the deep reserves of love a parent has for a child. I wished for a moment that I was still back there outside of town, that I could postpone coming home until things at home had calmed down, the baby off to sleep.

Maybe Julia hadn't even heard me come in, I thought. Maybe I could just step back outside for awhile until I saw that bathroom light snap off.

But it was the intensity of the baby's screaming that seemed pitched in anger, and Julia's staggered weeping coming out in twists of anger. I walked up the stairs.

When I opened the door, she was standing there with the baby on one arm, strangled almost over her elbow, while she was beating the child with her open right hand, tears running down her face, her arm swinging back and forth ruthlessly, time and time again against him.

Everything seemed lost, my own wife's sense somehow departed. Instinctively, I grabbed the baby. "What are you doing?" I said, yanking Rudy from her arm.

"Let me alone," she said, trying to take him back. She came at me like an animal, scratching at me as if this child she had been beating was her own salvation. "Give me my child," she said.

I can't describe her at that moment because rage had tortured her, turned her into something I recognized not as my wife, but as an exaggeration of some horrid possibility lurking in her character, just as it does in all of us. Something not simply Branderhorst, but greater than that. When she attacked me, I was nothing more than an enemy.

And that's when I hit her. I had the child in my arm, and I swung out with the back of my hand, catching her jaw with my forearm full force as she came at me. Her chin jerked upward and she staggered back until her leg glanced off the toilet and she fell against the bathtub as if she were shot, the back of her head banging first against the edge and then off the floor. She lay there limp and motionless, her legs spread beneath her housecoat, one arm thrown up over her head, the other beneath her, her body turned away from me.

And there I stood, holding the wailing baby, thinking I had killed my wife. My first thought—I swear it—my very first thought was an instinctive desire for self-preservation. I had to put the baby away and keep the children from seeing what I had done. My first thought was to cover up my own crime. When I remember it now, I could cry to confess it, but it was true—like a kid caught stealing fishhooks, I thought only to deny it had happened. I didn't even think of her, not at the very first moment. The older kids would wake up, I thought, and they'd come in and they'd know. And all the time the baby was there in my arms, its crying just as strong, just as rasping as it had been when I first heard it downstairs.

"Julia," I said, not shouting, but loud enough. She showed no signs of waking. "Julia, I didn't mean it," I said. But the baby's screaming alone was enough to keep me from thinking clearly.

I reached down for her face, felt her forehead, her neck, clamped my hand over her mouth and felt the breath still flowing. I looked around the bathroom, as if some remedy would be there on the shelf, something to reverse time, to relieve me of what I knew had happened.

I ran down the steps with the baby in my arms, the hand I had used against my wife now up against the wall to keep my balance, and I put the baby, still crying, in our bed downstairs and went back up.

What stays with me so horribly is my own mind's instinctive pursuit of an escape. I thought of a doctor immediately, even though when I felt behind her head there was no blood; the blow I had given her to the face left no bruise. I knew she might have a concussion from the violent bang of her head on the bathtub. But I still find it hard to believe how fast my mind ran into excuses, each of which fit the pattern exactly. "She had fallen in the bathroom and hit her head against the bathtub." That's what I'd tell them when I got her to the hospital in Meridith, and the nurse would have every reason to think that this respectable looking man who has just come home from a meeting at church was, in fact, nothing more than a wife-beater, and a liar to boot. All of that I thought completely through in the seconds that had passed since the moment I hit her. My mind—my guilty, filthy mind—ran through excuses as if it were leafing through a new book, at the very time that my wife lay there on the floor, still unconscious.

I knew she was breathing. I picked up a wet facecloth from the counter—why?—who knows why we do those things?—thinking maybe it was what should be done, maybe the cold would revive her. I put it on her face and picked her up in my arms so her head was cradled in my lap.

"Julia," I said, "do you hear me?"

I was so conscious of the older children just outside the door, so conscious, so defensive.

Her neck turned slowly, as if she might come awake.

I looked at my watch. Why?—as if to remember the exact moment?

"Julia," I said, "I'm sorry. You hear me? Do you hear me at all?"

The door swung open slightly, and there stood Buddy in his pajamas. "Daddy?—" he said.

"Go back to your bedroom," I said, yelling almost.

"What's the matter with Mom?"

"Go back to bed now!" I shouted.

He shut the door, but I knew he would be crying himself in a minute.

She wasn't completely limp. I held my hand behind her head and I could feel some motion there, some tension in the muscles. Finally it was all coming clearly to me. I sat there with my wife in my arms, one foot curled beneath my leg, holding the wet cloth over her face. I had hit her. At the very least, I had knocked her unconscious. I had beat my wife. I loved my wife. I swear I loved her. But somehow I had beaten her.

For a moment she was dead to me. The world itself turned over, and all the responsibilities of a life without her fell from the image. I could be tried, of course. I would be charged with abuse. I could plead not guilty, tell them about the way she was spanking the baby, but the picture itself was so horrible: child-abuse, spouse abuse, violence, hatred, cruelty.

"Julia," I said, "just nod your head if you hear me—"

I felt her head swing, and I could see her eyes swirl beneath her lids.

"I'm sorry, Julia. Forgive me, please," I said.

"My head," she said, and then she groaned almost inaudibly as she exhaled.

"I love you, Julia," I said.

Her eyelids squeezed tight shut, then fluttered open suddenly, and she stared at me, through me, as if she were trying to locate me in a dim memory.

"I don't know what happened," I said. "It's all horrible what happened."

She looked around the room. Her lashes were clumped with tears, and gray lines had formed along the edges of her cheeks where tears had left streaks.

And the longer I sat there, the more I began to understand of what had happened. I pulled her more closely to my chest, held her against me with both arms.

"What happened—Howard?" she said.

But even then, even when she said it that way, I was thinking that maybe I could lie, even to her. Maybe no one would have to know.

"You hit your head," I said.

"My head," she said, as if I had reminded her suddenly of something she'd forgotten.

There would be no bruise on her jaw. I could see nothing at all—no sign. I had hit her with the back of my wrist, with the sleeve of my coat as a pad. It was the force that sent her reeling backward, and the toilet that had tripped her, and the bathtub's edge that had knocked her unconscious.

"Did I fall somehow?" she said.

"You fell," I told her.

What is it in us that makes us want so desperately to have our own innocence. It is nothing more or less than the innate pride of self-preservation, some instinct that roils around in us and muscles its way out in the form of self-defense and the will to live. At all cost, save your own hide, it says, involuntarily. You really can't just stop breathing, I'm told. If you want to take your own life, there is no natural way of doing it—the only way is to employ violence against yourself. Is it that instinct for self-preservation that floats, lies before us like the last inflatable raft from a sinking ship? Is it just effortless instinct that makes us liars?

If it is, then there's something to Emil Branderhorst's old Calvinism.

By the time I brought her downstairs, the baby was fast asleep in our bed. Buddy was still whimpering back upstairs, but once I got Julia on her feet, I went up and told him that his mom had just taken a fall in the bathroom and that she'd be all right when he got up for school.

"It scared me, seeing her lying down on the floor like that," he told me.

I told him that it scared me too, but that now everything was all right. It was a parental lie, of course, made legitimate by the fact that my own son didn't have to know the truth. We do it all the time.

On the way to the hospital, she said that maybe it wasn't even necessary to drive over. "I've just got this headache is all, Howard," she said. "I'll be all right in the morning."

I don't know why I didn't just turn around then. I'd like to think it was my own dim sense of what might be an injury. I'd like to think that it was my concern for Julia's head right then, but I'm not so sure it was. We were in the car, we were already half way to town, we were going to the hospital. Things had to be checked out. Reason became inoperative in the odd necessity of completing what I had begun when we'd got her dressed and into the car. Maybe I wanted to tell someone. Maybe that's it.

"What happened anyway?" she said. "It's funny how I don't remember very much—that the baby was crying—"

Three times before I'd brought Julia into emergency in Meridith, each time for the birth of our children. The streets in town are empty; everything is dark except the floods outside the back door of the hospital, where this huge steel door is always open, the side door to the garage where the ambulance is parked. You come in from the deadness of night to the perfect order of the ambulance stall, and the whole thing has this surreal taste, as if you were part of an Edward Hopper scene. Julia walked evenly, my hand beneath her arm.

"What happened?" the nurse said, just as I had rehearsed it in my head. What could I tell her? Would it pay right then to say that I had clubbed her and sent her reeling to the floor where she hit her head against the bathtub. Even the nurse didn't want that kind of responsibility just then, not after midnight.

You can see doubt in people's eyes, and the nurse never once questioned what I had said, not for a moment. She filled out a report with a ball point pen, the erasable kind, and we went off to the x-ray room, where she felt around for the bubble at the back of Julia's head.

We ended up leaving quite quickly. The nurse claimed it probably didn't amount to much at all and that there would be no scar. She said to call in if Julia felt nauseous.

"I'm still not sure what happened," Julia said on the way home. "It's all gone—completely gone.''

"What do you remember?'' I said.

When the winds die at night, you can ride down country roads in so much silence that the car itself seems barely running.

My question turned her inward. She straightened herself on the seat and brought her coat up tight around her legs. Our stay in emergency was so short that the car never really got cooled.

But her silence shifted the conversation. When she didn't respond immediately, I knew she had stumbled upon the old issue, the matter of the church. But it wasn't easy for me to make that jump. The old issue seemed so pitifully small now.

"My brothers say they're leaving,'' she told me.

I glanced at her across the seat. Her eyes were on the dashboard in front of her. I had it in me to tell her yet. I had it in me to say exactly what had happened. It was all sitting there on the edge, waiting to fall out of me.

"That's what they say,'' she said, and she reached back with her hand and rubbed the back of her neck.

But I couldn't tell her then, because I knew exactly what she meant. "They were leaving'' meant she wasn't sure, and I knew what kind of courage it took for her to say that—not only to depart from the way her older brothers had chosen, but also to admit that she was coming back to me. It was an act of humility on her part even to hint of a breach between herself and her family. "They were leaving'' meant she had taken one anxious step away from them. No matter what she decided ultimately, there was a sense in which she had created distance between them and herself, painful distance.

So it wasn't a time for talk just then. You can fault the Branderhorsts all right, but they have this sense of dignity that stands up like a huge cottonwood, daring the very roughest weather the prairie can bring. Julia told me that she wanted us back together again in that one word *they*, but she didn't want me gushing over the fruits of her own anxious decision. She didn't want me touching her, not even my hand on hers at that moment. She didn't want me saying something, because another death had occurred in the separation she had made from her family. It was nothing but silence she wanted, not praise or some weak show of gratitude.

So I didn't tell her, and I never have. It's been easier and easier every day not to tell her. The next morning already I was thinking that to tell her the truth would be admitting not only what I had done but what she had done as well. It was easy for me to rationalize that not telling her was in fact protecting her from a memory that could haunt her the way my memory haunts me.

For awhile I fought with myself about not telling her about the whole truth of what I'd done—and what had happened. Late at night when the kids were upstairs we'd sit up together and watch the news, Julia wrapped in her bathrobe, sitting on the couch with her legs beneath her. Then she'd stand like she always does, yawning, stretching in silence, her way of saying that she's going to bed and she'd like me to come along.

"I'll be there in a minute," I'd say, and she'd smile.

And once she'd be gone to the bedroom, this urgency to tell her would rise in my chest like a sickness, making me shake. And I'd tell myself that I had to tell her somehow, that she had to know the truth of what had happened that night, to know how her own husband had hit her. Even if she didn't have to know, I needed to know that she knew. What I needed was forgiveness.

So today no one knows what really happened that night. No one knows but me.

And I know now what Heerema said in Beagle's funeral service; I know it better than I've ever known it before. He meant it for all of us, really. It's just that on the day of the funeral, only the Branderhorsts were listening.

Maybe you can hide out here on the plains.

"Lord Jesus," Vermeer would say, "come quickly."